Not Yet Loved

By
Caroline Paulette McDowell

Caroline Paulette McDowell 2008

PublishAmerica
Baltimore

First printing

All characters in this book are fictitious, and any resemblance to real persons, living or dead, is coincidental.

PublishAmerica has allowed this work to remain exactly as the author intended, verbatim, without editorial input.

ISBN: 1-60474-409-X
PUBLISHED BY PUBLISHAMERICA, LLLP
www.publishamerica.com
Baltimore

Printed in the United States of America

This work is dedicated to my wonderful husband, John T

Amber threw the book she was reading against her bedroom wall. After hitting the wall the book fell to the floor with a "thud." The silence that followed annoyed her even more than the contents of the book had. Amber wondered; why, in every book she had ever read, the girls were always beautiful, with perfect features, silky hair and sparkling teeth? They never needed braces nor had cavities; their skin was "dewy soft" and was always without blemishes even during puberty. And if they managed to get sunburned; well, they didn't blister and peel and become something close to an unsightly lobster; no, they turned "golden and tawny." What the hell color is tawny anyway? Even if these girls had a conflict in life, it always turned out of the best for them and all off their loved ones. Never an unhappy ending. She wondered why, just once, couldn't these girls have freckles or crooked teeth or fall in love with somebody ugly or poor? She almost laughed at herself over the story line that popped into her thoughts. "Fat girl falls in love with an unemployed trash collector who has three children by a previous marriage. "Now that's a reality," she thought. Reality, she was so sick of reality. Her reality surrounded her every waking moment of her life.

For Amber Harris, reality was looking in the mirror and seeing a mane of auburn hair that framed an oval face. Not an ugly face, but definitely not the face of a "roman beauty" either. There were freckles across the nose and cheeks. The eyebrows were nice enough but beneath them the green eyes were not "piercing" nor were they "crystal" or anything like that. They were green, as the grass of summer is green. They never stayed the same color for more than an hour at a time and there were little gold flecks scattered through the color giving them a cat like quality. The gold flecks only reminded her of the freckles on her nose. Damn freckles. When she was 12 years old she had tried for three hours one day to scrub them off her face; succeeding only in chaffing her skin, and then having to put up with not only the freckles, but with the teasing about her chaffed skin too. Now she smiled as she brushed her hair.

It was almost like thinking of another person when she thought about her childhood. She thought back now of the stories her Grandmama had told her about how her Daddy had actually stolen her from an orphanage. Amber loved these stories and had listened to them being told to her over and over. It was important that Amber never forget those first years.

Amber was the illegitimate child of a woman of not many standards and one Lance Denver Harris.

This woman didn't tell Lance of her pending motherhood and at Amber's birth, she left Amber on the steps of the old county home. Around the time that Amber had turned six months old, a cousin to Lance told him of the baby born and given away.

Lance Harris was no perfect specimen, but, he had been raised by a stern but loving father that believed one answered for ones' own conduct no matter what the cost. Lance had grown up admiring his father's strong moral and emotional background, and had sought to be as much like the elder Harris as possible for most of his life. It was in this state of mind that Lance looked up the mother of the child he had spawned. He asked her point blank if the story he had been told was indeed true? The woman acknowledged the fact that she had given birth to his child and yes, of course, she had left "it" at the Home. When hearing this story, he asked her for reasons for such actions on her part. She explained the whole thing very simply. She did not want a baby, could not find someone who would risk an illegal abortion, and she had no intention of marrying Lance or anyone like him; "like him" meaning poor. In addition, she had no real desire to even try and raise a child by herself; therefore, the most logical solution to her problem was to leave the "brat" where "it" would be safe. She didn't tell Lance of her pregnancy because she didn't want to hear all of the reasons he could come up with for them to marry, and she knew enough about Lance and his family to know that would be his first reaction to her "impending motherhood."

Lance wondered what a newborn baby did to rate being labeled a "brat." He was angered, then shocked, then sad. He made plans that very night to visit the orphanage to find out what "his bastard child" was like.

It was late December 1947, nearly Christmas Day. Lance had been home from the U.S. Navy for over two years but still hadn't purchased many new clothes. He put on the only civilian suit he owned, and much to his mother's distress, refused to tell her where he was going.

His mind wondered as he drove across town to the orphanage. He waited for forty minutes in the ancient office for the administrator of the orphanage to appear. While waiting he noted the smooth finish of the wooden door and wondered how many times the huge brass knobs in the center of the door had been turned.

He felt his pulse quicken as that knob turned now to allow Mr. Armand Holsinger to enter the room.

Holsinger was short, with skinny legs supporting a too thick torso. He looked as if he were top heavy and might tip over at any second. His skin was pale and too soft for Lance's taste. His white hair was well groomed and really the only healthy looking thing about him.

Lance shook hands with him and wished he hadn't. Holsinger's palm was clammy and soft. Lance wondered if his urge to gag was visible.

"I've come here to visit my child." Lance said bluntly.

Holsinger laughed and a pathetic looking secretary joined them in the office. She held a file folder that Lance guessed to be his child's records. Holsinger glanced at the file and tossed it down on the top of an already cluttered desk.

"And just what makes you think your child is with us?" Holsinger tried to sound threatening. All he succeeded in doing was to annoy Lance further.

"The baby's mother told me she left it here. Around six months ago. I want to see it." Lance was nervous and his annoyance was fast becoming anger. He hated being scrutinized by anyone.

Holsinger smiled and revealed crooked teeth that were discolored by years of smoking strong cigarettes.

"My dear Mr. Harris! You may as well leave and take your silly notion of visiting a foundling housed in our institution with you. You have no way of knowing you really have a child, and, if you do, there is no way you can gain visitation rights or anything else." He laughed and added, "Next thing I know, you'll think you want custody of the little bastard."

"The child is mine too, and I want to see it whether its' mother wants to or not. I have a right to the child. The child has a right to know who its' father is."

Lance's protests fell on deaf ears.

"Mr. Harris, I am a busy man. You are wasting my time and trying to break the law. Now, be off with you! I really had other plans for today."

Trembling with anger, Lance left the wooden office with its' wooden people who lacked any kind of compassion and slammed the door on his was out. Once outside on the porch of the old building he slowed down for a moment to think. Years later he would tell of standing there surrounded by the quietness of the afternoon and watching the shadows play across the grounds as the sun was disappearing behind clouds that threatened more snow for the small town. It was that then he decided to become a "Daddy." He decided it sad indeed for any little person to grow up in such a cut and dry atmosphere; much less a little person that might carry his blood through its' veins. He thought about his own wonderful childhood, although quite poor, he never lacked for warmth and affection from either of his parents. He had a child now and he had honor. And he would keep both. He would do the honorable thing by this child and the administrator and his rules of the establishment could be damned. He turned on his heel and asked the first attendant he met how to get to the nursery, or "wherever they keep the six month olds?" There were five young babies in the room. Lance stopped in his tracks. It had never really dawned on him that there might be more than one baby there. He glanced around the room and his sight fell upon a pile of curls lying on a tiny pillow. The curls were the color of copper lying in the afternoon sun. The same color Lance remembered his own mother's hair to be when he had been a youngster. The child was asleep. Lance picked the baby girl up, and she woke instantly and with sleepy eyes only half open, she smiled at him.

Years later Lance would smile at his daughter and say, "That was it. I knew you had to be my girl."

Lance Denver Harris' first crime in his life was kidnapping. Amid hysterical threats and protests of the attendants of the County Orphanage of Aston, Virginia, Lance walked out with a baby girl wrapped in a yellow blanket. He drove home grinning and wondering exactly how his mother would take to this, but it did not matter what she said, she would help him, he knew it. She just had to. This little creature was his "fault"; no, "it" was part of him, his responsibility and "it" had already smiled at him. He had made up his mind and he would raise "it" and do his very best by "it" from now on, no matter how shaky the beginning might be. And he would never call "her" "it" again.

"Just like a stray pup," her Grandmama would say for years to come. "He come dragging you in just like a stray pup! Said we just had to keep you cause you was his and he wanted you."

Sarahlou Harris hardly had time to overcome the shock of this little bundle her son brought home before the county sheriff came knocking on her door. He asked for the baby to be returned to the orphanage immediately, and, when Lance refused, he was arrested. It took every dime of his mother's egg money to bail him out of jail that night, and the baby was returned to the home; but, by seven o'clock the next morning Lance had already borrowed enough money to hire a lawyer and with the help of the town's only physician, Lance was granted temporary custody of his little girl while the proper authorities thought about the bizarre situation. It took nearly a year of debate and battle for Lance to be granted permanent custody of the tiny redhead. He started adoption proceedings in July of 1949. Amber turned two years old surrounded by the love and affection that only a Daddy and a Grandmama can bestow on a child.

By the time Lance was given custody of Amber, he had won the respect and admiration of nearly every adult in the small town. There wasn't a shopkeeper or business owner in town that hadn't seen Lance with his small charge strapped on his back. Lance once told Amber that she had probably had her diaper changed by every good hearted woman in the town while he was making his coal deliveries. A bottle warmed here, a diaper changed there, noon feedings at the diner by the waitress who had a crush on Lance anyway. Coal deliveries in the small town of Aston were never the same again.

These thoughts brought a smile to Amber's lips but stinging tears to her eyes.

Lance Denver Harris, her beloved father, her best friend was dead. For days Amber had tried to come to grips with the fact that Lance, at 49 years of age, had died unexpectedly at home, in his own bed, an apparent heart attack during sleep. All so neat and done. The papers made it sound almost boring.

Amber knew her own life would carry on. It had to and it would. However, she was having no luck at believing she would ever enjoy anything again. Her mind screamed at times at the injustice of it all. Lance had been so good; so caring; so wonderful to so many people, not just Amber. Her mind demanded reasons and there were no reasons. Her mind drifted again to the stories that her Grandmama Sarahlou had related to her.

Lance Harris was a self made man. He had grown up poor and was used to doing hard work just to survive. He had adored his own father and had often voiced a desire to "be just like Dad." However, Lance matured early and longed for more than the small farm just outside Aston could give him. For what was supposed to be one summer, Lance left home at fourteen years of age. He assured his parents that he knew what he was doing. That "one summer" turned into three years. He traveled from town to town doing odd jobs for as little as a glass of milk and a piece of cinnamon toast. He picked fruit in Pennsylvania and spread asphalt on the highways of Georgia. He lived as good as rented rooms with a shared bathroom and as bad as hobo camps where you shared everything. And he learned about living, about surviving, and enjoying every day of his life as it came to him.

Eventually he grew tired of not knowing for sure where his next meal would come from, so he lied about his age and joined the United States Navy. At seventeen, he was already over six feet tall and very muscular from years of manual labor. Actually no one really questioned him very far, and when World War II broke out in full force, no one really cared very much. Lance served in the Navy for four years and eleven months. He pulled duty on two destroyers and an aircraft carrier. He watched his friends die at his feet, and he had saved the lives of more than one man by the time he was discharged in 1945.

Even Lance was surprised that he survived the war. He returned to Aston to find crops failing and everybody and their brothers out of a job. The only factory near Aston had laid off most of the people working there, but Lance wasn't much for assembly lines anyway. Lance's father had passed away while he was on duty somewhere in the Pacific Theater, and his mother was aging fast, so Lance offered no protest when she insisted he move back to the farm with her. He was twenty-three years old, and had already lived a lifetime. Maybe the quiet of the farm was just what he needed after all, for a while at least.

Lance's mother more or less let him take over the farm and the disastrous finances that went with it. It didn't take a financial genius to know that, without some serious money coming in soon, Lance and his mother would lose the farm and most of the possessions they owned. Lance knew that he had to get him hands on something that everyone else in the world needed. In early 1946 that something was coal.

Lance bought a used dump truck with his "coming out" pay he had saved when he left the Navy. Anyone could go to the coal yards and buy coal by the ton or by the basket; but, having coal delivered was a real novelty and people would pay a few extra cents on the bushel to have it brought to their house. Some of his stops were for only a few pounds of coal at a time, but he never refused a call. Many of the aged people of Aston thought him a real "godsend." He would let them buy their coal a tiny bit at a time, bring it right into their living room if needed, and thusly, helped them overcome one of the more difficult chores of their daily lives. He would often work till midnight mapping out his delivery routes to accomplish a time efficient system. He rose by five in the morning to tend to the farm chores before he left with his truck. With money he made with his coal deliveries, and his crops surviving, Lance could see the light at the end of the tunnel by the end of his first full year home. There was never much money left over, but at least he and his beloved mother would not lose their land or home.

Life was beginning to be good again for Lance, and he enjoyed being stationary. His mother had a renewed zest for life and together they made a home. However, Lance yearned for "something" in his life to make it complete. It was over this "yearning" that Amber had been haphazardly conceived.

Lance met Inez Chandler, Amber's mother, just after he returned home from the service. They met in a bar and Lance took her home after a two hour lecture on all the reasons she shouldn't be there in the first place. Lance was interested in stable companionship and eventually, a loving wife with whom to build a family. He thought Inez to be the most beautiful creature that he had ever laid eyes on. And beautiful she was. She was tall for a woman, but still dwarfed by Lance's stature. She was thin with small but firm breasts that always seemed to strain against whatever blouse or sweater Inez chose to put on. Her raven black hair fell to her shoulders and framed an oval face with a softness that certainly did not match her disposition. There was nothing else soft about Inez Chandler.

Inez had run away from her own home at thirteen and turned her first trick by the time she was fourteen. She had been caught by the local authorities and placed in a foster home, but was promptly thrown out by the lady of the house for "seducing" her son. Seducing hell, he was seventeen; she was fourteen. Anyway, Inez left town in the middle of the night with over four hundred dollars she had stolen from the "bitch" that threw her out and had headed for New York before the social workers had time to pick her up. Her deep brown eyes would sparkle every time she spoke of the dreams she had and the plans she would put into action when her dreams came true.

However, none of her dreams included love or marriage. None of her dreams had come true by the time she met Lance Harris, but they still did not include the day to day drudgery of being a farming, coal hauler's wife. They certainly did not include being poor the rest of her life. Lance had a hard time dealing with the fact that for some women, love just isn't what counts. When they first met he had been sure that his sincere love and compassion would be enough to tame her. He vowed to be patient, he cared nothing about her past, just her future. His first attempts at making love to her were shy and controlled; almost to the point of being clumsy. He "courted" her with old fashioned manners and attentiveness. He feared she might break under his rough touch. He lover her, with his very heart and soul, he loved her.

They had been sleeping together for nearly a year when he asked her to marry him. He wanted her to help him make his dreams come true. In return, he promised to love her forever, provide her with a home and to protect her from any and everything that might dare to try and harm her. She laughed in his face and told him to ask again when he had money in the bank, a mansion on a hill, and even then not to count too heavily on immortality in the form of offspring. She wasn't the motherly type, she told him. He saw her only a few more times after that night, each time begging her to reconsider his proposal. When she dropped out of sight without even a good-bye, Lance cursed being a poor man, and vowed to not only put an end to his poverty, but to never again share his soul with anyone. And he was cautious from that day on.

Little had he known that for him and Inez, it was a little late to be cautious. Amber had already been conceived and Inez had already planned to rid herself of the inconvenience of an unwanted child when she disappeared.

With Lance's vows to end his poverty came the idea that would indeed make Lance one of the richest men of his time. It hadn't take long to discover that coal was in demand everywhere and one man with one truck could scarcely begin to make all the deliveries that were needed in Aston County. And what if you could deliver not only in your own county, but, all over the state of Virginia? Maybe someday in other states as well. His dream was to be rich and now he had an idea to make that dream come true. His next step was to gamble. And gamble he did. He bought two more trucks by mortgaging his first one and hired two friends who had been out of work for some time to drive them for him. The rules were simple when you worked for Lance. Be honest, be fair, and do your best. He asked nothing of an employee that he did not ask of himself.

That had been the beginning and before his death, Lance Harris was a wealthy man. However, he never loved another woman. He never married. He rarely trusted and by the time his daughter was two years old he had begun to hate Inez Chandler. He vowed Inez would never get close to their child....HIS child.

Lance found out about Amber's existence in the winter of 1947, gained custody of her in 1948 and adopted her in 1949. By her sixth birthday in 1953, he had landed the local power company's contracts to deliver coal to their production stations, and not only had dozens of dump trucks on the road, but, a fleet of semis hauling coal from the hills of Virginia around the clock. He had built coal yards on both sides of the city, had controlling interest in thirty coal mines. He was active in road and mine safety programs all over the state of Virginia. He had seventy-five men working for him in the field and another sixteen in his offices. Every man that worked for Lance Harris considered him a personal friend. The closest of these men was Eric Tolliver. Eric was Scottish, born and breed, and proud of it. He was only twelve years old when he came to Lance to bargain for a job.

Eric had explained to Lance very matter-of-factly that he could do and would learn to do any task ask of him. He was from a very large, very poor family and they needed even the pennies a day that Eric might earn to keep their home running. He could sweep floors, clean out truck beds, run the sorters at the coal yards, anything! Lance took kindly to the boy's attitude and let him work for three hours each day after school and all day on Saturday.

Eric worked mostly in the sorting bins at first, making sure that the conveyor belts didn't get snarled on a large piece of coal. Eric learned fast and made observations that some grown men missed. One day in particular, Eric had noticed a frayed belt on the largest conveyor. He brought it to Lance's attention and ultimately saved costly repairs and down time. Lance shuddered to think about what could have happened if the belt had actually broken while in motion with ten tons of coal on it. Lance was so impressed and grateful that he "promoted" Eric to "Maintenance and Repairs." The biggest advantage for Eric was the fact that Lance took more time to get to know the lad, and started taking Eric home with him for the evening meal. The advantage for Lance was the youngster took his position very seriously and instituted a preventative maintenance program that would set records for safety for years to come.

Eric spent more and more time at the coal yards and devoted more and more of his life to Lance Harris and to the learning of the coal shipping business.

Eric had been delighted when he met Sarahlou and Amber. He rejoiced with the family when Lance gained full and legal custody of his little girl. He had been instantly fascinated by the tiny creature, and when he wasn't tending to his chores at the yards, he was running errands for Sarahlou. He often tended Amber while her Grandmama was baking or washing, or some other time consuming chore. Amber was always good natured and smelled of soap or talcum powder, unlike his own little sisters that cried from constant neglect and wore clothes soured with yesterday's spoiled milk. In comparison to the stench of vomit and whiskey at home, Sarahlou's kitchen always smelled of apple pies in the oven or fresh baked bread cooling on the sideboard. Her floors shone and there was always a brightly colored quilt in the corner for baby Amber to play upon, although no one had much luck keeping her on it for very long at a time. Eric loved the Harris family, their home, their business, and especially their Baby Amber.

By the time Amber turned six years old, if she wasn't with Lance or Grandmama, she was following Eric around the coal yards helping him tend to his duties. She would come home black as the night, with some exciting adventure to tell her Grandmama.

Eric finished growing up watching Amber mature. He was relaxed at Lance's side and was never intimidated by the "boss." They were friends. Eric was the one person Lance had voiced his insecurities about raising Amber to, and the one person who hadn't told him how crazy some of his ideas were. Eric just listened and although still a child himself, he had served as a sounding board for many of the early decisions Lance made. At fifteen years old he had already become smart enough to never agree nor disagree with Lance; he just listened. That was what Lance needed. Someone to listen, the way a true friend listens to you when you pour out your heart. And likewise, Lance had served well as confidant to Eric during his times of turmoil. Eric's father died of a heart attack and a few weeks later his mother ended her own life with a razor blade. It was Lance that stepped in and took care of details that Eric could not face alone. When Eric's younger brothers and sisters entered foster care, it was Lance who saw to it that their birthdays did not go by unnoticed and that Christmas was special for all them every year. It was Lance who listened to Eric when the prettiest cheerleader in the world broke his heart and it was Lance that insisted that he finish high school, and wrote him every week during his hitch in the Army and saved a place for him with the company upon his return.

By the night of his twenty fifth birthday, he and Lance had known each other and worked together for thirteen years. On this night Lance and Sarahlou hosted Eric at their home for a special birthday dinner.

Eric arrived at Harris Manor just before six. He entered the huge hallway that he himself had helped Lance remodel. Every time he entered this house he remembered the fit Sarahlou had thrown when they had moved into the town proper from the farm. This evening there were no fits, just hugs and kisses from both Sarahlou and Amber....God, how Amber was growing.

After dinner, and the cake, and the hugs were all over, Lance asked Eric to join him in the library. This usually meant business and even though the clocks were striking 9 o'clock, Eric was eager. He loved the business. It had become the bigger part of his life since his return from the service. His family had scattered as they had become of age to leave foster care and there had been little communication among the siblings even before his entrance into the Army and none since his return home.

Lance quietly handed Eric a glass of brandy and a legal document. Eric sipped his brandy before opening the folded paper. The document was short and to the point. It stated that one third of Harris Enterprises now belonged to Eric Tolliver and that henceforth the company would be known as Harris-Tolliver Enterprises, Inc. Eric was in shock for a month. Lance's generosity was matched profoundly by Eric's devotion to making the business the most trusted, most efficient coal transporting company in the land.

Lance and Eric had worked and played together for a total of twenty years at the time of Lance's death. Eric's admiration for Lance had never been a secret. He, like Amber, was numbed by the injustice of fate. He had been at Amber's side for days; doing anything he could to comfort or help her. He wept openly with her and had been consistently kind and gentle. He had watched Amber grow from infancy, the daughter of his best friend and mentor. He loved her as his own. Or was it as "his own?" His thoughts of Amber troubled him deeply. Even before Lance's death he had been acutely aware of Amber's physical maturity and her mental innocence. "My God," he had often thought, "doesn't she know what men feel when she enters a room? Doesn't she see every head turn to watch her? Can't the little fool see how I feel?"

Eric loved the freckles Amber hated. Her hair always smelled like violets touched by musk. Her skin was soft and "just clean." She almost always had a smooth clean shine to her face, a face never covered by makeup. Actually, Amber couldn't wear makeup. She had once discussed this matter with Eric while waiting for her father to return to his office. Without even knowing it, Amber had nearly driven Eric out of his mind.

Eric had walked into the room and found Amber eyeing her face in a mirror while brushing her hair. Embarrassed at being caught, she had been quick to explain that she was watching for some "hideous bump" to leap out of her skin because she had just been visiting the local Dime Store and had tried out at least three of their finest facial foundations. "I'm allergic," she announced. "And I know I should be more careful, but it's such fun." While making her announcements, she had moved very close to Eric. "Do you see anything?" she asked him. She had stood only inches from him. He had felt the warmth radiating from her fevered breasts which were not inhibited by the presence of a bra because her shoulders were sunburned and the straps hurt. Her breasts, though small, were perfectly formed, firm and begging to be caressed. Her waist curved into nearly nothing and her hips in short shorts were enough to make any man crazy. She smelled clean and real, not like so much cheap perfume. She was so innocent, so trusting. Eric had touched her neck and acted like he was inspecting for "hideous bumps" while in truth he wanted to smother her throat with kisses. He didn't of course. Partly because he knew Amber would bolt like a frightened deer, and partly because he was fifteen years her senior, and partly because he did truly love her very much, and MAINLY because she was his best friend and business partner's daughter and no smart business man ever put something like this between himself and his partner. He also figured that if Lance knew his desires for Amber he would just flat knock his brains out of his head onto the floor and then walk through them. So, he stood there, the aching in his groin refusing to be ignored, torturing him both physically and mentally. His mind had already raced beyond the moment and he had already dreamed of what it would be like to possess her. He wanted to climb between those silken thighs, to mount her and to plunge himself into the softness that he knew would be there. It might be even better if she did struggle a bit at first, a little better if she were frightened at the pain of his entry. He would take her for his own and never let her go. He would plant his seed in her and keep her marked for his own. He would watch her during the pain of childbirth, over and over he hoped. What the hell, they were rich and cold afford one child after another. He would be somewhat gentler with her when he mounted her while her belly was swollen with his children. She would be required to bear many children.

He would have sex with her right up to the day the child birthed, even if he had to mount her from the rear. He hoped it would be painful and she would sweat so that he could lick her salt from her back. Her breasts would swell with milk when the babies arrived. He would watch them nurse her breasts and then mount her again.

He had cursed himself over these kinds of thoughts more than once. He didn't even understand his overpowering desire to possess Amber. When had this started? He knew this was not just a normal desire for sexual encounters with her. He loved her, but, more important he wanted to be sure no one else would ever touch her.

He had crashed back into reality with cold sweat on his brow. He smiled and swore to Amber that he did not see anything to mar her pretty skin. He then turned from her and nearly ran from the room to avoid Lance's approach; knowing that Lance would have read his turmoil like an open book and perhaps beat him to death on the spot. For several weeks after that day Eric avoided close contact with Amber. This was the child that he had tended as a baby. She considered him her best "hug" in the world. Now those hugs that buried ripe breasts into his chest were driving him mad.

And now…. Now with Lance gone, Eric had to be ever present for Amber. He couldn't run and hide every time she walked into the room. She had shown her appreciation for his attentiveness with lingering embraces. She cried against his chest never knowing the pounding in his heart was not because of the grief they shared, but because his blood nearly boiled with anticipation of touching her body without clothing to inhibit his advances. Amber was completely unaware of the fire she was igniting.

In her room, Amber stared at the mirror and thought now about the first years of her life. There were such pleasant memories. Those first years had been spent on the little farm outside the city of Aston. She could remember when Lance had first purchased the house she lives in now. She remembered the evening they named it simply Harris Manor. It had taken nearly a year for Lance and Eric Tolliver to make it ready for Sarahlou, Amber and Lance to move into. There had been so much excitement then. Her Grandmama had lived on that little farm for entire life, and it took nearly a month to convince her that they would be somewhere even near comfortable in the city. Lance persuaded her with the fact that he really needed to be near his offices since the work in the yards went on around the clock now, and even then, she still had not been sure that a "heathen" city was a safe place to raise a child. Lance was somewhat inclined to agree with her, but decided with Sarahlou for her main influence in life there would probably be minimal problems with Amber. And he was correct. Amber had thrived no matter where she was.

She had learned much from Lance during those first years. After teaching her to walk and to talk and to feed herself, Lance concentrated on the important things to teach his young daughter. He taught her to smell fresh water and how to treat your elders. He taught her how important it is to be honest with yourself and with the world around you. He taught her how to look people directly in the eye when you are speaking to them, and to expect the truth out of everyone you meet. And if you don't get everything you expect; well, that is just part of life too. "Life isn't always fair," Lance would tell her. He told her that even before she was old enough to understand English. "That's why your Mama isn't with us, because life just isn't always fair." Before she was five years old Amber instinctively knew that you rolled with the punches or you got punched in the mouth. You learn to duck and you didn't cry just because you got disappointed. She learned about the inner peace one finds when one fulfills responsibilities handed to them as a result of their own actions or by someone else's doing. It always felt good to "Do the right thing."

Lance was honest with himself and with the world around him. He taught Amber very early on to be totally honest no matter what the cost. Lance loved the God of this great universe and, although he had no organized method to his devotions, he did practice his own particular brand of religion with a consistency that impressed even the strictest clergymen. Amber learned well from Lance and even at six or seven years old she could size up most people with uncanny accuracy. She took stock of the way her Daddy treated everyone around him. She could talk to him about anything. He was always soft spoken and complete in any answer he gave her. Complete, that is about anything and everything except Inez Chandler. On the subject of her mother, Lance was a closed book to Amber. He wouldn't even discuss her existence. His standard reply to Amber's questions came in the form of an apology. "I'm sorry I did not better choose your mother for you. You do not need her anyway. You have me and Grandmama. Even Eric loves you like his own." A few years later Lance would add the name "Lillie" to the list of people Amber had to love her instead of her mother. Although she never said so out loud, Amber felt her father was wrong. But, that was it; one of those punches fate threw that she had to take on the chin and try not to cry. But Amber did cry; when no one could see or hear her, Amber cried. She cried for the mother she did not know and would never know.

Amber walked to her hope chest and carefully opened the lid. Right on top of her favored treasures was a little sign reading "Lance Harris and Daughter." A friend of Lance's had made the sign as a gag gift for him while Amber was still the wee baby he carried in his back pack while he delivered coal. No one was even surprised when he actually hung the little sign in his yard. It was Lance and his daughter against the world after all.

Now it was just Amber Harris and nobody. She sighed and tucked the little sign back among her cherished keepsakes. Someday she would show it to her own children. Children she vowed to cherish. Often during her childhood she had wondered why her mother did not love nor want her. Lance had no idea how his refusal to discuss the issue with Amber had scarred her soul. Perhaps even deeper than his own. He knew he loved her and had thought that would be enough. But, then no one could have possibly known the heartache that lay in store for Lance Harris' bastard daughter. No one could have predicted the coming torment for Amber. She had been cast aside at birth by an unloving mother, and by far that was the kindest thing Inez ever did for her daughter. The worst things were yet to come.

Amber finished brushing her hair and walked to her bed. She threw herself across the bed and sobbed silently into her pillow. She would be strong tomorrow. Right now she would cry herself to sleep, again.

She did not even realize that she had slept until the knocking at her door startled her. It was seven o'clock in the morning. The knock was produced by Eric Tolliver. Without even thinking about her gown, she crossed the room to the door.

"I'm on my way to the office. Is there anything you need?" His eyes fixed on her green eyes still swollen from crying the night before. Her face was pale and somewhat puffy from lack of rest. Eric noticed everything about Amber and this morning that included the fact that she did not have a robe on over the sheer night gown that she was wearing. He tried hard to control his thoughts and to regulate his breathing.

"I'm fine, Eric."

"Are you sure? You know you can call me anytime."

"I'm sure. I'm going to town myself today as a matter of fact." She took a deep breath and held it briefly before she exhaled, then spoke with false confidence.

"I've got to get back on the ball, Eric. I can't stay in my room for the rest of my life. Daddy wouldn't stand for it for a minute, we both know that." Tears dimmed the bright green eyes and her lips trembled.

Eric's admiration for her soared. She tilted her head back and studied the ceiling for a moment in order to hinder the flow of salty betrayal about to invade her cheeks. She cleared her throat and spoke again.

"Why, even when Grandmama died, Daddy was the first to insist that I get back into the swing of things. I had to attend the school play the very weekend after her funeral; remember? Daddy said Grandmama would never approve of my pouting around. Life will go on for us, Eric, it has to."

"That's my girl," he murmured. He stepped toward her and as so often this past week, she opened her arms to receive his embrace. He took her in his arms and immediately his heart pounded. Her body beneath the sheer gown was nearly more that he could bare. Her hair brushed soft against his cheek as she pressed her face into his chest. Couldn't she feel the pounding of his heart; the warmth in his groin? That warmth that now radiated to his thighs, making it difficult to stand motionless when what he desired was to arch forward so that their bodies would touch in all those special places. His stomach was weak with desire for her. And it was more than desire. He was actually afraid. The mixture of this fear and desire turned into a special kind of torment. He knew things could not continue in the manner of late, but, he also knew that he hated to betray her father's trust in him. And right now she was so vulnerable. She was truly mourning her father's death. She would not be "over" this as soon as the exhaustion of the funeral arrangements was over. She might not be "over" this for a year, maybe never! There had been such a special bond between this father and daughter. Perhaps because he had raised her alone, Eric really didn't know. He did know that he had respected Lance, and he respected Amber. He did not want to destroy her trust in him, nor risk their friendship. Could he declare his feeling without confusing her? God he had to have her. He would have her, before someone else could capture her love or favors, he would have her.

Couldn't she see at all? Surely she was not so blind. She was a grown woman standing in the arms of a grown man. And at this moment his "manhood" was about to declare him nearly insane with desire. The sheer gown rustled softly as Amber shifted only slightly against Eric. The material offered no protection for her body. Her warmth against him branded Eric's skin and brought to attention every single nerve in his body. His voice was noticeably throaty, and, when he spoke, Amber was aware of the difference in the sound. She tilted her head back and looked into the dark blue eyes of the man that she trusted most in the world. She did this without actually stepping back and this made matters even worse for Eric because now her breasts thrust firmly against his already pounding chest. One of the few times in her life Amber misread what she saw on another's face was now. She mistook Eric's look of anguish for one of grief over the loss of her father, instead as one of frustration and desire. Eric Tolliver was not a man of steel. He shoved her from him gently and asked her to sit down. He took another deep breath and spoke shakily.

"I need to speak to you about the business and what is to become of us now that your father is no longer with us."

Amber braced herself for the discussion. The deep breath she drew in again pitched her perfect breasts toward Eric in an extremely erotic fashion. He sighed and drew in his own breath trying to calm his growing need to take her in his arms and kiss her till she fainted. Little beads of sweat dotted his forehead but if Amber noticed she said nothing. Eric placed his hands on her shoulders and was tempted to shake her. Instead he looked into her green eyes and tried to read the emotion behind the misty cloud of color there. As desperate as he was for just a hint of readiness on her part for an overture from him, it was not there. She really had no idea that the warmth of her body against his was enough to make him crazy. This very fact only proved to make his desire worse. If she could entice so completely without even trying, he wondered what she could do to a man if she really wanted to please him. And he knew he could make her want to please him; he was sure of that.

Eric leaned forward toward Amber's mouth. His lips found hers partly open, not from passion, but from surprise and ready to voice a protest that was stifled by his mouth on hers. Amber had never been kissed in such a fashion; and, after getting over the initial shock of his kissing her in the first place, she was again shocked by what she felt and how much she liked it.

His kiss was stronger and warmer than any she had ever known. She was confused and little frightened, and then confused again. She didn't even know for sure if she should be angry or not. Why was Eric doing this now? Didn't she have enough to deal with? Her mind raced with thoughts that had no relationship whatsoever to the lingering kiss. Then, without warning, she was aware that they were standing again and she was pressed tightly to Eric's body and there was an intense heat radiating from his groin area. There was no mistaking the meaning of his embrace.

Amber pushed against Eric and tried to move free of his hold. His arms were around her like steel bands, holding her tightly against his aching body. The small protest from Amber's throat might as well have been a plea for more, because the sound of it served only to heighten Eric's determination to teach her all about what she was doing to him.

His tongue found the recesses of her mouth warm and moist. His hands traveled down the center of her back to her hips. He pressed her closer to him still. She began to think her knees would surely buckle beneath her. She turned her head to take a breath and when she did his mouth followed the lines of her neck downward, drawing invisible lines of heat along her throat. The shoulder of her gown gave way to the slightest tug and Amber didn't even know when it fell to the floor. She again tried to voice a protest but his hands were firm at her waist and pulled her again closer to his aching groin. At this point her own body betrayed her and when his tongue found the nipples of her breasts, they were already rigid with desire. Her shock now gave in to Eric's expert handling of desire.

Her murmured to her, telling her of the years that he had watched and wanted her. He told her of the teasing he had gone through, of the way he wanted her and dreamed of possessing her; body and soul. He begged her; he promised her the world if she would be his. "Amber, marry me. I'll protect you for the rest of your life." His kisses were like fire licking at her skin. Her breath was ragged with needs of her own; desires that until now she had never really dreamed of experiencing. Eric took her hand and placed it firmly between his legs. She gasped at the hardness she found there and drew her hand away but did put her arm around his neck. His hands moved swiftly to her breasts and kneaded them softly, rubbing each nipple until she thought surely she would faint. Finally she pleaded, "Eric, please…Stop!"

"I can't." He groaned the words through kisses one after the other. "I do love you. I need you. I must have you. Marry me!"

This second mention of marriage brought Amber out of the trance she was falling into at his command. She struggled with real force and Eric let he go. He did not want to rape her, just to possess. If she were totally frightened, it would be no good for either of them. He did love her and God, Almighty, he wanted her. Someday if he had to, he would force her, but not this day, and not if there was any other way. At least now his feelings were out in the open and for that he was truly glad.

"Eric, I've never…. I mean I never dreamed that you and I would. I mean I just don't know what you want of me." Her face was crimson from embarrassment as she bent down to pick up her flimsy gown. Once it was back in place over her body she still felt naked against Eric's stares. His eyes followed her now as she moved to a chair and sat down. She was very near tears.

Eric enjoyed this surge of power he had just discovered. He would have Amber, but he could wait. He smiled for the first time. He knelt beside the chair and took her hands gently in his.

"Okay, Baby, I'll back off. But let me court you. Give us a chance. Let me prove to you that I love you as much as I want you. I know you think this is sudden, but it isn't. I have ached for you a thousand times since you were thirteen years old. I have been afraid to approach you. I would have in no way offended Lance, and I have no intention of risking our friendship. But you are alone now and I know Lance would rather see me taking care of you; marrying you, than to see you waste yourself on one of those lame brains you carry on with from school. You have no idea how I have hated to see you walk out of this house with some of those specimens you have picked to favor with your company."

"Eric, the boys I date have all been very nice."

Eric laughed. "Yes, boys! That is my point! You need a man and a grown man at that. One that can make you feel the way you just felt. You cannot deny that you wanted me and you cannot deny that it was the first time in your entire life that you felt that way!"

Amber tensed. "Just a minute Eric! I do not need another man telling me what I feel and how to think. I have got a brain and I intend to use it for a change. Daddy taught me how to think but half the time he refused to let me make any of my own decisions."

"I'm sorry, Amber. I really am. I did not mean to imply for a minute that you're not able to pick and choose what is best for yourself. I only hope you will decide that I am best for you. I do love you. I will live to keep you happy." His face was beaming. His smile was gorgeous. Amber had never noticed his perfect teeth before. All these years she had known him, she had never seen him as the truly handsome man he was. His wavy hair shone in the sunlight that was now making its way through her window. His dark complexion was flawless and his eyes sparkled when he smiled.

Amber smiled and relaxed a bit. What a complex man she thought. And what a man at that. He had awakened more desire in her body than she had known could exist. She thought the idea of a romance with an older man might be just what she needed, but she was smart enough to know she did not want to risk a life long friendship for a silly fling. She was by no means sure that she was sophisticated enough to handle what Eric had to offer, but the adventure in her made her determined to find out.

She asked Eric to leave and he obliged only after he promised to never let her rest until she married him or at least had an affair with him. Amber laughed for the first time in a week and then told him she would meet him downstairs in a few minutes. When he closed the door, Amber turned to face her mirror. There were several red splotches on her neck that always appeared when she was excited or angry about something. She laughed out loud. She touched a spot on her throat as she remembered the hot force that caused the splotches. This certainly was not the silken skin of a roman beauty that had just been aroused beyond anything she had ever known in her life. What this was; was her skin. It was her skin that had tingled at Eric's touch, her skin that now, this very moment, much to her surprise, longed for more. This feeling was new to her and she liked it.

She dressed quickly and brushed her hair till it shone in the sunlight. It was almost fall and already the leaves were stacking up in little mountains out in the yard. Amber gazed out her window and for a moment and remembered how she had always loved to build tunnels in mounds of leaves and pretend she was going to the center of the earth. She took a deep breath and headed down the stairs. She wondered what else life would offer her today.

When she entered her living room Eric looked as if nothing had happened between them in her bedroom. In fact he looked angry. The reason for his sober appearance was soon obvious.

The woman sitting in the large easy chair by the fireplace was a stranger to Amber, however, the woman recognized Amber immediately. She stiffened noticeably when Amber came into the room and it was obvious that she was nervous about meeting with Amber. Eric was furious and was not doing a very good job of hiding that fact. When he greeted Amber, it became obvious he was not going to introduce the woman. Amber decided to speak first. "Hello, I am Amber Harris. Is there something I can do for you?"

The visitor stood. She was tall for a woman and Amber admired the way she had chosen to put her clothes together. The stranger was an artist when it came to accessorizing an outfit.

"I know who you are," she was almost curt. "I mean, Amber, I am Inez Chandler. I know this is a surprise for you, but I read about Lance's death in the paper and I wondered how you are doing."

Amber didn't speak. She just stood there, frozen, as if captive of some horrible time capsule.

"Amber, I know you must hate me. But I tried to see you before, I really did. Lance didn't want me to be near you and as long as he kept the money coming in, well, I couldn't have gone against his will anyway."

Amber looked as if she had been hit full force in the face. "Money!" She couldn't tell if she was whispering or shouting.

Inez was immediately caught off guard. "Yes," she stammered. "Lance suggested the money, Amber, he really did. And he was determined to keep me away from you with or without it. What harm did it do to anyone for me to enjoy some of his good fortune?" Her voiced trailed off into the air as she began to realize that the only word Amber heard was "money." Her face flushed and she looked a bit helpless to Eric, but he had no real sympathy for her. He had watched his friend suffer over this woman for most of his life. And now Amber was to suffer more.

Amber's mind was racing with thoughts. She actually wanted to scream at this woman. "What harm indeed?" Boy, Amber could have certainly answered that one for her. Her mother had been bought off. All the years Amber had doubted her own worth as a person, all the years she had longed for a woman to discuss the things she had heard about from friends, the years of watching her father struggle to raise her alone; all those years were because this woman could be bought and paid for. Her mind flashed to the days when all her friends had shared their lives with their mothers, when she had longed to have a woman to talk with about all the silly things young girls want to discover. How could a woman turn her back on her own child, take money to stay away from that child, and now on top of everything else, just waltz back into the child's life and expect to "get acquainted?"

Amber shot a look at Inez that made her feelings quite clear before she even opened her mouth to answer any question about her desire to get to know her "mother."

"You are about twenty years late. I really am fine by the way, and now I would like for you to leave my home."

Inez tried to protest. "Amber, please wait before you make a permanent decision."

"Not now Inez!" Amber's face was ashen…her entire world was swimming around her. Suddenly everything she thought safe and sacred was changing. Her father had deprived her of a chance to know her mother, and now her she was, admitting that all it took to persuade her to stay out of sight peacefully was money. Suddenly Amber knew she wasn't sure of anything anymore.

Eric read her stricken face and stepped into the conversation. "Exactly what do you want after all these years? Surely you can't expect Amber to fall into your arms at this late date? Why don't you go back were you came from, wherever that is. Why didn't you just stay the hell away from her altogether?"

"What I want is none of your business, Mr. Tolliver." Eric was obviously surprised by the recognition.

"Oh yes, I know who you are. Just as I know plenty of other things about your lives. Lance was not totally innocent in all this. I repeat the money was his idea. He did not want Amber's loyalties divided and he was insecure about his abilities to raise her. There was no way he would let me near her and he was powerful enough to get most of what he wanted, which included keeping me as far away from Amber as possible."

"Just a minute, both of you. Let's not pretend I'm not in the room, okay? I really want you to leave. At least for now. I'm not sure that we have much to discuss but it is my decision."

Inez tried once again to protest, but now Eric turned on her and without any thought to protocol seized her by the arm.

"There is nothing for you here Miss Chandler. Why don't you leave before I get the maid to call the police to help me throw you out?" Amber fought to control tell tale tears.

"I suppose you consider yourself a gentleman like Lance Harris grew to be. Go and get help to throw me out so you don't get your hands dirty. Funny, if Lance had been worried about the rest of his anatomy getting dirty, we wouldn't be standing here discussing our darling bastard daughter, now would we?"

"Get out!" Eric nearly shouted.

"Okay, I'll go. But there are a few surprises left in life, Amber, don't forget that."

Amber's cheeks flushed first red, but then turned snow white as if every drop of blood had been drained from her entire body.

"Surprises Inez? Right now I can't think of anything out of you, life, or anything else in this world that would surprise me. Frankly, it doesn't make a hell of a lot of difference. Whatever Lance Harris was or was not, he was my father and he did his best to raise me. He left me enough to get through this world on and I know how to use it. As for you, you weren't there when I needed you and it makes no difference to me now that you aren't here. I don't need you now. In fact I doubt if I need anybody. I am a grown woman and I intend to act like one from now on. Now will you please just leave? And Inez, do us both a favor will you? Don't try to mess up my image of my father. He wasn't perfect. That is obvious. His taste in women was lousy. But he raised me and that is what counts now. So don't waste any more time telling me it was his entire fault that I don't have a mother."

Inez Chandler made a sound in her throat that could have been a sneer or a groan before she turned and walked out. The front door slammed. Knowing that Inez was completely out of the house Amber sank into a chair and openly sobbed. Eric knelt beside her and took her into his arms. Soothingly he stroked her hair and smothered her neck with kisses.

"Don't Amber; she isn't worth even one of those tears. She won't be back. You certainly stood your ground. I am so proud of you. Please Baby, don't cry."

Amber raised her head to face him. He tilted her head back and kissed her fully. He kissed her with compassion and with genuine sympathy for her distress. There was no lust as there had been upstairs in her room. Amber recognized this and much to Eric's delight she kissed him back. From the depths of her very soul, she kissed him back.

This embrace was interrupted by one Lillie Hasglow. Lillie, a Spanish born lady of around 55, had been the house keeper at Harris Manor for nearly half of Amber's life. She had been around 55 ever since Amber had known her and Amber guessed that Lillie would go to her grave with her real age still a secret. She had come to Harris Manor just a year before Sarahlou died and had quickly become Sarahlou's closest ally. They had been very much alike, Sarahlou and Lillie, both desiring more than anything else to make Lance Harris a comfortable man and dedicated to seeing that Amber was a happy child. Together they had accomplished both. Although technically domestic help, Lillie had enjoyed a position as part of the family from nearly her first week in residence at the Manor. She like so many others was stricken by Lance's passing. And with his passing, Lillie was now devoted totally to Amber's needs. She sought to protect her at least as much as one can protect an adult, from anything that might cause her pain. Harris Manor had been her domain alone since Sarahlou's death and she had run the house smoothly and without a hitch. Today's invasion had left her near hysteria. She had been told of Inez Chandler when she first arrived at the Manor years previous, but she had never laid eyes on the woman; not even a picture. When she realized who she had allowed to enter Amber's home, knowing the way Lance felt about the woman, she lost all control. She was on her way to Amber's side when she realized that Amber already had someone at her side. Very much at her side.

Realizing her presence, Amber straightened in the chair and Eric immediately stood up, looking a little like a child caught in a cookie jar. He smiled at Lillie, nonetheless, and moved to the coffee pot sitting on the sofa table. He motioned to Amber and she nodded affirmatively, saying nothing because she knew that Eric knew how she drank her coffee. There were many things Eric knew about Amber, and she was quickly beginning to realize that.

Lillie was excited. "Amber, I did not know who that woman was. I am so sorry I let her in your home. Your poor Papa would flip in his grave if he knew she was right here in this house." Lillie was near tears as she spoke.

Amber smiled and stood to embrace Lillie. She patted her on the shoulder and soothed the older woman with confidence. "Lillie, there is no harm done. At least no permanent harm. And it is not your fault! Now shhhh, you have done nothing wrong. And as for Daddy, well, he would understand our position, I am sure of that."

"Well, she will not pass through that door again; I can promise you that. At least not without your approval first."

"Very well, Lillie. But please do not worry yourself. I doubt if she will come back here."

Amber had long ago learned that it was easier to go around Lillie than it was to change her mind. And if Lillie had made up her mind that Inez would never pass through the doors of Harris Manor again, well, that might be just as well.

Lillie was leaving the room but she paused again to hug Amber once more and to wink her approval at Eric. Eric blushed. Amber blushed and Lillie giggled. As far as she was concerned there was nothing like the love of a good man to heal a woman's wounds and the Good Lord knew young Amber had many a sore wound lately. Then she spoke teasingly, "If you two are going to carry on that way, you had better close the door."

Amber started to bury her face in her hands but spied a pillow and tossed it gleefully in Lillie's direction.

"Out of here, I say.! Before I decide to throw a cushion through you!" Lillie's exit was quick and graceful. Barely outside the door she called back to Amber, "By the way, Darling, your breakfast is ready and waiting for you…That is if you are up to eating these days."

Amber turned around to find Eric smiling in her direction adoringly.

"We have to talk you know. I really had no idea about the way you say you feel about me. All these years you have nearly been a member of my family. It is hard to think of you in terms of a lover." Her smile told Eric more than her words did though. Her smile said she most certainly could consider the possibility of him as a lover. He moved closer to her and relished in the sweetness of her smell. His eyes smiled before his lips did and he pulled her into his arms gently. "I have to get to the office and take care of business while we still have one to take care of. We will talk over dinner tonight, okay? I'll take you someplace special. Lillie needs the evening to rest anyway; what with all the company you've had this last week. I'll be back around six." He kissed her gently and let her go.

"Already you are taking me for granted. I want to talk romance and you want to leave." She was trying to fake a pout but her lips refused to cooperate and she broke into a smile before she could accomplish the full affect. Eric moved her back into his arms and held her close for a moment. "Never, my love. Never will I take you for granted, not for even one minute of one day. I do love you, Amber. Trust that, please. But I really do have to go to the office and get busy. There are a lot of loose ends that need tying up and a lot of associates that need some reassuring since your Daddy isn't here to talk with them now. The world needs to know that in spite of how awful we may feel, Harris-Tolliver is still on the ball and ready to deliver." He kissed her forehead and released her. "I'll phone you around noon, okay?" He was now in the hall outside the library door pulling on his coat to protect himself from the brisk wind that was now howling around the corners of the ancient Manor home. Amber walked with him and helped him with the sleeve of his coat. He hugged her once more and as she held the door for him she could not help but wonder if the turmoil outside the house was any indication of the turmoil to come to the inside of the house. She closed the door gently and turned in the hallway to survey her surroundings. She smiled and thought briefly about the discoveries that she had made this very morning. She was especially intrigued by the ones that she had made about herself. She could be strong when she had to, and she was quite capable of capturing a real man's attentions. She had finally met her mystery mother and found that perhaps she hadn't missed as much as she had always feared she had. Eric had surprised her but he had awakened the real woman in her. And her father. She was a little disappointed with the knowledge revealed by Inez Chandler but she could handle disappointment a little at a time. And she had done quite well putting Miss Chandler in her place. She mused for another moment about her father before she headed to the kitchen for the breakfast Lillie had promised and for a talk with her. Eric was to be taken very seriously about his ardor for her. She had noticed that right away during their second embrace this morning. She was still innocent enough to giggle at thinking about her own physical attraction to a man's body. Even now, thinking of the ways Eric's body had hardened at her touch, she tingled. She would enjoy exploring the unknown quantities of love making with Eric. She knew she would. But she wanted to talk with Lillie about these things. The time for loving Eric would have to be exactly right and she wasn't at all sure how to tell about such things. And she wanted to talk seriously with Lillie about Inez. She did want to know more about this woman, even if she couldn't face her objectively. Even if she hadn't missed much by not knowing her, Amber would always be curious about the mystery lady.

Amber walked into the kitchen all set to feel Lillie out further on the subject of Inez Chandler. If anyone in the world knew about the things Amber needed to know, it was Lillie. Lance and Sarahlou had trusted Lillie from the day she had entered the household. There was nothing Lillie didn't know. Perhaps with Lance gone now, Lillie would feel free to open up about what she knew of Amber's heritage.

"No Mam, absolutely not!" was the only reply Amber could get out of Lillie even after an hour of begging, pouting, and threatening.

"But why Lillie? Why wouldn't Daddy just let me know who she is? Why couldn't I meet her? It would have been a lot easier with him around than it was this morning."

"Your Daddy couldn't know everything. But he did know enough to keep that woman away from you Amber Child! She ain't anything but trouble for everybody she knows. That includes you child. She doesn't love anyone, not even herself and she is as dangerous as a rattlesnake in the summer time. She hurts people, Amber. She hurt your Daddy so much that he never loved or married or trusted another woman after their affair. Oh, yes, he told me some, but not all and even if I did know, your father ask me to keep it to myself and that is exactly what I intend to do. I've never told anyone what I know and I'm not going to betray his trust just because he lays dead and buried. You are wasting your time and mine. Why don't you go upstairs and pretty yourself up for Eric. He may be back anytime and you ought to look you best for him.

Lillie gave Amber a very knowledgeable look. Amber blushed brightly and smiled sheepishly.

"What do you think of that Lillie? I personally am still a bit shocked."

Lillie laughed and shook her head slightly back and forth the way a person says "no" silently. "Why child, I have known for years that he took a shine to you. Ever since you started to bloom, maybe even a little while before that. It shows all over him every time you walk into a room he is standing in. It all started back when you were still a child trapped in a woman's body. The poor boy would break out in cold sweat watching you prance around here in those short shorts and halter tops. He loves you and he would be good to you. He will be good to you because he loves you and because he loved your Daddy."

"You really think so Lillie?"

"Yes, I really think so."

"Well, I guess we are about to find out. I am going to start seeing him socially. I mean, well, you know what I mean, I'm going to date him." Amber's cheeks turned pink again as she smiled.

"Lillie, I felt things in his arms that I have never felt before. I always thought it would be only after marriage that I would submit to a man's demands on my body but after this morning, I'm not so sure anymore. Lillie, I was ready to make my own demands on my body today. I wanted to make love to Eric. I really didn't know it worked that way Lillie. It scared me half to death but I like feeling the way I did. Do you know what I mean Lillie? Am I awful?"

Lillie laughed aloud and embraced Amber gently wanting to erase her self doubts the way she had done for the last ten years.

"No, no child you are not awful. You are still growing and it is good that you got the good sense to be honest with yourself. I guess you needed a Mama more than any of us realized. You are beginning to be a real woman, and it is time for that. You are plenty old enough to be a woman. In my country you probably would have a daughter of your own by now. Just be careful and do not make any promises that you do not want to keep and do not let your heart be broken needlessly."

Amber sat back in her chair and traced the wooden grain of the huge oak table with her finger. She looked at Lillie with the green eyes that so often had brimmed with tears these last few days.

"Oh, Lillie, it is not possible for my heart to ache any more than it has over the last week. I am over broken hearts for good. They are not fun and I am used to fun. I miss fun. Being this miserable can't possibly be healthy."

Lillie sighed heavily. The she touched Amber's cheek softly with one finger. "Amber, when it comes to affairs of the heart there is never a guarantee. Learn that and learn it well. I will hope for you and I do think Eric Tolliver is good and loves you, but there are no guarantees. I know that well."

"Well, we will see, my sweet Lillie. Thank you for talking to me Lillie." She headed for her room to get ready to go into the town proper. She had much to do today before her dinner adventure tonight with Eric Tolliver.

Once inside the offices of Harris-Tolliver Enterprises, Eric Tolliver was an entirely different man. He was not nervous nor was he unsure of anything. He knew this business, he had grown up watching Lance Harris become one of the most successful men in the state right from this office and he had done his homework for twenty years to enable himself to be where he was today. There were ten other people in the office and all of them respected Eric for his brains about the business and they appreciated the way he treated each one of them, which was in fact the very way that Lance Harris had taught him to treat his colleagues. Once inside this domain he did not even think of the altercation that he and Amber had with Inez Chandler. At least not until he entered his office and found her sitting in a large leather chair looking out the window that overlooked the coal yards. She seemed aghast at the sight of coal dust in the air and the smell of diesel fuel emitting from the exhausts of the trucks lined up behind the loaders. Eric was surprised but he did not allow it to show. He was also angry and this he allowed to show without a qualm.

"What the hell are you doing here? I thought Amber made it quite clear that you are not welcome around here. I second that motion whole heartedly. What do you want anyway? Amber can't possibly be very important to you and your money tree died a few days ago. I won't pay you to stay away. Amber is a grown woman now and you can't threaten me with the same trash you used on Lance for 19 years." She smiled. Something she had not done this morning. "You got a light for a cigarette?" she said.

Annoyed, he lit the cigarette. He didn't know why. When he got close to her and actually looked into her eyes he could see a definite resemblance to Amber. Funny, Amber's coloring was Lance's alright, but the way her mouth and nose were shaped was much like Inez's. Eric mused at the thought of telling Amber she looked like her mother. He decided quickly that doing so would not be a very good idea.

Inez spoke softly.

"Actually, what I want is really no business of yours. Let's just say I'm curious as to how my daughter turned out. Lance did quite well by her I find."

"A hell of a lot better than you did by her." Eric left no doubt of his loyalties.

"How I did anything is of no concern to you. It is obvious that you favor Lance and feel he could do no wrong."

"Not perfect, Miss Chandler. But he certainly tried to do the right things in life. He worshiped Amber and Amber felt the same about him. This is certainly a fine time for you to show up, you know. And YES, I liked Lance Harris. As a matter of fact, I loved him and I feel no need to justify that to anyone, least of all the likes of you. And as a matter of another fact, I love Amber and I intend to marry her if she will have me, so how you do is my concern especially if how you do is going to have any affect on Amber whatsoever! I certainly do not intend to let you hurt her any more than you already have. I hope I make myself clear."

"Well, that's cozy. You already own one third of the company and you can marry the other two thirds. Then you will be the big shot in Aston all by yourself. You won't even have to share the limelight with Lance. Tell me, have you laid her yet, or are you saving that for the wedding night?"

Eric's face became crimson, partly from her candid manner, but mostly from sheer anger.

"For God's sake, I just this morning declared my desire to court Amber. And besides it is really none of your damn business as to whether I have or have not touched Amber. If I have do you really think for an instant I would share the news with you? What exactly do you take me for?"

She laughed in his face. "What I take you for Mr. Tolliver, is exactly what you are and that is almost as corny as Lance Harris was. Maybe that is why he kept you around all these years."

"Lance KEPT me around because we worked our asses off together making this company what it is today. Jesus H. Christ, listen to me. You come into my office uninvited, insult me and a man dearer to me than my own father was, insult the woman I love, your own child, and I stand here and defend my status in the world to you. Who do you think you are and just what the hell do you want? Why don't you just go crawl back under whatever rock it was that you came out from under?"

Without warning, Inez Chandler's eyes clouded with tears. She changed suddenly and her voice broke when she spoke again.

"I want your help, Mr. Tolliver. I know I'm late as hell, but I do really want to know about Amber. I know she will never love me and that is okay. I don't deserve her love. I should have stood up to Lance. I should have tried to buck his money and his power. The courts will sometimes forgive people for being young and foolish which is obviously more than you will do. I have already gotten off on the wrong foot with Amber and I just thought you might talk to her for me because I know she has always been willing to listen to you. I always promise myself I am going to tread softly with people but things just seem to automatically fall into place to make people hate me. I really don't know how I make enemies so fast." She paused for what seemed like a long time. Then she added, "I have no one in the world, Mr. Tolliver. I never have had anyone. It gets pretty lonely sometimes."

Eric was caught totally off guard by her tears and the candidness of her words. She sounded so sincere.

"Where have you been all these years?" he asked cautiously.

"I left Aston twenty years ago, after having Amber and leaving her at the home. I wanted a new start and thought I'd be able to get that somewhere up north. I never planned to return. Things didn't go to well. I worked a few jobs, turned a few tricks for about two years, and when I hit bottom I came back here and looked up Lance. By then he hated me for living and he ordered me not only out of his life, but out of Aston as well. I fought him for a day or two, but he was so bitter I knew we could never make things work out. He didn't believe a word I said about anything. Then out of the blue his lawyer appears and offers me money to just disappear. It was serious money and I was desperate. He wouldn't let me near Amber, I couldn't fight his power, nor change his mind about me so what was the use? I took the money and ran. I lived good and Lance kept the money coming in order to keep me at a distance. When he died I figured I had absolutely nothing to loose by looking Amber up. I didn't really mean to hurt her. She has a lot in common with her father, once you hurt her you might as well forget it. There is no forgiveness in her heart for mistakes made by the young and stupid either."

Eric was really taken by her words. He was really listening. When he spoke, he spoke slowly, thinking out the words as he uttered them.

"You have to give Amber a chance. She is really a warm and loving person. You are correct. You got off to a bad start with her but stick around long enough to let her cool off. And don't pick on her father. She worshiped him while he lived, and now that he is dead, he has risen to sainthood. And there is nothing wrong with that. When it came to fatherhood, Lance Harris went the entire route. There was nothing he wouldn't have done for his child."

Inez dried at her tears and cleared her throat.

"Will you give me some more advice, Mr. Tolliver? Please? Will you help me get to know her without hurting her anymore."

"Call me Eric. I will talk to her. I am to have dinner with her tonight in fact. I will see if I can approach the subject with her then. Where are you staying?"

"No where yet. I can't thank you enough, Mr., I mean Eric. I really appreciate this. I think I will check into the Imperial Hotel here in town. You can call me there after you talk with Amber. Call anytime, it doesn't matter how late. I'll be there."

"Fine, I'll try and make it before nine. Or if I have any luck, I will ask Amber to call you."

"Oh, that would be grand! Thank you again." Inez was suddenly a bit breathless and she took Eric's hand for just a moment. For the first time he really looked into her eyes. The were deep brown and shaped like Amber's eyes. Her skin was olive gold and smooth. She hardly looked old enough to be Amber's mother. He remembered she was closer to his own age than Amber was. Her hair was raven black and she wore it smartly cut in the latest fashion. It was short but curled wistfully toward her face. Her makeup was applied with expertise. She looked much younger than her years and she was ultra feminine.

She was starting for the door when Eric, without thinking, blocked her exit. He stammered for a moment, then asked, "Have you had lunch? It is almost noon and hell I haven't accomplished anything all day and probably won't for thinking about you and Amber, so you might as well join me for a quick lunch and then I can drop you off at the Imperial."

"Oh, Eric, I'd love some lunch and especially with you. You are so kind. Amber is a lucky girl to have you in love with her."

She was totally impulsive and Eric loved that kind of freedom. There was something about the total non-commitment in her personality that was appealing. She was as vibrant as any young woman he had ever known. She was wise and although she did most of the talking, she had a way of making Eric feel he was important, perhaps like he was the only person she had ever talked to in this manner. He found himself really liking her and thought it no wonder that his life long friend had love this woman. Whatever else Inez Chandler was, she was beautiful and she was a woman. All woman. She leaned forward and quickly kissed him on the cheek. He felt the warmth of her body briefly and it stunned him slightly. She was a real woman, not just the ogre that he had always thought her to be. She was not sub-human. She was a real human with a real problem. She had real feelings and perhaps was really hurting. He could imagine himself helping her. He liked the idea. In fact he wanted to help her.

They left the office and walked briskly to his car. He opened the door for her and watched her legs as they bent beneath her to allow her to sit on his front seat. He liked what he saw, then admonished himself curtly. This was Amber's mother, for God's sake and he did love Amber. It was Amber he wanted, more than anything, he wanted Amber.

Lunch with Inez was delightful. They talked about everything. She was open and honest about her relationship with Lance and she no longer scorned nor condemned him. She was just honest about her feelings about being married to a poor man and about being tied down in one place all her life. She still didn't want to stick around in one town for more than a month or two at any one time. She had been nearly everywhere in the eastern part of the United States and had lived out of a suitcase as much as not since Amber's birth. She liked the way she lived and not until just recently missed a family life or some permanent ties. She did know what it meant to be lonely and she honestly had worried about whether Amber would be lonely now that Lance was dead. She was not completely heartless and by no means did she plan to hurt anyone on purpose. Actually she didn't really PLAN anything, not even a trip to the local supermarket.

After dropping Inez at the Imperial Hotel, Eric returned to his office. His first chore there was to call Amber and finalize arrangements for their date. "Date". suddenly Eric was unsure of himself. He felt too old for Amber. Inez Chandler's perfume lingered on his lapel and he could smell its' aroma as Amber answered her phone. The sound of her voice was all he needed to reinstate his conviction that Amber Harris was all he needed to make his life complete. He hesitated and then spoke.

"Hello there. Hope I didn't interrupt anything. I just needed to confirm our date for this evening. You know I have known you all of your life and this is the first time that I will have you all to myself. All of a sudden I feel like I am about to date my kid sister."

"Are you trying to back out on me now, Eric Tolliver?" Amber's voice was teasing but Eric's mind was racing. Why did he feel so out of control. He hated feeling this way.

"You know better than that? I love you but we have a lot of serious things to discuss tonight. I want no regrets for anybody. Can I come by the house early?"

Amber giggled. "You have never asked what time you could come by before, why so formal now?"

"It will be different now Amber. If I come by now and catch one of your college punks there with you, I will want to kill him even more than I have in the past. Amber, honey, will you please take me seriously?"

"Yes, yes I will." Amber tried to pout but even over the phone Eric knew she was smiling.

"Be here by five. I want to try Dorsey's and if you get there later than six you have to wait in line forever. Is that okay with you?"

"That's great. I'll see you at five."

Dorsey's. Lord, he wasn't even hungry after this lunch but then again he figured that neither he nor Amber would have an appetite once he brought up the subject of Amber's mother. God, why did Lance have to die and leave such a complicated mess?"

Amber had hung up the phone and thought for a few minutes before she yelled to Lillie. "Lillie, I'm going out with Eric tonight; what should I wear?"

"Why child, you have been out with men a hundred times and you never ask Lillie for help before. What is wrong with you?"

"Eric is going to be different Lillie. I know he is. Things have just got to be real special. You know what I mean don't you, Lillie?"

"Oh yes, Lillie knows what you mean. You want sex appeal but no sex, that's what you want."

Amber blushed bright red and tried to hide the laughing as she spoke.

"My word, Lillie, is it that obvious?"

"You bet it is, but that is okay, Honey Child. You just be your own sweet self and Mr. Eric Tolliver won't stand a chance. You make sure that is what you want though, you hear? You have had some mighty fine boys come a calling on you.

"That's right Lillie. And boys they were. They have no more decision about them and their futures than my old tom cat does. Eric is a man, Lillie. A real man and I already respect him and love him in many ways. He is my friend, always has been. He made me feel so different while I was in his arms this morning. I didn't know what to do but it felt so good, so right? I think Eric likes being in control. I've never imagined him so strong."

Lillie smiled an old knowing smile. "Well, I sure should hope not! You got no business imagining his strength!!"

Amber blushed again and threatened again to throw something at her.

"You are supposed to be helping me, not giving me a hard time and embarrassing me you know?"

"Okay, okay, let's see here."

Lillie opened Amber's closet. It, like her life until a few days ago, was neat and well organized. Red garments on red hangers; blue garments on blue hangers and so on. Shoes were stored in boxes labeled with colors and notations as to whether or not they had a matching purse. Amber could be dressed five minutes if she had to and took great pride in how she looked at all times.

"AHA, wear this!" Lillie almost made a command of the suggestion. "This" was a simple sleeveless dress in blue knit, cut low at the neck with the bodice hugging the waist. The hem struck Amber just above the knee. "This will show off your shoulders and your legs. Men like skin, Amber, remember that."

"Oh, Lord!" Amber sighed before she giggled and headed for the bathroom to draw her bath water. Lillie laughed and started looking in the shoe boxes for the blue shoes that she knew Amber owned that matched the dress and for the purse that matched the shoes. When she found them it was as if she had found gold after a long search. Amber liked the way Lillie shared her excitement. Lillie had always regarded most of what Amber did with enthusiasm. Amber wished for the millionth time that Lillie had been her mother.

Amber climbed into the bathtub and relaxed in the water. She made a mental list of things she absolutely must get around to in the morning. The things that just could not wait any longer.

On the top of the list was to call her college dean and confirm her return to classes. The dean had been most understanding when Lance died and had arranged with all her professors for her to take her finals in the privacy of his office and all on the same day. She had gone into the finals with a 4.0 average, but finals were the week of Lance's death and when she exited the exam room she couldn't have repeated the contents of even one exam if her life had depended on it. Even so, by the grace of God, she had passed all her tests and was able to maintain a 3.0 average. She had always strived for perfection in order to be as much like Lance as she possibly could. She wondered what she would devote her energies to now that her beloved father was gone. Perhaps Eric, then again, perhaps herself. She thought briefly of changing her major from journalism to business administration. After all she was now two thirds responsible for the welfare of Harris-Tolliver Enterprises and the people that worked there. Then on the other hand, neither Lance nor Eric had college degrees and they had made the business the success it was to this very day. The she wondered if she should finish college at all. No contest! Lance Harris taught you to finish what you start and she only had about thirty more credit hours to finish and she would have her degree. She wasn't about to let her Daddy down just because he was out of sight. Top priority was to go to work at the offices of Harris-Tolliver and start getting acquainted with the way the REAL world turned round and round. The days of Daddy writing a check for her allowance and the covering of her bills were over. She was lucky indeed that Inez Chandler picked Lance Harris to be indiscreet with.

Inez Chandler. Boy, that was a different subject. No one in the world had ever frightened Amber the way Inez did. Amber didn't know why, but an awesome dread had come over her when the woman had left in a huff this morning. Amber wondered if the fact that he mother rejected her so totally at birth was why she remained so confused about how to feel about the woman. She had always wanted to meet her mother, but when the meeting finally took place it had been nothing like her imagination had promised. It was so strange. Inez was angry at someone too, that was obvious. Amber wondered. "Is she mad at Daddy or me or perhaps even herself?" Was Inez jealous of the way life had turned out for Lance and Amber? Did she wish she had stood by him while he was poor? Amber wished for a moment that her Irish temper had not taken over so quickly this morning. But, perhaps it was for the best. Everyone else seemed to think so anyway. Inez probably wouldn't return.

Lillie called from the bedroom.

"Amber, will you quit daydreaming and come on. It is almost four o'clock."

"Daydreaming, I wish!" Amber mumbled low enough that Lillie would not hear. She dried and slipped into her robe. She brushed her hair fiercely so it would shine, and let it fall down her back and wished it were any color but auburn. She dressed quickly, then sprayed her favorite perfume on the back of her neck. She touched her eyelashes with mascara, and decided she didn't dare use any more makeup, took a deep breath and went downstairs to wait for Eric. She had barely settled behind the large oak desk when Eric arrived. She stood up and he whistled, crossing the room to embrace her. How quickly their countenance had changed. Amber had never imagined Eric behaving this way. Amber blushed when she smiled and Eric noticed right away. He loved her innocence. She was so unlike any woman he had ever dated. He cherished the thought of her innocence and ached for the day she would succumb to his teachings. He would end her innocence and relish her always. He nuzzled her neck and breathed deeply as the fragrance of her perfume invaded his senses.

"You smell good, and you look grand, my sweet. Better than you have looked for days. Did you rest today?"

She pulled away from him. "I feel good. And we have a dozen things to talk about. We'd better be on our way."

"Okay Simon!"

"Who is Simon?"

"You are, you know, Simon LaGree!"

Amber smirked and called out to Lillie. "We are leaving now, but I'll be home early, okay?"

Lillie laughed out loud. "Amber, you are the lady of this house now. You give orders, you don't have to follow them. You don't need my permission to come and go. You do that as you please!"

"I know Lillie, but I think I want to answer to someone. I feel a little less alone in the world if I do. Old habits are hard to break. I'm jut not quite used to all this independence yet. I'm not even sure that I like it."

Lillie hugged her gently and kissed her on the cheek. "Don't be late and I'll wait up for you. Tonight and always. Do be careful, both of you."

Amber hugged her tightly before taking Eric's arm and letting him lead her to his car. Once in Eric's car, her mind wandered. It was a typical September afternoon. The leaves were starting to turn, painting the hill sides at least a thousand different shades of red and gold. Once out in the country, the air smelled of new mown hay and Amber's early memories tugged at her thoughts. She remembered the years of her childhood spent on the farm outside Aston city limits. Lance had never sold the land although he didn't personally farm it once the business demanded his full time attention. He had let a family by the name of McIntire take over the care of the place. The arrangement was typical of many of Lance's business agreements. The kind that make your accountant and lawyers crazy. The McIntire family were to farm and care for the property. The were to maintain the buildings in good condition and keep the land healthy. They were to live in the home and treat it as there own. They were to care for the small cemetery where Lance's father and mother were buried. Lance would not disturb them or question their judgment. He rarely saw them over once or twice a year and that was only because be came out to hunt or fish or sometimes just walk briskly through the fields. He liked to feel the good earth beneath his feet once in a while. Their bargain was struck vocally and sealed with a handshake. Just a handshake between two men that trusted each other. And so it had been for the last 14 or 15 years, Amber really couldn't remember. She did remember that the McIntires had one child. She thought a son. She made a mental note to visit the farm to ask Mr. And Mrs. McIntire if their arrangement could stand as it had with her father. She hoped they would trust her as they had her Daddy. She had watched Mrs. McIntire weep at Lance's funeral but before she could make her way to Mrs. McIntire and thank her for coming, she and her husband had disappeared in the crowd. She would go to the farm this weekend.

Eric spoke first. "Hello, Miss Harris, I'm Eric Tolliver. I think I'm with you this evening, however, at the moment I am not at all sure about that."

"Eric, I'm sorry. I don't mean to be rude. I just have so much on my mind ant the afternoon is so beautiful, it is just easy to let my thoughts ramble. I was thinking about the old days, Eric. I mean the OLD days of the farm. When we were still all together, me and Daddy and Grandmama and you. Remember how Daddy brought you home for dinner every evening? I bet he did that for two or three years. Grandmama loved you dearly. I miss them so much Eric. Will the pain ever stop? I have so many decisions to make and I'm so confused. I've got so much to do and all of it should have been done yesterday. And now I have you to consider; and Inez. Lord, she shocked me this morning."

Eric noticed the tears very close to escaping from beneath the inch long lashes that framed her eyes. He took a deep breath and then spoke softly but firmly.

"I am glad you brought her up. Amber, I am going to make a long story short and say simply that I had lunch with Inez today. I was really quite surprised by her in many ways."

Amber was stunned but curious.

"Well, welcome to the club. She surprised a lot of people. What did she have to say? What is she like when she isn't angry? I am assuming she wasn't angry."

Thanking his guardian angel for keeping Amber from hitting the roof of his car, Eric spoke more gently now.

"She is a complicated woman, honey. She is genuinely upset by the way you two hit it off this morning. Don't get me wrong, I don't think she will ever be my favorite person after what she put your daddy through, but I swear Amber, she is human. There is something about her that is downright appealing. I can't explain it, but I found myself wishing that she and I could be friends. You know what I mean? Maybe you should try and get to know her a little better. If you can meet without either of you losing your tempers, I think you would find her interesting, it nothing else."

Amber stared at him without speaking so Eric continued.

"Amber, she swears the money she took was Lance's idea and since she showed up so soon after his death, maybe she is telling the truth. She has no one in the world and you know something, she is actually afraid you might be lonely now that Lance is gone. She was really worried about you and came to see about you, only her own messed up emotions got in the way, just like yours did Baby. I think you should try. It can't do any harm, can it? You're a big girl now. You have a mind of your own and there is no way your loyalties can be divided now. If there is room in your pretty little heard for one more, give it a serious thought. I'm supposed to call her tonight at the Imperial House and tell her if you are interested in seeing her now or ever. I told her you might give her a call yourself. I hope I didn't step too far out of bounds by telling her that."

He hesitated and tried to calculate just how Amber felt about all that he was saying. There was no reading the cool green eyes now. There was a trace of pain or was it anger? For a moment he was a bit worried. Then Amber spoke.

"There is no denying that I am curious about her. I always have been. I'll

45

call her myself. Thank you anyway, but it is about time I took things concerning me into my own hands." Then without showing the slightest effort, Amber changed the subject. It was as if Inez Chandler had not even been mentioned. Lance Harris would never be dead as long as this girl lived, she was so like him in so many ways.

"By the way, I am going out to the farm this weekend. Do you want to go with me? I am going to talk with Mr. McIntire about their staying on at the farm with the same kind of agreement that Daddy had with them."

"No, I have a ton of things to attend to this Saturday and besides the younger McIntire and I have nothing in common. In fact we do not even like each other."

"Why?"

"I'm not sure. Lots of reasons and no reason at all. He is just a cowboy trapped on a farm and he comes off a little cocky sometimes. I guess he is okay; he just isn't my type. We just never seem to have anything to say to one another. His folks are nice though. Old man McIntire was ready to retire when he took over the farm for your Daddy. I figured he would be long ago dead, but I guess he is still going strong and then again I guess the young McIntire does most of the manual labor involved in keeping the place successful. Anyway you go out and see them and enjoy yourself. The place hasn't really been the same form me since your Grandmama quit baking goodies in the oven and you gave up the blue jeans you wore every day for a year. Boy times do change don't they?"

Amber smiled and squeezed his hand. Maybe they did have a lot in common, she and this handsome man.

They had pulled onto the parking lot of Dorsey's when Amber announced that she would be going back to school when the quarter started in January. "I'm not sure anymore about what I want to do. I am thinking that journalism will be only a secondary interest for me and that I am going to start working in the offices right away. But, I do have to finish what I started in school. I won't disappoint my Daddy by being a quitter now. Do you think I should change my major to business administration? I might have to go a little longer and pick up a few things I missed with a journalism major, but it shouldn't be that many subjects."

Eric was instantly excited. "Are you serious about working at the offices?"

He couldn't believe his luck at having her where he could watch her all day long. He could make sure no one else even had a chance to win her affection. He would possess his darling Amber and maybe much sooner than he had expected. His spirits soared.

"I am really interested. I don't expect you to just humor me either, I want you and Mr. Fargo to teach me all there is to know about the entire business. I am very serious about this. I'm already older than you were when Daddy taught you, now it is your turn to return the kindness. I will know everything. I will stand proud in Daddy's tradition."

"Okay! Baby, the very idea is wonderful. We can be together always, working side by side; but, you must know that I am serious when I say that I will take care of you and you don't have to work anywhere. Surely you will want to stay home when we have children."

Amber's heart quickened slightly and she became tense.

"Eric, in the first place we haven't even gotten past the first date, much less getting married and making babies. In the second place, I thought my Daddy would always be here to take care of me too. Let us imagine for a moment that you and I marry tomorrow and have twins the next day, and on the next day you drop dead in your tracks. What becomes of me and twins then? No…No Eric, I tell you I am tired of knowing nothing about how to take care of myself in this world. I am tired of being afraid and not knowing what direction I am going in. From now on I am going to take charge of my life. I really am." She paused. "Do I sound convincing?"

"Yes, you do. I was sitting here wondering why you can't just be sexy and adorable and crazy about me, but you make really good sense." He leaned forward and kissed her gently. "I am living for the day that you will marry me though, you might as well know that."

"Please, Eric, slow down. We have all the time in the world. Let's just enjoy each day as it comes for a while."

Eric sighed and tried to look wounded. "Okay, okay, Simon. Let's go eat. I'm starving for love and affection and you want mashed potatoes and gravy. What a cruel world."

Amber smiled and Eric loved that smile but oddly it reminded him very much of another smile that he had observed this day.

Undoubtedly Dorsey's was built by someone in love. The ceiling was a huge glass dome allowing the night sky to be visible to those below. The windows were open, allowing the evening breeze to drift over the dance floor, bringing with it the sweet smell of Jasmine and Mint that grew in the large garden just outside the main dining room. The indirect lighting was reflected in the mirrors that were suspended from the ceiling by invisible wires. They produced an optical effect that made the rows of glasses above the bar seem miles and miles long. They sparkled like a million stars. The waiters were instructed to make every customer feel like he or she were the only person in the entire room. Was it the soft music, the wine, the atmosphere, Eric's attentive ways or the combination of it all that made Amber relax? She didn't know but she was completely at ease for the first time in days. Maybe even in her life. This wasn't such a bad idea after all; Eric was a good person, he was kind and gentle. At the end of their last dance Eric held Amber long after the music ended.

"I love you Baby, I truly do. Tell me you will love me."

Amber looked into his eyes, tears brimming in her own.

"Soon Eric," she whispered. "Give me time okay?"

"I'll give you forever if that is what it takes."

During the drive back to Harris Manor, Amber actually fell asleep on Eric's shoulder. Eric drove with one arm around her shoulder. He stroked her smooth skin and longed for the day there would be no material between them anywhere on their bodies. His mind raced with thoughts of her total submission to him. He would be careful with her at first, he knew she was still a virgin. He had watched Lance protect her for years and besides, if she had been experienced at sex, this morning's encounter in her bedroom would not have ended without their satisfaction. Her body had told him of her desire for him. She had been surprised by own body and he knew it. He didn't want to hurt her a lot but God, how he wanted to penetrate the depths of her very soul. He trembled slightly and realized that small beads of perspiration had materialized on his forehead. He shook his head slightly and tried to clear his brain. His movement roused Amber. She immediately straightened and asked, "Are you okay Eric, you look funny."

"I'm fine Amber, I'm fine." He wiped his brow with his hand and cursed, "Damn!"

"Eric, what is wrong with you? I'm sorry I dozed off. I'm just really tired. I didn't mean to be rude."

Eric laughed out loud and pulled the car to the side of the road. He set the brake and turned in his seat to face Amber.

"Listen, Amber, I am a man…a grown, healthy man. You are a woman. A sexy, warm, gorgeous woman. You are not just Lance's little girl anymore. I want you Amber, you hear me? I've been driving along this road fantasizing about us for the last ten miles. You are driving me insane with desire and you don't even have sense enough to know it. How the hell have you survived without getting raped by one of those college brats you hang around with? If I didn't love you, I would take you somewhere and rape hell out of you myself right now. But, I DO love you, I want you to be my wife, I want you to have my babies, to be mine willingly, forever, not just for a one time fling. And you tell me you need time, well, God knows I have got lots of time. I have wanted you for years. And I am willing to wait for as long as it takes to win you, but for Christ's sake don't be so damned shocked when you catch me in a cold sweat and my gut tied in knots over desire for you. This is real Amber, very real, very physical. You know that. You felt it this morning. It is time you grew up and faced the fact that if you are going to run around looking and smelling and feeling the way you do then I am going to want you."

He was barely inches from her when he finished. Amber sat literally frozen in her seat. He leaned to her and kissed her fully leaving her breathless. When she spoke she could barely whisper. He was glad. He wanted her weak.

"Are you finished?" she whispered.

"Yes, I am, at least for now."

"Then please take me home Eric. I don't want our first time at love making to be while we are double parked in this dumb car." She leaned forward on her own now and kissed him with fire on her lips. He trembled starting in the pit of his stomach, ending at the finger tip that touched her cheek. "My God, woman, I'll marry you right now in the middle of this road, just say the word."

Amber kissed him again, more gently this time. She was a quick study. She wanted him to want her and thrilled at the taste of salt on lips. The nipples of her breasts hardened and tingled with desire.

"I told you soon. Now, let's get on home."

Eric sat up straight and placed his hands on the steering wheel. He sighed softly and grinned. "Okay, at your service. Next stop, home."

The lights were on in the hall at Harris Manor. Lillie didn't have to speak. Amber had already found the written messages Lillie had left on the hall table beside the phone. One; call the McIntires tomorrow. Two; call Dean Phillips tomorrow. Three; call Inez Chandler at the Imperial Hotel. Tonight, it doesn't matter how late.

Amber's mood changed instantly. She looked at Eric but decided that her earlier announcement of independence was indeed a fact of life she should start work on and, that she should face the issue of Inez Chandler on her own.

"I'm going to call Inez now, Eric. We had best say goodnight for now. Will you call me in the morning?"

"Of course I will. You call me after while if you need me, okay? And, Amber, I hope you will need me. Always."

She leaned forward for the kiss that he obviously was ready to place on her moistened lips. He kissed her gently but even so the agony of desire rose almost instantly for him. He had never been so obsessed with passion and the need to possess another human being. He wanted no other person to be able to claim any of her affection. It was a thought that haunted him night and day. He wrapped his coat around his shoulders and ran for his car. As Amber watched him leave she saw the wind whip at the empty sleeves making them flop obscenely from one side to the other. The sight reminded her of the emptiness that she was now feeling within her very soul. She was afraid of Inez Chandler. She knew not why, but she was. She walked to the phone and placed the call to the stranger that had so recently invaded and confused her life. The voice that answered promised to connect her with Inez Chandler's room. The phone rang only one time before Inez answered it.

"This is Amber. I got your message to call." Amber felt at a lose for words and felt like her sentence was just hanging out there in the air.

"Oh Amber, thank you for calling. Did Eric tell you I talked with him? Amber, please, could we talk again? Just for a few minutes."

Amber hesitated, hoping that Inez could not tell that the tears she was shedding were falling down her cheeks into the very receiver of the phone.

"Inez, I just don't know. To tell you the truth, I just don't need much more turmoil in my life at this time."

Inez's voice cracked a little. "Amber, please, if we had just met as strangers, if I hadn't told you who I am, we could have talked. I know we could have. About who you are and about who I am. Hell, about the weather. I know it is too late to play "Mama" to you, but we could be friends, at least acquaintances. I know I was terrible this morning. I promise to play is straight with you if you give us a chance. What can one time over lunch possibly hurt?"

Amber was still reluctant. "I just don't know."

"Give us a chance and if you say the word tomorrow after lunch, I'll get out and stay out of your life for good. I swear I will."

Amber could hear the staggered breathing as Inez also tried to hide the fact that she was weeping.

"Tomorrow, Inez. I will call you. We can have lunch or something. I have to come into town anyway to run several errands. I will pick you up around 11 o'clock at the Imperial Lobby. Is that okay?"

"That is great!"

"I will see you then."

Amber placed the receiver back into its' cradle quickly to make sure Inez Chandler did not know the little girl on the end of the line was going to set down right in the floor and sob for the mother that did not exist in her life. It was not a good night for Amber. She hardly slept and when she did sleep she had fitful dreams about Eric and Lance and Inez. In her dream all three seemed to be sinking into some kind of mire or swamp, all of them reaching for Amber and begging for her to help them to safety. She stood on the edge of the swamp unable to reach any of them. She could not save them and had to watch each of them sink from sight struggling for air as the ugly mud covered their faces. Near the end of the dream she stood alone in the mud looking for her loved ones and finding no one, she began sinking herself and choking on the filth as it covered her face. Amber woke at the sound of her own screams. She was afraid to go back to sleep. Suddenly she felt trapped but she didn't know why.

The alarm rang at 7 a.m. and Amber was dressed by 7:15 a.m. She went downstairs to find Lillie humming in the kitchen. Amber's "usual" toast, coffee. and juice was sitting on the table. Lillie sat down at the table with Amber and smiled.

"You going to tell me all about it?"

"About what?" Amber teased.

"About last night with Mr. Eric Tolliver, you know about what! Don't be a fresh smarty pants with me, young lady.

"It was wonderful Lillie. I really do believer Eric loves me, but I need more time. I am not in love with him, Lilllie, I didn't even consider such a thing to be possible until yesterday."

"Ah, yes, my sensible Amber. That is very good. Take your time always when dealing with men and the ways of the heart. You got lots of time anyway. I do so want things to be right for you Amber."

Amber looked at the lady and saw the look of genuine love that touched her very soul. If anyone in this world did care about Amber's welfare, it was Lillie Hasglow. "Lillie, did I ever tell you that I wish you were my mother? Did I ever tell you that I love you, Lillie?"

Lillie looked stunned for just a moment. For years she had wished that she had been the woman that gave birth to Lance Harris' child. She had loved him practically from the day he had placed Amber in her care. Never had she known such a caring and gentle man. She had lived at Harris Manor for ten years and had spent every waking moment seeing to it that Amber and Lance had a good home. And she had loved Amber instantly also. The child had been taught manners and kindness and practiced a gentle loving faith in mankind that she had never seen before in a child, or even many adults for that matter. She did truly believe Amber to be gifted in many strange ways and she had always treated Amber as she would have treated one of her own if God had chosen to bless her with children of her own. These words from Amber meant a great deal to her. She finally managed a reply without breaking into tears.

"No, darling, you never told Lillie those things before…I…I love you too, but I, well I never thought of myself as your mother. I would never have minded though. Lord knows I've always thought the world and all of you and your Daddy. I don't have to tell you that I will always be here for you Amber, always."

"You are the dearest person in the land Lillie, and, Daddy thought so too. I know he did. He coached me all my life to treat you with respect and kindness."

There was no hope for Lillie to hide her tears at this point. "Your Daddy was a special kind of man. You remember that, and remember that you were lucky to have him to raise you. You follow in his footsteps and be as much like him as you can. You do that and you will do yourself proud. You really will." Her tears wet her face as she tried in vain to stop crying.

"I know I'm lucky and I feel good about sharing the responsibilities he left for me. We will make it, Lillie. I know we will. Between Eric and Mr. Fargo, I will learn everything I need to know about the business. Harris-Tolliver Enterprises will go on and be as good as Daddy ever wanted it to be."

Lillie dried her tears on her apron. "You bet it will." She smiled now and stroked Amber's copper colored hair. She patted her affectionately on the shoulder and then ask, "Did you get your messages last night?"

"Yes I did. Thank you very much."

"Did you call that Chandler woman?"

"Yes I did. I am going to have lunch with her today."

Lillie bit her lip and her mood changed instantly. "Your Daddy will flip right over in his grave!"

"Please, Lillie, this is probably the only time I will ever see her. She did give me life even if it was against her will. I really want to know what she is like, not just what everyone else says she's like. Maybe I can learn enough to satisfy all the doubts about myself I've had all my life. Maybe nothing and I will wish I hadn't even gone, but I can't just act like she isn't in town. Please try to understand that I have to talk with her this one time. Listen, I gotta run. And don't worry so much, okay?"

Lillie didn't answer Amber; she just hugged her and watched as she almost bounced through the kitchen door.

Once inside her car Amber wasn't nearly as sure of herself as she would have Lillie to believe. But she had things to accomplish. And she would accomplish them. She had vowed to herself to take charge of her life and she was going to do just that. She really had no choice, no one else wanted to be responsible for her life with the possible exception of Eric and she wasn't so sure that she could put up with Eric's hovering over her all of the time.

First she registered for classes at the college. If she got finished before the lines started at the admissions office then she would have time to see Mr. Fargo and tell him of her plans. She wanted to make sure the McIntires knew they were welcome to reside at the farm for as long as they wished. The terms would be the same as those they shared with her father. Nothing in their lives should have to change. She wanted to visit them one day soon herself but she didn't really want to discuss business with them, that was what Richard Fargo did best so she would leave that up to him. Then she would go and visit Inez Chandler. Today was the day. Today she took hold of her life and accepted her fate as it came to her. From now on she was Miss Amber Harris, not just Lance's little girl. Eric had put it aptly last night. She was on her own and the world would have to get used to the idea, including Eric. In fact, most of all Eric.

Registration for classes was a breeze. Dean Phillips was very kind and helpful. As it turned out, Amber decided to keep her declared major in journalism and act on faith that she could learn what she needed to know about Harris-Tolliver Enterprises from Eric and Mr. Fargo. She smiled with the thought of viewing the world from her Daddy's office. Eric was certainly going to be a willing teacher. Her classes this quarter were all in the afternoons and she could spend every morning at the offices. She could take enough hours this quarter to enable her to graduate at the end of the winter quarter. Her credentials were already impressive and chances were good that she could have a job at the local paper if she wanted to pursue it. She really hoped that she could be active enough at the shipping yards that she wouldn't have time for or need a job. She certainly didn't need the salary from either position but she had to do something with her time. She had made Eric promise that she would not just take up space at the offices; she wanted to seriously work and make a contribution to the company or she wanted nothing at all. A college graduate and the executive of one of the best coal transporting systems in the country at 20 years of age; the strict discipline of the parochial schools and entrance into college at 16 was about to pay off. Amber felt alive and good about herself.

She arrived at Richard Fargo's office at 9:30 a.m. She was told that he would be in very shortly and to wait for him in his office. She took a seat while his office girl fixed her a cup of coffee.

The office was decorated in Amber's idea of typical attorney. There was lots of rich looking wood. A bookcase filled with volumes of leather bound books that looked like encyclopedias covered an entire wall from floor to ceiling. His desk was wood also, with a black leather inset in the top. The swivel rocker behind the desk was also black leather. There were degrees proudly displayed on the wall directly behind the desk. On the desk there was a picture of Richard's wife and two children. The children, one boy, now in pre law school and, one girl, about Amber's age but already married with a baby of her own on the way; looked like a pleasant combination of their parents. They looked happy in the picture. Amber wondered why she and her father never had a picture taken together. She wished they had. To the right of the family portrait stood another picture. It was actually an enlarged snapshot taken about three years ago. The picture was of Richard and Lance. They were in a boat and had just caught a huge fish. They were proud of their trophy and it showed. Their smiles were relaxed and happy. She missed Lance so much already! What was she going to do in the years to come?

She sipped her coffee and sat the cup down on the glass topped end table and was about to pick up a book when Richard Fargo entered his office in a flurry. He was a small man but he filled the entire office the instant he came into the room. He welcomed Amber warmly. He was loud but he was not rude.

"Good morning, Amber. To what do I owe this visit?"

"I came to talk to you about the farm and the McIntires. I'd like for them to stay there if they want to and I'd like to meet them if you don't think it would be too much trouble."

"Of course! I'll call Mr. McIntire today and discuss the terms of his agreement with your father."

"I want the arrangements to remain as they are, if that is okay with them."

"Good, I'm sure they will pleased to hear that. And meeting them is simple. Just drive out and see them. Or if you would prefer a formal introduction, I can take you out there myself."

"No, oh no. I'll go on my own. I just wanted to make sure they wouldn't feel I was intruding on their privacy or anything. I know Daddy didn't go out very often and I just don't want to get off to a bad start with them. I'll go out this weekend. I've given a lot of thought to the farm lately. I'm anxious to see how the farm looks these days."

"I know you will be pleased with the way the McIntires handle things. Your father always was."

"Well, I won't take up any more of your time. I'm on my way to lunch. I'll be in touch. I am going to take an active part in the business, Mr. Fargo. Do you think that is a good idea?

"Yes, I do. Your father would like nothing better." Richard hesitated.

"Amber, this is none of my business. I know that, and I say this as a friend, not just your attorney." He paused again, obviously wishing he hadn't started.

"Go on Mr. Fargo. You don't offend me. You have always been straight forward with my father and I expect you to do the same for me."

"Well, okay. Eric tells me Inez Chandler is in town."

"Yes, she is. In fact when I leave here I plan to see her. She is my lunch date."

"You have got to be kidding!" The small man was instantly alarmed and suddenly he seemed much bigger to Amber. His next sentence nearly exploded from his mouth.

"What on earth for?!" he demanded.

Although a little shocked with his reaction, Amber tried to stand her ground without being rude.

"For sir? FOR nothing. She is my mother. She gave birth to me, regardless of the circumstances, and I would like to know a little more about her. Maybe I can learn something about myself. She is not a demon, Mr. Fargo. I am twenty years old. I can handle this, I really can."

"I know Amber, I know. I have no fear of your capabilities." His face was red and he was genuinely embarrassed. "It is just that…she hurt your father so badly. You know he never married and I have always suspected that it was because of her. She is trouble Amber, everywhere she goes she leaves a trail of broken hearts."

"Well, I will be careful. Besides it will probably be just this once. You know I am dealing with a few hang ups of my own over this. I wish Daddy would have discussed her with me. Maybe then I wouldn't be so curious and wouldn't need to put myself through this meeting today."

"Perhaps you are correct, dear girl, but he couldn't. He just couldn't."

"Well, I'm going. When you talk with Mr. McIntire tell him that I'll be out to the farm on Saturday afternoon. I'm really looking forward to meeting with them again."

Amber walked to her car puzzled by the overall concern over her meeting with Inez. Her thoughts changed quickly when she noticed a piece of paper on her windshield. She picked it up and read a note from Eric. It read simply; "I love you Simon. Eric."

Apparently he had seen her car on the street and stopped in traffic to leave the note. She tucked it into her purse and smiled. "He is crazy," she thought to herself. "Crazy and a bit wonderful."

Amber arrived at the Imperial Hotel at 10:45. She phoned Inez from the lobby instead of going to her room. "I'll be right down," Inez had said but Amber waited for nearly thirty minutes before Inez finally made her appearance. And what an appearance.

There was no denying that Inez chandler was beautiful woman. Her figure was perfect and she knew how to dress in order to accentuate all the positives. Her dark hair and eyes shone in the sunlight and her makeup, although more that Amber thought appropriate, was applied expertly. As she entered the lobby she hardly looked forty years old and even young men turned to look at her. Inez flirted openly with all of them. Amber was shocked by her behavior but secretly wished that she had the confidence to do such a thing. Inez walked to Amber and took her hand.

"Hello, Amber. I am so glad you decided to come."

"So am I. Are you hungry?"

"Yes, I am. You have any suggestions for lunch?"

Amber was hesitant but said, "No not really, I thought maybe someplace quiet so that we can talk." Amber had hardly finished the sentence when Inez interrupted.

"Then let's go where Eric and I went yesterday. It was so nice. And maybe we will run into him today. I bet he eats there often. Everyone knows him. It was so much fun being with him."

Amber flushed. She suddenly knew what all the cheap novelists meant when they said a character "gushed." Inez made her lunch with Eric sound like a date and the Liberty Café was hardly Amber's idea of quiet and she certainly didn't want to "run into" anyone. She wanted to talk about her birth and find out a few facts about this woman. Inez stood waiting for

Amber to answer. Amber shrugged. "Okay, the Liberty Bell it is. I hope we can still find a seat."

For all her determination to be in control of her destiny, Amber was way out of her league with Inez Chandler. Lunch was a disaster. The restaurant was crowded and noisy. Several of the people there knew Amber. The women stood and repeated condolences to Amber over her father's death, and the men insisted on an introduction to her lovely companion. The name Inez Chandler didn't ring a bell with any of her father's acquaintances and Amber found herself glad it didn't. There wasn't time to ask any of the questions that she ached for answers to. Amber didn't even know for sure the true date of her birth. She had always celebrated the "approximate date" stated on the birth certificate issued by the orphanage. A small matter, true, but important to her. She wanted to know why Inez hadn't told Lance of her pregnancy, why she hadn't just left her with Saralou instead of making things so hard for Lance by leaving Amber at the orphanage? Why hadn't she married Lance and why had she stayed away from Aston all these years? Amber felt that Lance would not have continued to turn Inez away forever if Inez had continued to make an effort to see her child. What had Inez done to Lance to make him so bitter in the first place? What was so awful that even Lance's friends seemed to think they should protect Amber from it now that Lance was no longer here to protect Amber himself? What was the big secret everyone seemed to be keeping from Amber?

Inez was totally ignorant of Amber's uncomfortable state of mind. She talked about her journey to Aston, styles of clothing and the newest hair dos. It was as if they were next door neighbors that saw each other every day. Each time Amber tried to start a serious conversation about the past, Inez broke into another tirade about either the local tastes or the lack thereof, and even the weather. By the time they finished lunch Amber was not only miserable but furious. On the way back to the Imperial Hotel, Inez chatted about "what a marvelous time" she had.

"We must do this again, okay? Oh, Amber we can be friends, I know we can. You can introduce me to all your friends. This will be a whole new beginning for me." Inez was "gushing" again. Amber had the urge to throw up right there in the car.

Amber sat stiffened and angry. There was no telling Inez how she felt and if she could have told her, Amber doubted that Inez would seriously hear a word said. Amber could barely get a word into the conversation. It was almost as Inez was being this way on purpose. The entire point of their rendezvous had been missed. None of Amber's questions had even been asked, much less answered. None of the pain she felt had been relieved. None of the frustration had been erased. The same doubts and fears plagued her now as they always had, maybe even worse. How could this woman sit and look at her and not even say something like; "Gee, you grew up fast." or "Gosh, I'm sorry I missed your whole life." Something. Anything, almost anything would have helped. But she said nothing. Just nothing. No mention of her birth or the circumstances surrounding her affair with Lance. Didn't Inez know why Amber agreed to see her in the first place? Did her tears and pleas over the phone last night mean nothing? Were they just part of a ploy to get her own way? Lillie had warned Amber. Inez Chandler was completely blind to the way she hurt people, or maybe worse, she knew but did not care.

"We must do this again soon," Inez said as she lifted herself from Amber's car. She leaned back into the car and patted Amber on the arm before closing the car door. Amber hesitated and avoided looking Inez in the face.

"I'll call you," Amber lied. She didn't say when so that she would not make the lie any worse than it already was. She had wanted, no needed to ask Inez so many things. Now Inez was bouncing off to have her hair done with no thought of Amber's pain and frustration. They hadn't even started a decent conversation. Amber watched her walk through the swinging doors of the hotel. "Good bye, Mother!" she said through the tears that streamed down her cheeks. "Good bye!"

Amber sped away from the curb and moved her small car into traffic. A horn blasted at the rear of her car and Amber could see the angry words of the driver. They were mostly about her inability to drive and where she must have obtained her driver's license. Her own hostile feeling emerged and she pushed the accelerator to the floor. She wanted to run. She wished she hadn't been so stupid. Why hadn't she listened to the people that warned her? Only Eric had not given her a rough time when she spoke of seeing Inez. Boy, did she have a news flash for Eric. Among other things she had some serious doubts about his capability of judging character. Christ, he had thought Inez to be sincere! What a joke.

When she pulled into her garage she braced herself for the thousand questions Lillie would have about her luncheon with Inez. She really preferred not to discuss it. She entered the house through the kitchen door. Lillie was no where in sight and Amber silently thanked the Lord for small favors. She thought to herself, taking deep breaths and trying to restore some calm to her nervous system. "I have time for a bath and to collect my thoughts." There was fresh coffee on the stove and she poured herself a cup of the warming liquid and sat down at the wooden table. She looked around the room. The kitchen was a large room with spacious cabinets made of white oak. Lillie kept them neat and orderly, waxed at least once a week. This was as Sarahlou had done things and Lillie, out of respect for her hadn't even rearranged the order of the spice racks. The floor was red ceramic tile and shone like glass. The windows above the sink were huge and open most of the time to allow whatever breeze that might be stirring into the kitchen. Up until Lance's death this kitchen had been the hub of all activity at the house. It seemed there was always someone coming to the house on business and at least once a week Lance had entertained someone of importance. He had enjoyed dining with friends and Lillie had created feasts fit for a king at the drop of a hat on more than one occasion. Her talents for cooking and organizing a dinner party were envied by all who knew her. The windows were open now and the smell of the freshly cut grass blended with the rich aroma of the brewed coffee. It was probably the last time this year that the grass would need cutting. Amber actually relaxed in the chair and stared into space letting her thoughts run in every direction.

How could her life change so in a mere time span of two weeks? Fourteen days? Her beloved father gone forever, her second best friend vying for a love affair with her, and she half tempted to oblige him; actually more than "half" tempted. She had now met her mother and was more lost for control of her feelings than she had ever been. Funny, just twenty four hours ago she had announced her independence. She was going to take control. That had been her plan and at the time it sounded like such a good idea. Now her she sat, wishing she knew how to control her emotions, much less her life. The secrets of the past nagged her every waking moment, the present frustrated her and the uncertainty of the future scared her to death. There had to be some way to solve these problems. Surely everyone in the world didn't feel this lost. If they did the world would surely grind to a halt. Was this part of "growing up?" Admittedly her adolescence, except for the absence of her mother, had not been painful. Oh sure, there had been boys that walked all over her heart, and her ever present freckles had been a source of annoyance all her life, but seriously, between Lance, Sarahlou, and Lillie, she had never doubted that she was loved at least by them and she had never wanted for comfort in any way. Even at the beginning, when times were hard, Lance had protected his daughter from the pain of doing without. She remembered when she started the first grade of school. Lance had the power company contracts but finances were still not as stable as they could have been. He had everything he owned mortgaged and had borrowed even more money on personal notes. He escorted Amber to school on her first day. Once there he noticed that most of the little girls, even the poorest ones, had dresses with ruffles and many had bright ribbons in their hair. He went home and asked his mother if she could sew? When she laughed out loud and replied "of course," he announced; "Fine. I want ruffles for Amber. And hair ribbons too." He spent the rest of the afternoon scouring every second hand shop in Aston looking for a reconditioned sewing machine. In those days a dress for a child could be made for fifty cents and Amber never went to school again without ruffles and color coordinated ribbons. She was amazed by the fact that often when she went to bed her Grandmama would be sitting with a piece of cloth spread out on the table and when she got up to go to school she would have a new dress or jumper hanging on her door knob to wear. She wondered now how many nights she had gone to sleep with the soft hum of the sewing machine in her ears. What love and devotion went into those ruffles. How she missed that dear lady. And after Sarahlou's death, Lillie was every present to serve as buffer for Amber's disasters. Amber though about how hard it must have been for Lance to raise her without a real partner of his own. Oh, financially life had worked out, but there were still so many gaps, so many times her must have felt entirely alone. What do you do when you want to discuss a decision and there just isn't anyone there to discuss it with? Then again why did he choose to stay alone? Why had he made raising Amber look so easy? Lillie and Mr. Fargo had warned her about Inez and she hadn't listened. Perhaps Lance had chose the smart route after all; protecting her from Inez but still it did not soothe her heartache now.

She drew in a deep breath. She renewed her desire to take control. She had to make decisions and be person enough to stand by them, no matter what the cost. She did decide she would never depend on Inez Chandler for anything. She would conduct herself like a lady and ride with the tide. After all wasn't that a pretty good philosophy? And it wasn't too hard to live with either. She must get on to more pleasant possibilities also. There was Eric to consider. She smiled, and then she blushed. Her Daddy was gone and she would deal with her loss day by day. He had been a good teacher and a wonderful father. She had been lucky that he had loved her. Now she would go forward. She had a brain with which to think, a home of her own, she would never have to worry about money, and she could even have a career if she wanted one. Lordy, there were about forty million people in the world worse off than she was right now. She had Lillie and Eric and even Mr. Fargo to care for her. She had a life, responsibilities to herself and to others and she would be busy and hopefully productive. She thought out loud. "I'll miss you Daddy. But you don't have to be right here in my sight for me to know that you loved me. I'll miss you, God how I already do. But very much of you is still alive for me. Right here in this house, your offices, your history, your memory. Knowing you loved me will have to be enough. Inez exists but that is about all. The past is buried with you Daddy. No more futile searches for the secrets that you kept all those years. No more kidding myself into thinking Inez wants a future with her daughter. If she wanted that she would have started it today. I've made it this far in life without a mother. I just don't need any more complications in my life and frankly I think that is about all Inez Chandler will ever amount to. If she calls I'll tell her there is no future for us and is she is foolish enough to question my decision, I'll simply explain the way I feel. I should have done that in the first place. I should have listened to you Daddy. I should have listened." Her self lecture and conversation with her Daddy was over and her coffee cup was empty. She got up to refill her cup and the phone rang. She picked up the receiver to say hello.

"Hello Simon. How's your day been? You find my note?"

"Yes, I found you note, you silly person."

"How was lunch, Amber?"

"Let's just not discuss lunch okay?"

"That bad?"

"Yes that bad and worse."

"Inez seemed so sincere when she and I had lunch. What happened?"

"Nothing happened. That is part of the problem. Absolutely nothing happened. I wanted to discuss my birth and she talked about the weather in Ten Buck Two. I wanted to hear about her and my father and she was too busy trying to start a new love affair to talk about an old on. She flirted with every man in town. It was just awful."

"Darling, you sound jealous."

"Oh, cut the crap Eric. Jealously has nothing to do with my feelings and you know it. Inez and I didn't talk about one serious thing. Like where has she been all my life. Like nothing. We talked about hair styles and who is who in Aston. It made me physically ill. All these years I dream of meeting her and what do I hear? I hear about how good looking all the men in the dining room are. God, why did I ever think I needed her in the first place.?"

"Eric recognized her vulnerability. He could hear her pain.

"Hey, Simon, I'm sorry. That was a low shot. Honest, I am sorry. You in the mood for a movie tonight?"

"No, not really. When Lillie gets back from wherever she is I am going to discuss some things with her. Eric, I've been thinking about redecorating part of the house; to suit my own tastes. What do you think?"

"I think that would be terrific. Course I'd rather you sell the house and move in with me, but if you insist on keeping the house make sure you design a nursery. I hope we have lots of need for a nursery."

"Eric Tolliver, you are truly depraved."

"That is what being in love with a redhead does to a man. It is all your fault. Can I at least stop by tonight? I need your signature on a couple of invoices anyway."

"You can come by, but don't bring any business with you. I'm coming to the office in the morning. I've scheduled all my classes for the afternoons and I am going to spend the mornings at work with you."

"Hey, you got my vote for that. You will love it. You can share my office until we revamp an office of your own."

"Great. Eric, I am serious about learning things. I really think it is important for me. I need your help and I do not want you to leave anything out. I can't take Daddy's place or yours, but I do intend to make a place of my own. Understand? Will you help me?"

"It will be fantastic. You know I will help you. You and me working together to carry on the Harris Tolliver legacy forever. Lance would love it. I know he would. I need the help and who better than you? I've been doing the work of two and a half people around here and you will fit right in. You already know everyone. They already care for and respect you. Your Daddy hand picked every one of them and they miss him almost as much as we do. Actually, you probably have as much coal dust in your veins as I do. You have made me a happy man. The only time I will be happier is when you tell me that you will be my wife."

Amber laughed and Eric continued. "It is good to hear you laugh Amber. I love to hear you laugh. I love you."

His words sobered her. "Oh, Eric," her voice was almost a plea. "You are so dear to me too. I'll see you later this evening."

"Okay, Baby, I'll be there soon."

Eric hung up the phone first. Amber stood holding her receiver. It was almost as if when she hung up she might loose him. Why was she so suddenly confused about her relationship with Eric? He was a dear friend and had been all of her life. She could think of no time that he had ever hurt her in any way. He was handsome, openly loved her and he certainly had awakened in her a desire to be a woman. A complete woman. She respected him. Yet almost as quickly as her mind decided to consider him a lover, something else clicked and warned her of impending sorrow. Almost like a premonition of some sort. But she didn't believe in premonitions. She hung up the phone. "Dumb!" she thought.

The sound of Lillie's car in the drive captured Amber's attention. She walked out to the drive way to meet the happy lady. The back seat of Lillie's care was loaded with groceries. She had been to the hardware store and bought paint rollers and pans, masking tape and new paint brushes. She had stopped by the bakery because she hadn't had time to bake fresh bread or Amber's favorite chocolate chip cookies. She had stopped to pay the utilities and was in hysterics over the phone bill. Amber had made several long distance phone calls the evening of Lance's death and the bill was just now catching up to them. The memory brought stinging tears to Amber's eyes and she quickly concentrated on something else. The last package Lillie produced was small, wrapped in bright paper. It was a gift for Amber.

"Lillie, whatever are you doing?" Amber eyed the bright paper and Lillie suppressed a giggle. Lillie knew Amber had always adored surprises. This time was no exception. It had probably been five years since Amber had received a present for no reason at all and she hurriedly opened the small box. She found inside a small locket on a fine sterling silver chain. The locket was a square with a tiny shooting star carved on it. Inside the locket the engraved words read "Nearly my child, nearer to my heart."

"Oh Lillie. This is so beautiful. Lillie, I love you so much. Promise me you will never leave me. Say you will stay with me forever."

The middle aged Lillie put her arms around Amber. "I'm not going anywhere, Amber. I'll be by your side always. I promise." Lillie, like Amber, was in tears and to hide the fact she tried to laugh and said, "besides, I got no other job offers, you know!"

"Job! Job nothing, Lillie Hasglow! This is your home and you know that. I want to take care of you too. Always!" She hugged Lillie ever tighter now afraid that any moment she might disappear like everyone else that she had ever loved. Lillie sensed Amber's desperate need for someone in the world to love her and was more than happy to comply. "We will take care of each other," Lillie whispered. Then gruffly she added, "Now, help me get into the house with this stuff before half of it spoils and I have to beat you."

Amber released her grip around Lillie's shoulders and smiled through her tears. "Okay, okay. Eric will be by in a while and I want to talk to you about how we are going to redecorate part of the house before he gets here anyway. I don't want him in the way and trying to clutter up my thoughts about this. I see you have already got a few tools to get started with."

"Oh yes. I do, and you will kindly notice that I have TWO of everything. One for you and one for me."

"Fair is fair, I guess." Amber faked a heavy sigh but was actually looking forward to the physical labor of love she was about to begin. She wasn't even sure about everything she would do but she wanted it to be something drastic. She needed to make a statement, needed to leave her own mark on the world and the Manor House was as good a place to start as any. She had always loved being "Lance's little girl" but now Lance was gone and she sometimes feared without him she would have no identity at all. She would make one for herself.

Lillie paused. "Amber, may I ask how your luncheon date went today?"

Amber stiffened visibly. "Actually Lillie, it was awful, just like you told me it would be. Maybe someday I will learn to listen. I didn't get a word out of Inez about the past."

"Maybe it is best that you don't, Child."

"Well, maybe so. As a matter of fact, I was sitting here talking to myself just before you arrived and I've about decided to let the whole matter drop. Lillie, I am a person whether Inez Chandler loved me or not."

"Yes, yes you are little lady," Lillie was suddenly excited. "You are very much a person and maybe it is time you faced the fact that there are some things in life that you just can not change. And perhaps that is for the best too. You are the daughter of a man that loved you with all his heart. You were loved more by one parent than most people would be loved if they had a dozen parents. You just need to believe that and let the rest go with the past and forget it." Her little speech finished, Lillie picked up the last of her packages and went into the house. Amber followed her, wondering if this was how a scolded puppy felt. She didn't mind though, she was glad Lillie cared.

"I think you are correct Lillie, and I can live with a decision to let the past rest now. I really can. I think the more I find out about Inez Chandler, the less I am going to like it anyway. I don't need her, she disappoints me, and I am just not going to see her again."

It was nearly five o'clock.

"Lillie, I'm going to freshen up a bit before Eric gets here, okay? We will talk in the morning about redecorating since it is already so late in the afternoon. I have lots of ideas but I really want your advice before I get too serious."

"Fine dear. You go on. I've got lots to do here. Mr. Templeton gave me a new recipe for cinnamon rolls that I'm going to try today."

"Great! I'll be your taste tester after my bath."

Lillie tried to look menacing but wasn't too successful and she told Amber to "Get" out of the kitchen. Amber hugged her once more before she left the warm room. Life was going to go on and it was going to be good. Lillie was humming a song by the time Amber turned the corner to go upstairs. Amber decided that someday very soon that she would be that content.

Amber rested in the tub full of hot water and suds and daydreamed about her future. Did she want marriage and children or did she want to be a successful business woman and carry on in the Harris tradition? Or was it possible to have both? Actually, with Eric, both might well be very possible. She chased a bubble that was resting on her leg down to the end of her toes before it popped. She had done this several times when she heard Eric's voice. He was at her bedroom door! He called to her as he opened the door.

"Hey, Baby, it's me. Lillie says you've been up here for an hour. You all right? "The door to her bathroom was open and when he realized she was still in the tub, he froze but not for long. He smiled. She was bubbles to her breasts and her hair was piled in curls on her head. She reminded him of the prettiest soap advertisement he'd ever seen.

"Eric, get out of here. Lillie will flog us both!"

"Oh come on, I used to help bathe you all the time," he teased and came still closer to the open door.

"Eric, I'll throw something at you I swear."

"Good, stand up and take aim, okay?"

"Eric, please!"

"You are beautiful. Are you ready to marry me? If you don't say yes I am getting into the tube with you right now." He bent to untie his shoes.

"Eric Tolliver, get out of here and let me dress. I am not about to accept a proposal of marriage setting in a tub full of soapy water. Now get. You are a beast!"

Eric laughed and moved back into the bedroom. Amber rinsed quickly. She buffed her skin to a soft pink glow and wrapped a towel around herself. She was pulling the pins out of her hair when she walked into her bedroom. Her hair fell in soft waves around her face and served s a cloak around her shoulders. Eric stood and looked at her with obvious adoration. She flushed immediately.

"Eric, please leave. For gosh sakes, Lillie is right down stairs. I'll be down in a minute."

Eric didn't leave. Instead he crossed the room to her. "Will you listen to me for a minute, Amber. And hear me well. I love you. Heart and soul I love you. I want you with every ounce of energy in my body. I'll be good to you. I won't hurt you. Not now, not ever." He touched her shoulders and brushed her hair back from them in much the same fashion one would handle a piece of crystal, taking special care not the break it. He leaned forward and kissed her shoulders, her neck, her forehead and finally her mouth. The ache, the desire, the warmth, the love he held for her; they were all present in this one kiss.

"Lillie went back to town. We are alone. Love me Amber," he whispered now hoping to break the spell that was taking over his entire being. He kissed her again, this time using his tongue to force her lips apart. Her mouth was sweet and warm and he groaned as he pulled her closer to his body. One hand found her breasts. Again he kneaded them gently to arouse her. His other hand crept down her back to her hips and under the towel. The skin beneath was smooth and firm. When she felt his hand on her naked buttocks she tried to move but only succeeded in getting closer to him. He held her tightly, kissing her so hard and long she could hardly breathe. He picked her up and carried her to her bed. The towel was nowhere in sight and Amber heard his pants unzip. Her mind raced with thoughts and one of them was to wonder as to how Eric managed to do so many things with his hands at once. She didn't have time to dwell on these thoughts however. Eric's shirt was unbuttoned, and exposing his perfect shoulders, strong chest and narrow waist. His chest against her already sensitive breasts felt good but still she protested.

"Eric, Eric, listen please. I'm not sure I'm ready for this. I don't mean to tease you, I just…"

His mouth was over hers again and both his hands were on her body with soft touching caresses that left little streaks of fire on her skin. He moved his head down. His tongue found the nipple of one breast. He held the nipple between his teeth and rubbed his tongue back and forth over it till Amber began to squirm under him. One hand traveled down to the soft tuft of hair between he legs.

"You ARE ready," he whispered, his voice husky with desire. "Trust me. Love me."

He raised himself upon her entirely now, on knee pushing her thighs apart. Amber held her breath as he laid himself against her. When she felt the actual hardness of his penis against her leg, she panicked. She pushed against his chest with both hands. Her struggle only heightened his desires as he had often dreamed it would. He grabbed both her wrists and pinned her arms down to the bed above her head, this leaving her breasts totally at the mercy of his mouth, his chest, his free hand. He kissed her again.

"Easy Baby, I'm not going to hurt you if you relax." He kissed her neck, her shoulders. He murmured sweet endearments between the kisses. Still she protested.

"Eric, don't please don't. I've never done this."

"I know Baby, I know that. That's the best part. You will be totally mine. No other man has a part of you. No other man ever will." Now he was looking at her. She noticed small drops of moisture above his brow. The moisture at his hair line had caused small wisps of hair to curl. His blue eyes sparkled. All the while he spoke, his hips were moving in rhythmic fashion and each time he moved, the hard protuberance he possessed came closer to actually penetrating the essence of Amber's womanhood. He kissed her again, still holding her wrists so tightly that all circulation to her hands was beginning to cease. She trembled each time his penis inched closer to actual entry. The heat licked at her thighs and she could feel the actual moistness of her own desire that was quickly overtaking her.

"Amber, you want me, you know that you do and I know it. I can make you want me more than anything else you've ever wanted. Don't fight me and I'll let your hands go and teach you how to enjoy this." Amber did not respond. She was frozen in time thinking that this moment would not ever be over. He let her hands go so that he could move freely. He kissed her throat, her shoulders and traced an invisible line down her body to the middle of her abdomen. His kisses lingered a moment at her navel and when his mouth moved to her thighs, she cried out in shock. Again he murmured endearments to her. His hands were holding her thighs apart as he slowly and deliberately kissed every inch of her skin. He worked slowly up from her thighs, one hand expertly exploring her vagina. When her legs no longer needed force to keep them apart, he directed full attention to the now moist outlet of her passion. He looked at her once more before his actual attack on her clitoris. Her face was flushed, her cheeks streaked with tears, but yet there was a resolute look that told him that she was resigned to losing her virginity here and now. She would protest more yet, even beg, but he would not have to rape her forcibly. She was afraid, probably of everything; the pain of his entry, his follow through to his own ejaculation and maybe even of getting pregnant. He wondered for a fleeting moment if it would be possible to leave her pregnant this very first time, this very night. God he hoped so. He would still those fears now. His fingers found her clitoris already rigid from the teasing of her breasts with his mouth and hands. Her thighs, like every muscle in his own body, were tight with anticipation. She was moist and warm and he intended to make her want him to take her. He wanted her to need his entry into her soul as much as he needed it. He moistened his fingertips and gently touched her over and over causing her to squirm beneath his touch. He smiled. Without warning he bent forward and began to probe her clitoris with his tongue. He wanted to taste all of her. Amber froze in time. She thought surely her heart would stop beating. His tongue moved back and forth, working her into a frenzy of need. She groaned when his hands moved back to her breasts. His fingers found her nipples already rigid and throbbing. He could feel the pounding of her heart. This was the way he had wanted her for years. Now she would be his. Now she knew the meaning of desire. The muscles of Eric's body ached as he tried to control his mounting passion. He began a journey back up her body, leaving invisible traces of heat against her skin with his kisses as he moved back into a position that would leave his pounding groin against her thighs. He kissed her fully on the mouth, using his tongue now to explore the sweetness of her mouth. She kissed him back, now placing her hands at the small of his back.

"Hold my hips," he whispered to her.

"Oh, god, Eric," she was silently weeping.

"Don't fight it Amber. I'm going to take you now. We can't turn back now, even if I wanted to and I don't want to. Let me do it now while I have enough control left in me to be gentle. I don't want to hurt you. Let me take you now, while I can be slow. Hold me Baby, hold me tight!" His voice was almost a groan, desire claimed his soul, and the perspiration had started to form little streams running down the side of his face. He maneuvered his hips back between her thighs. The weight of his body kept her legs apart and his penis lay at the entrance of her vagina. She tried to back away but the bed held her fast against him. When she stiffened, her breasts arched against his chest even more firmly. The hair on his chest tantalized her now sensitive nipples even further.

"It's now baby, it has to be now!" He had already felt the wetness of her desire with the head of his penis. "You are ready, I have made you ready. It won't hurt for very long." He began to inch his way into her. She gasped, not moving, tears wetting her face and falling onto the pillow. He kissed her. "I love you. I will be your slave if you want. But I am going to have this, whenever I want, I am going to have this. Help me. Take hold of my hips and pull yourself closer to me. Come on. Pull me!" Amber followed his instructions, trembling uncontrollably. "Good! Good!" he groaned. His penis came against her virginity and she cried out in pain.

"Hold on Amber, hold on."

"Eric, it does hurt. Stop, please stop."

"NO, not now, no way." His breathing was irregular and sweat now ran freely down both sides of his face. Droplets fell on Amber's neck and on the pillow. He withdrew a tiny bit and relaxed the weight of his chest against her, he kissed her with fire and the passion he had held for her since he had been a teenager. Just as Amber relaxed, thinking that he had indeed decided to let her remain a virgin, Eric plunged himself through her hymen with such force that she stopped breathing. A burning pain ripped through her flesh and she begged him to stop. Warm blood oozed from her slowly.

"The bad part is over, Baby. Hold me now. Relax. Give, give." He began to move back and forth inside her with forceful strokes, his throbbing fullness filling her completely, each stroke hurting only slightly less than the one before. He watched her face. The fear, the pain, the tears; it was glorious! "Help me, Baby," he moaned.

"No Eric, please let me go!" There was desperation in her voice. Eric raised and thrust himself deep within her causing a brand new pain and then stopped, holding himself deep inside her, knowing she was in pain. He looked as she had never seen him before. He breathed deep and slowed to calm himself. The he spoke to her softly. "Amber, the worst is over. Relax; let me show you how beautiful this can be. You did want me, I know you did. You know you did. You can't go back to being a virgin now, even if we stop and never start again. For God's sake let me make your first time a beautiful memory. Don't end it like this. Baby, I'm shaking all over from just trying to be good to you. I am not going to leave you feeling bad, I'm not. Help me though. God, I need you, damn you I need you now!" With these words he thrust himself yet deeper into her if that was possible. She ached and could feel the throbbing of his manhood move even deeper. He kissed her neck and nuzzled his face into her hair, drinking the scent he had loved for so long.

"My God, how I love you. I have loved you for years. I'll never hurt you." His eyes were azure pools. His mouth smiled before it came down on hers again. He kissed her gently, waiting for her to respond before he began to move within her again. The aching of his need was making his skin chill and then turn hot again. She returned his kiss. His tongue parted her lips and this time it was her tongue that explored, much to his delight. "It's going to be good, Baby!" he said.

She looked at him, still crying. Eric nibbled at her earlobe and his breath came more labored and hot. "I want you to say it. Say 'now', Amber. Say it. Don't let me down now, please."

Amber kissed him fully. In a voice that was barely a whisper she submitted to his power. "Now.", she said. Then a statement that was more a plea than a command, she said, "Eric, do love me, love me forever. Don't leave me alone anymore."

"Oh, Baby, Baby," he groaned as he began to move again, in and out, gently at first, then with more and more force. His passion climbed to heights of ecstasy he had known with no other woman. Amber was the first virgin he had ever taken; all the more reason to worship her, but he was better fulfilled by the overwhelming power he felt. His expert handling of his mounting desires was about to give way to his own animal need. His body was bathed in sweat and he clung to Amber tightly. Her world too, was filled with excitement. Her body had become radiant with desire. She wanted the intrusion of his body into her, and had become enthralled with the fullness between her thighs. She had begun to meet his rhythmic thrusts, pumping her hips with a new found courage and force. She trembled as climax approached, never dreaming anything between man and woman could be so fulfilling. She began to throb and could no longer move. Eric felt her throbbing heart and began to moan. A few more thrusts and his own orgasm began bringing his soul down like an avalanche falling from a mountain top, slowly at first and then picking up momentum and speed as it nears the valleys. He thrust himself once more; hard, deep within her and let himself go, leaving himself deep inside her womanhood. He collapsed on her body and did not withdraw from her as the life forming fluid oozed from his body into hers. He lay atop her keeping his semen deep within her, hoping that she would this very first time at lovemaking become pregnant. He so wanted to possess her always, to leave his visible mark upon her forever. Amber lay beneath him, breathing hard, face flushed, eyes closed. He had totally satisfied her needs. The needs he had so skillfully created. There was still some burning between he legs, but she was now too content to become overly alarmed by that. Amber felt Eric's weight shift as he finally withdrew from her. She opened her eyes to find him looking down at her. He kissed he brow, her eyelids, her nose. "I love you," he whispered. The full realization of what they had just shared hit Amber full force and her eyes clouded with tears again. Before she could speak, Eric put his finger to her lips. "Shhh, don't Amber, don't spoil any of this. There is nothing wrong here. We enjoyed this. Amber, I love you and I have loved you for years. I'll marry you and I'll protect you. I'll never ever forsake you. Trust me. No piece of paper could have made the way we feel any more sacred. Please, Baby, don't tell me you're sorry. It will break me into pieces if you do. Please, don't be sorry."

Amber's lips trembled but she smiled. Eric kissed her gently. Her moist skin felt cool now against his heated chest. She kissed him now with more confidence than even she knew she had. Her desires had been created and fulfilled by this man. His skills at lovemaking were indeed beautiful and she was no longer afraid of commitment to him. Eric was aroused by her touch, by boldness of her kiss. His hands traveled back to he firm, still aching breasts and then to her hips. His passion had produced the same rigid fullness as before, begging for release. This time when he mounted her, he neither begged nor coaxed. He placed his hands beneath her hips and pulled her body up and against him with one swift movement. He slammed his manhood into her with no mercy this time. The entry caused less pain but still burned.

He licked her nipples and tugged at them with his teeth, hurting her yet thrilling her at the same time. Amber became moist enough to readily accept his second penetration into her flesh. Eric's movements were deliberate and forceful now. Their souls soared together to heights of ecstasy they were sure no one else would ever know. Their climax came together leaving them totally exhausted. They lay limp on one another's arms and fell into sweet, restful sleep. Before drifting into sweet slumber, Eric's only thought was that he had for the second time this hour poured his semen into his beloved Amber. He was delighted. He would never protect her from pregnancy.

Amber woke in a darkened room. Eric was gone! Her heart leaped. How long had she slept? Where was Eric? Why had he left without waking her? She rose from the bed and wrapped the sheet around her naked form. Her soreness and the blood stained sheets were a stark reminder of the evening's events. Her mind weak with apprehension, she made her way to her bathroom. She showered quickly, put on her favorite robe and cautiously crept downstairs. It was just past midnight but all the hall lights were on. Apparently Lillie was in bed. She made her way to the kitchen where she found freshly baked cinnamon rolls and fresh coffee. The coffee was warm. There was one rose in a bud vase on a tray sitting in the middle of the table. There, in a chair, slumped over the table lay Eric, face down on his arms. He was sound asleep. He was fully dressed and unlike Amber, he looked calm and relaxed.

"Eric?" The word came from her throat a hoarse whisper. He raised his head and smile. "Eric, what is going on?" Amber was trembling and very nervous. He rose from the chair and walked to her.

"Amber, Baby, I've been waiting for you to wake up, that's all. I got up so Lillie wouldn't find us together in bed. She is out with Mr. Templeton from across the street. She said she would be late and I didn't want you to wake up in the house alone. Besides I wanted to see you again. I didn't want to leave without telling you how much I love you and to thank you for what we shared tonight. It was beautiful and so are you." Amber's face became scarlet at the very mention of their lovemaking.

"Oh, Eric, I am so confused."

He was holding her now, pressing his hard body close to hers once more. She did enjoy the warmth he stirred within her.

"You are not confused. You are a woman. A wonderful woman. And tonight you discovered what love can be like." He kissed her softly. She looked up and smiled at him. "Are you hungry?" he asked. Surprisingly she was. "Yes, yes as a matte of fact I am starving." Eric laughed with her.

"Sex does that to you. James Bond always ate a bowl of corn flakes after he ravished his damsels. Myself; I prefer cinnamon rolls and coffee." He poured coffee and bowed gracefully to Amber. Amber laughed and hugged him.

"Eric," she smiled at him. "I'm not sorry. Scared to death, but not sorry."

He looked down at her reverently. "Thank you, Baby, thank you." He held her close and sent silent prayers of thanks to the powers that be for his darling Amber. She was his and his alone.

Days turned to weeks and weeks to months. Amber's days were busy with learning the shipping business inside and out. And she was sharp too. Many times Eric smiled with pride at the way she handled herself at a meeting or a bargaining session. Her classes were easy for her, and her nights were filled with bliss. She loved Eric and had become almost as anxious for their lovemaking as he was.

She heard from Inez only twice during the months leading up to Christmas. Inez called a week after they shared lunch. She wanted Amber's company on a shopping trip. Amber lost the nerve to tell her the truth and made up an excuse for not joining her at the new shopping center. Then about a week later, Inez called again to ask Amber is she could borrow some money. Amber had stood frozen to the phone. She had talked to this woman a total of four times and this fourth time, the woman wanted money. Amber met Inez in the coffee shop of the Imperial Hotel. "Where are you going Inez?" Amber ask weakly, almost afraid Inez might tell her the truth.

"Oh Amber, honey, I'm not even sure myself yet. I'm going back to New York for now though. Then maybe out west for a while. I'll send back your money as soon as I get settled."

"Forget it," Amber said. "Just consider it a going away gift."

"Inez laughed. "Seems like I'm always on my way out of this town."

"Yes and out of my life," Amber thought but dared not say it out loud for fear the sadness of her heart might leak out to her voice. Inez sensed Amber's very thought and blushed.

"Well, you don't really need me much anyway. We certainly don't have much in common, now do we?"

"No, I guess not."

"Well, thanks for the loan," she was getting up to leave the table.

"I told you to consider the money a gift." Amber paused and then almost as an afterthought she added, "Good-bye, Inez."

"So long Amber. You're a nice kid. You really are."

"I'm not a kid, Inez, I haven't been for some time now." Amber didn't even know why but for some reason it seemed important to establish her adulthood, especially now. Inez didn't notice, like so many other things about Amber she never noticed.

"Well, anyway, whatever, you are really nice."

And that was the end. Without ceremony or care, Inez Chandler turned and walked out of Amber's life with no more regard that if Amber had been any other stranger. Amber sat for a few minutes awed by the total lack of commitment Inez seemed to have toward anyone or place or thing. Amber was still puzzled by the first phone call she had received from Inez begging for the chance for them to get to know each other. And what about the way she had talked when she had lunch with Eric? Was this all some sort of show for someone else's benefit? How could she change so drastically so often? When she did have a chance to really talk to Amber, their relationship had been the farthest thing from Inez's mind. Amber was still sitting in the coffee shop when Inez breezed through the revolving door, hailed a cab and rode away. It had been surprisingly easy for Amber to watch her go. She did not weep. Her own self doubt was gone. It truly no longer mattered that her mother did not love her and never had. Amber took a deep breath, finished her coffee, and returned to work. It was done.

With Lillie's help, Amber re-did two thirds of Harris Manor in colors and materials and furniture that suited her own new image of herself. Only the kitchen, library/den, and Lance's bedroom escaped Amber's changes. The kitchen was Lillie's domain and Amber let her do as she pleased with that room. The library/den and Lance's bedroom remained exactly as he left them and served as part of Amber's own shrine to his memory.

Classes were boiling down to graduation and she would graduate with enough honors to make Lance Harris proud indeed. She would begin working for the Aston Daily Newspaper in the spring. She would write a small column which would publish once a week. It would be enough to keep her style sharp but not enough to make her so busy that she neglected Harris-Tolliver Enterprises. In fact nothing would ever make her so busy that she would neglect the business that was now so much a part of her life. At last she understood why her father and Eric could work till far past midnight on bids and cost estimates. She knew the thrill of bid openings that announced her company the winner of contracts that had taken a thousand hours to prepare. She walked with pride into her office daily and looked each morning out over the very coal yards she had played in as a child. The noise and the dust never bothered her. Then she would look across the hall to the door bearing the name of the man that put the finishing touches on her growth into adulthood. She was very happy.

The first year anniversary of Lance's death was marked with sadness by all who had known him. Amber wept when the office staff wore black arm bands to again announce their mourning of the fall of their leader. That autumn rushed upon them even faster than the last one had, and before she even had time to notice, November and Thanksgiving gave way to the Christmas rush. Both Lillie and Amber loved Christmas and this year would not be dimmed as last year had been. The entire house testified to the fact that Lillie loved to decorate for Christmas. Eric was drafted to put up the outside lights and though he complained the entire afternoon about it being "too early for all this," as soon as it got dark, it was Eric that insisted that Lillie and Amber be at attention out in the yard as he threw the switch to turn on the lights. He stood proudly as the colored lights formed a bright halo around the entire house. He hugged Lillie tightly, and when he turned to take Amber in his arms he noticed the mist of tears that clouded her vision. His sensitivity to Amber was extremely keen. He took her in his arms and whispered, "Don't cry, Baby. Our missing out on the joys of life won't bring Lance back to us. We skipped last Christmas because it was so soon after we lost him, but now, well, now it has been over a year and it is time we enjoyed what is left of our lives. Lance would be the first to say so, you know that."

Amber raised her head and looked at him. The colored lights behind them cast a glow around Eric that made him seem almost angelic. They had been sleeping together for nearly a year. The flowers, the small gifts, the notes, the constant, adoring attention that he gave her were unbelievable. In bed he took her to heights of ecstasy that most women only dream of. He was forever attentive and never demanding, or at least he hadn't been lately. His eyes sparkled and his wavy hair was a bit tousled by the breeze. A soft snow was beginning to sprinkle them. Lillie had run into the house and put on a Christmas album on the stereo and the yard was bathed with soft music proclaiming the joy of Christ's Birth. A snow flake landed on one of Eric's eyelashes and Amber tiptoed to kiss it away. She then looked him in the eye and smiled as a solitary tear rolled down her cheek. "Eric Tolliver," she said with her voice trembling with emotion, "Is it too late in our relationship to tell you that I love you?"

Eric's face froze for a moment. He looked as if he had just seen an angel. "Amber, I have waited over half of my life to hear you say those words." He laughed, he picked her up and swung her around and around in the yard. The he let out a yell that would wake the dead and indeed it did bring Mr. Templeton from across the street out onto his porch.

"Eric! SHHHH!" Amber tried in vain to quiet him. "You will disturb the whole neighborhood!" But she was too late.

"Hey, Mr. Templeton. She loves me. She just said so. Come on over. We're going to celebrate. I am anyway. Lillie has got hot chocolate already poured. Come on over! She loves me! She is going to marry me!" He stopped suddenly. "Oh, my God! You are going to marry me aren't you? Tell me right now or I'm going to drop dead so help me. Right here in front of you on your own front lawn. It will be all your fault. Say yes, Baby, God, please tell me yes!"

By now Lillie was back outside to investigate the racket. Amber laughed. "Yes, yes, yes. Now will you be quiet? Before we get arrested for disturbing the peace." Eric grabbed her, kissed her and then very seriously thanked his patron saint in heaven above for is good fortune. Amber watched him for a moment as he actually said the prayer, then she bowed her head and also said simply, "Thanks."

They spent the rest of the evening singing Christmas carols with Lillie and Mr. Templeton. They discussed when they would get married. They decided they would enjoy one special occasion at a time. Amber's graduation would be December 9th, then Christmas and New Year's Eve and they would marry in early spring. The sooner the better as far as Eric was concerned. Lillie had the social event of the year planned in fifteen minutes. She was thrilled by the idea of their marriage. She liked Eric and she knew he loved Amber, although she noticed with some uneasiness a very possessive attitude in Eric sometimes. But, perhaps in this ever changing age that was natural. His love for Amber could overcome what faults he might have and he really was basically alright in Lillie's book. Even Mr. Templeton was caught up in the excitement of the evening and even got so bold that he actually hugged Lillie in from of Eric and Amber. Lillie immediately scolded him for all she was worth, but everyone present knew that she truly loved his attention.

Amber graduated quietly, with honors and the editor of the newspaper eagerly awaiting her first installment of her column. Never mind waiting until spring he had said. We have room for your talent now. The Christmas season was in full swing and was as perfect as any Christmas season could be. A foot of snow fell over Aston two weeks before Christmas and the Yule Spirit had a hold on nearly everyone Amber met. Amber shopped with care for all her favorite people. For Lillie a golden locket much like the one that Lillie had given to her. Inside the locket were the words "More that a mother, my friend." She had also bought her a coat with gloves, purse, hat, and boots to match. And to top that off she bought a small television for the kitchen. Lillie loved the new soap operas and now she wouldn't have to miss anything while she was busy in the kitchen. And Amber figured that Lillie would be busy once she and Eric were married in the spring. Already they entertained business associates together and many times it was at the Manor House and if not for Lillie and her talents, Amber had no idea what she would do.

She and Eric had decided together to share their joy with everyone that worked for Harris-Tolliver Enterprises. Business was fantastic and profits were nearly doubled compared to the figures of the previous year. They decided to give every employee a one thousand dollar bonus check with his or her paycheck on the payday just before Christmas. Even their payroll officer didn't know about the surprise. They hand wrote and signed every check and slipped them into the pay envelopes. It was truly like playing Santa Claus and Amber loved it. They had worked to nearly three in the morning to accomplish their good deed. They came to work on payday a planned two hours late. When they did arrive they were greeted with a standing ovation by the office personnel. Later in the day Amber received a dozen red roses along with a bottle of scotch for Eric from the yardmen and truck drivers. The entire day was festive and everyone reminded each other to be thankful for their blessings.

Amber bought Richard and Mrs. Fargo new luggage. The Fargos were leaving in January on their second honeymoon. Married for forty years, they had never been out of the state except while Mr. Fargo served in the Army and now it was their children who were giving them the much deserved vacation. Amber hoped her marriage would be much like theirs. Amber didn't want to wish her life away but she couldn't help but hope for the day when her love would be forty years old and still going strong. How very reassuring that must be for Mrs. Fargo.

She bought Mr. Templeton a new Bible with his name engraved in gold on the cover. It was one of the editions with the very large print. Mr. Templeton had become very casual as of late and spent more and more time sitting at the kitchen table at the Manor House. Amber had overheard Lillie reading to him in the parlor many times. She had heard Mr. Templeton say how much he enjoyed reading his Bible but lately "they just don't print things as big as they used to." When Amber showed the Bible to Lillie she had been thrilled. Amber was letting Lillie know that she approved of Mr. Templeton's presence at the house so often. Lillie was by no means in love with Mr. Templeton, but she certainly did enjoy his companionship. Or did she love him?

Amber had shopped for several days for the McIntires. They had fast become friends in the year since her father's death. Amber had visited them at least once a week and liked them very much. Jack McIntire seemed ancient and was much like she imagined her father would have been if he had lived to be an old man. For him she bought a pipe rack and multi-colored afghan for him to snuggle in while napping on the couch. "He falls asleep on the couch in the winter and under the oak tree in the summer,"

Ada had said on nearly every visit. For Ada she had chosen a bright red and white checkered tablecloth for her country style kitchen. She also bought her a sewing basket that doubled as a foot stool. She knew Ada would be delighted with it. The young Mr. McIntire proved to be somewhat difficult to buy for considering that she had never actually met him. Although her visits were at least weekly, Jason McIntire was always tied up somewhere on the farm or was in town taking care of business, or away at some horse show or auction or something. She finally decided on his gift anyway.

She bought him a statue of a mare with her new foal. It was bronze and she loved it herself. She hoped he would enjoy it and told him so in the polite but friendly note that she attached to the package. She teasingly addressed it to the Phantom McIntire. And on the day that she delivered her treasures, he was gone as usual. She laughed and told Ada that she was really beginning to believe that Jason was a figment of their imaginations. They laughed with her and presented her with a gift for herself and for Lillie. It was a basket full of canned goods from the farm. It had canned green beans and corn and pears and home made jellies and jams. There were pounds of homemade cookies and candies. Also for Amber, there was a picture that Ada had found in an antique shop. The picture was of a large man and a tiny girl walking down a path through some trees. They were holding hands and the man was pointing at something in the trees for the little girl to see. "It reminds me of you and your Papa," Ada said. Amber knew right away she would treasure this picture always. She hugged Ada and was not ashamed of the tears that escaped her eyes.

"Thank you, I can't wait to show Lillie. I'm so glad I have gotten to know you both. You are such good people."

"You come here anytime, Amber. You are family. This is your home too, you know. You were a babe learning to walk right here in this kitchen and my how you did strut. You remember that, when all else goes wrong you can come home to your roots and gather your thoughts. Remember what I'm saying to you now, you hear?"

Amber smiled and hugged the wonderful woman again. "I hear Ada and I thank you."

When Amber arrived home, she hung the picture up in the library where she spent much of her time when at home. Lillie was impressed by the picture and delighted with the basket of goodies. She would taste something and immediately call Ada for the recipe. By the end of the week, Ada had spent at least an hour a day on the phone with Ada. The two ladies were much alike, thought Amber one day after she overheard Lillie talking with Mrs. McIntire.

For Eric's gift Amber had thought and shopped for weeks. She wanted something really special for him. She had already purchased a watch for him but she couldn't stand keeping it a secret and had already given it to him. The words "Beloved Teacher" were engraved on the back of the watch and she had watched Eric swell with pride as he slipped it on his wrist. She had been glad she had given it to him in private, but now she was at odds with what to buy him for Christmas morning and now the day was only a week away. He practically lived at Harris Manor now and he would be moving in publicly once they were married so it seemed kind of silly to purchase something for his apartment. He had impeccable taste in clothing and had most of his clothes tailor made in fact, so that left clothing off her list of ideas. She thought seriously about something really extravagant, like maybe a new car, but decided against it for fear Eric would get angry over her making such a decision without him. She was beginning to get frantic as the week before Christmas wore on. At noon three days before Christmas she left work to go shopping determined not to come home without something for Eric. Finally just when she was about to give up, it hit her. Eric loved to hunt when he had the time. He and her father had gone on many hunting and fishing trips together and Eric had always had to borrow a gun. Why hadn't she thought of that before? First she went to the only gun shop in Aston. Her choice was guided by the elderly gun smith. The weapon she bought was one of the finest made and quite beautiful to look at. It was a 12 gauge automatic shotgun with a walnut stock that had been hand rubbed to a glass smooth finish. The steel blue barrel was almost mirror like when you looked into it. The trigger was of gold and the gun smith assured her that the weapon was a limited edition manufactured at one time in Belgium and no longer in production. Time would only add to the value of the weapon. This appealed to her sense of uniqueness and she bought the gun without another thought. Then she went to the kennels on the south end of town. She picked out two beagles whose heritage was to be envied by all. All she knew for sure was that the puppies were little darlings, marked exactly alike and Eric would love them as long as they knew how to bark. And bark they did. All the way home. Lillie nearly had a heart attack but agreed they were darling little creatures. They cornered Mr. Templeton with a joint plea to hide the pups at his house till Christmas Day. The squirmy pups loved the snow and delighted everyone watching them. "I just know Eric will love them. He hasn't owned a pet since her father died and that was when I was still just a baby." Suddenly Amber was acutely aware of their age difference but dismissed the thoughts the same way that she always did when something troubled her conscience. She shook off her feeling of morbid apprehension and held on to the happy thoughts.

The rest of the week was spent preparing for their feast on Christmas Day. Mr. Templeton had bought Lillie a gorgeous shawl and a pearl rosary. He had shown them both to Amber and she had agreed that Lillie would be delighted with the gifts. The old man had blushed when Amber complimented his good taste. He thanked her for making him feel so welcome in her home.

Eric took Amber Christmas tree shopping two days before Christmas. The selected a ten foot pine and Eric had to struggle for three hours to get it to stand up straight in the living room. Amber laughed and teased him and took several uncomplimentary snapshots of him, much to his dismay. Finally, once the tree was in place the four of them; Eric and Amber, Lillie and Mr. Templeton, spent until long after midnight decorating the tree. They drank hot toddies and sang songs and counted their blessings time and time again, each time counting the people they were spending the evening with as one of their most dear blessings. While together neither of them would ever be alone. Amber was truly happy with her surrogate family.

Lillie walked Mr. Templeton back to his house for one last nightcap and a toast to the season by his tree and for what Amber suspected was a little privacy of their own. Eric and Amber sat on the floor looking up at the giant tree. Several strings of lights blinked on and off giving the room a soft glow. Eric leaned over to kiss Amber softly. "Tell me again," he whispered. Amber smiled and told him for the hundredth time since the first time she had whispered the words to him on the lawn, "I love you." She added, "You will tire of hearing me say that before our lives are over."

"I'll never be tired of hearing it, never." He pushed her to a prone position on the floor and kissed her hard.

"Eric, not here!" She had come to know what that particular kiss meant. He raised quickly to his feet and immediately picked her up in his arms. She squealed in fake protest, and he climbed the stairs two at a time. He dropped her on her bed and fell on her all in one motion. She giggled and continued to fake a struggle, until his mouth found hers. Then there was no protest, fake or otherwise. If love affairs were ever made in heaven, then surely theirs was.

Eric had Amber's blouse unbuttoned and her braless form was his to behold. He loved to sprinkle her body with his caresses and kisses before ever making entry into her soft flesh. Her body was his now, given openly and willingly. His ever present tenderness and love for her keep their lovemaking a delight for them both. Amber had learned quickly how to please him and was eager to do so. She met his thrusts with forceful purpose and always seen to it that his desires were fulfilled completely. Not once since their first sexual encounter had she refused him. In fact she discovered rapidly that it delighted him is she made the first overture toward their sexual activity once in a while. His ego soared and he devoted his entire being to her fulfillment. Now as they begun their lovemaking Amber was as usual eager to please him, to let him know that she wanted him and needed him. He kissed her, experiencing the same yearning deep within that he always did. Their bodies joined without the slightest hesitation. Eric's desire demanding relief and Amber's own passion meeting those demands with confidence. Her skill at lovemaking developed naturally and without inhibitions and she truly delighted Eric. At the moment of orgasm, they lay exhausted, smiling, kissing, wishing they did not have to move and longing for the day they would not have to hide from Lillie. Amber lay with her head resting on Eric's shoulder, her body moist with perspiration. Her chest still heaved with the short breaths she was taking. Eric spoke first.

"God, how I do love you," he said.

Amber smiled. "I think you just love my body.'

"Alas, does it show?"

Amber laughed as she raised herself off the bed. "Beast!" She walked across the room. Her skin shone in the dim lights. Her breasts moved only slightly with each step. Her silhouette was nearly perfect. Her hair fell down her back and formed a protective blanket around her shoulders. Eric sighed

as he watched her. "I can just look at you and want you all over again."
Amber turned to face him.

"I'm glad," she purred. She walked back to him and leaned over to kiss
him. Her breasts brushed against his chest, her hard nipples leaving little
trails of heat across his skin. He put his arms around her and pulled her
down on top of him. As he forced his hardened shaft into her again, he
moaned. His smile was teasing when he spoke. "I'm going to die young, but
happy." He made love to her with an intensity that drained them both. Once
satisfied for the second time, Eric carried Amber to the shower. The showered
together, frolicking like children in the water. Amber did truly love this man.
He was strong, good, kind and he made her glad to be a woman. What
more could any woman want? They dried each other, dressed and headed
back downstairs. When Lillie returned to the Manor, she found Amber and
Eric asleep on the floor in front of the Christmas tree. The lights were still
on, blinking brightly, quietly casting a warm glow over the entire room. She
covered them with a blanket, unplugged the Christmas lights and crept off
to bed with her own fantasies to dream about and her own brand of fulfillment
achieved.

Christmas Eve was something out of a storybook. The "foursome"
attended church services at the ancient church on the corner of the street.
The walked home in nearly 18 inches of new fallen snow. They shared
nightcaps with the neighbors and threw popcorn to the pigeons kept awake
by the Christmas carolers and late night sleigh riders. Lillie handed out at
least two gallons of hot chocolate to the neighborhood children. When Lillie
and Mr. Templeton retired to the kitchen to make sure they had everything
they needed for Christmas Day dinner, Eric turned to Amber and took her
gently in his arms. "I want to give you your Christmas present now. I can't
wait until tomorrow. Besides I want you to be wearing it at church tomorrow.
I have already asked Father Keiner to announce our banns after services."

Without unwrapping the package Amber knew it would contain her
engagement ring. Their final announcement to the world that they intended
to marry. She was suddenly nervous. She didn't even know why. Ever
since her father's death Eric had been at her side. Guiding her, helping her,
loving her, by her own requests teaching her. He loved her, she knew he
did. She felt as if she might suffocate. She felt a small chill. Total commitment

to him both in bed and in her mind had been a pleasure. But, somewhere hidden in the dark side of her brain there was a message that just wouldn't surface and become plain. Was she looking for a replacement for her father and friend she had lost? No, no she knew better than that. Never did she desire to sleep with her father and she did desire Eric's body. Her father had always been good to her and indulged in her fancies, whatever they might be, but he had been too busy building an empire to dote on her like Eric did. Eric took part in everything Amber did. If they were not at work, he was either at Amber's side or he was off on some errand for her. She opened the package slowly. The card was hand written by Eric. "For my friend, my lover and my wife." The ring was outstanding. On a white gold mount stood one perfect solitaire diamond. It was the largest diamond Amber had ever seen. On the band of the ring were twelve smaller black diamonds, six on each side of the solitaire. The contrast was breath taking. Amber smiled up at Eric and without speaking, her awe was evident. Eric smiled. He was pleased with his choice. He took the ring from her had and placed it on her left ring finger and kissed her fingertips. "Now everything is official," he teased as if the fact that they had shared their bed for several months meant nothing. The ring fit perfectly, as well it should have considering all the devious ways Lillie had sized Amber's ring finger for Eric. She looked at the marvelous piece of jewelry on her hand and admired the way it looked, almost as if she were looking at a hand belonging to someone else. She looked back at Eric's face and could only manage a whisper to him. "Thank you," she said. He smiled and kissed her. "The best is yet to come for us, Baby, I promise. I love you."

"I know you do Eric, I know you do. Amber almost sighed aloud feeling the weight of responsibility, ever present, unrelenting. Eric's love for her was almost as much burden as it was blessing sometimes. Eric watched her face and started to speak but Amber was saved from the confrontation by the ringing of the phone.

Amber answered the phone and was stunned when she heard the voice on the other end of the line. That voice belonged to Inez Chandler. Amber was instantly uneasy and it showed in her flushed face, making Eric anxious to know what was going on. Inez talked in hurried fashion.

"Amber, there is no place in town to stay tonight. Everything is full up. I never dreamed so many people would be coming to Aston for the holidays. For that matter I never dreamed I'd be coming either. Anyway, Amber, honey, please; can I stay at your place. Just for one night? I know it is a terrible thing to ask on such short notice and on Christmas Eve too, and I know you have lots of plans for tomorrow that do not include me, but I can be up and out of your way very early I promise. I am really in a spot Amber dear. Guess someday I will learn to plan ahead, won't I?"

What made Amber say yes she didn't know. She would never know. Their last encounter had been horrible and Amber had no desire for putting up with Inez's antics on Christmas Day. Lillie would flip. Amber would look back on this night for the rest of her life and wonder what possessed her to agree to allow Inez Chandler into her world for even one evening.

Inez arrived moments after Amber hung up the phone. She had only a small overnight case with her, proving she didn't plan to stay long anywhere. She was in Aston for the weekend only. She had meant to arrive earlier, but had been delayed by bad weather in the north. Amber was uncomfortable the minute Inez took off her coat. Her uneasiness was obvious. It was already far past midnight but Inez was wound up like a ten day clock and would not hear of retiring to the guest room. She caught sight of Amber's ring and demanded an inspection. "Well, my, my!" she exclaimed. "Eric you certainly have good taste in rings."

Eric placed his arm around Amber's shoulders and agreed that not only did he have good taste in rings but women as well. Amber felt herself anger over the assumption that she had nothing to do with the choice of her ring, even though she hadn't. Why was it just assumed that she had no part in deciding her own fate? Amber offered Inez a nightcap and she accepted. When Amber left the room to get more ice, Inez directed her attention to Eric. "Thank you, Eric. For sticking around I mean. I feel so inadequate around Amber."

"Why don't you give her a chance? Why don't you open up with her the way you did with me when we had lunch. Talk to her about the things she wants to hear from you. She was really disappointed when you were in town before, you know?"

"Yes, I know. I'm just so sure she will hate me the same way Lance did if I open up and really tell her the whole truth. Why is it so important to her anyway?"

"I don't know, but I do know it is; and you owe it to her to give it to her straight if you are going to keep hopping in and out of her life like this."

The dark eyes of the older woman met Eric's and he experienced that same weakness he had felt when she looked at him in his office nearly a year ago. She moved closer to him and spoke softly. "Eric Tolliver, would you believe you are the only man I have ever just talked to in my life? You are the first man that ever gave a damn about anything I had to say." She stood only inches from his body and, though no real overture was made by her, Eric felt strangely uneasy. Perhaps it was because she looked so much like Amber; he didn't know. Perhaps the nightcaps were getting to him, something certainly was. His head spun and he fought to control his breathing. He cleared his throat and spoke deliberately weighing each word as he spoke. "Lance gave a damn, for a long time he gave a damn."

"You are wrong, Eric. He worried only at first. Then when I made my crucial mistake, he was finished. There was no explanation good enough for him; no turning back, no matter how much I might have suffered, nothing was enough. That is the truth Eric, I swear it is." She looked alone and genuinely sad. He suddenly had an urge to put his arms around her and soothe part of the hurt away. He stood close to her not knowing what to do with his hands. He actually longed to run away from the entire situation so that he would not have to face the confusion he felt.

Amber returned with the ice for their drinks in time to notice how close their bodies were but she was too tired to think about it. Considering Inez's way with men it wasn't surprising. The aroma of the rum in his drink replaced the linger of Inez's perfume in Eric's nostrils and he was glad.

"Well," Amber finally spoke. "How have you been, Inez?"

"Fine, really fine. As a matter of fact, better than I have been in years. I have something for you Amber." From her purse she produced an envelope. Inside was a cashier's check for the money she had borrowed from Amber. Amber was impressed. "I told you to consider that money a gift. I really don't need this."

"Oh, I know you don't need the money. But I'd like to start fresh with you if that is possible. Amber we are both adults. You made that clear to me when I left before. I want to be totally honest with you. I know the years got away from us and they can never be replaced. When I visited here last year things between us got off to a bad start and then got worse. I know we will never be best buddies but can we at least act like we know each other? I would have liked to be your friend, but if that isn't possible I'd settle for acquaintance. I've been afraid that you are enough like your father to judge me without forgiving and I just can't take anymore of that. Please try and understand my side of this situation Amber. If you are still willing I will talk with you about the things you want to talk about. I really will."

Eric bowed his head wanting to avoid looking at either woman. Amber faced Inez and tried to smile. She took a deep breath and answered with caution. "I don't know if we can follow through with a relationship of any kind, Inez. To tell the truth, it is not as nearly important to me as it used to be." Eric gasped almost out loud in disbelief. Never had he heard Amber speak so cold or calculating. He suddenly felt that if Amber could hurt Inez, she would. Even when angered at rival executives at a bargaining table, Amber was always coaxing with demands. Never had he imagined her being headstrong or close minded. Perhaps Inez had been correct and Amber was too much like her father to deal with Inez fairly. Eric was slightly frightened of this side of Amber. She continued to speak, knowing that her words had already shocked both of the people listening to her. Listening; that was the key word. Amber liked that. It was about time! She spoke slowly and deliberately.

"There is one thing I would like to know. I want to know exactly what you did to my father. He lived the rest of his life without ever loving another woman after you, do you know that? He trusted only a few close friends and none of them were women. What Inez, what on earth did you do to Lance Harris? He fostered a hate for you that was unnatural. I grew up not allowed to speak your name, did you know that?"

Eric took a deep breath and crossed to the other side of the room. He stared into the fireplace. He rattled the ice in his glass. He wished he were someplace else. Amber noticed his uneasiness. She wondered for a moment why all this hit him so hard. For the first time in a long time she felt in control of a situation and she enjoyed it. There were no tears left to cry over Inez Chandler and that felt good too.

Inez said nothing. She opened her purse and pulled a folded, very faded document from it. She handed it to Amber. Eric drew in a sharp breath. He had advised Inez to be honest with Amber but he wondered if this might be a little too honest. He braced himself with another glass of rum and waited for Amber's reaction. It seemed to him like it took a long time for her to read her birth certificate. When he found the nerve to look at her he saw that she was smiling. She had read the first line and finally knew her real date of birth. She was actually a month younger than the orphanage records had estimated. Her smile quickly disappeared and Eric recognized the look in her eyes; he had seen that look every time Lance Harris ever spoke of Inez Chandler. The anger, the pain, the horrible disbelief was exactly the same.

Amber's voice was barely audible. "Oh, my God!" There it was in black and white; the reason Lance Harris went to his grave hating Inez Chandler. The reason he refused to forgive Inez Chandler the mistakes of her youth. "I have a twin brother?" Amber's voice trailed off into the air weakly. The room was silent except for the crackling of the logs in the fireplace and to Eric the silence was deafening. He became aware of the uneven breathing and the bright splotches becoming visible on Amber's throat. He wondered for a moment if she were going to faint. Inez was visibly shaking when she finally spoke. "Yes, Amber, you do. Lance Harris also had a son."

"Where is he now? Why didn't Daddy take him from the home?"

"He wasn't at the home, Amber."

"Then where was he? Did you choose to raise him yourself? Why him and not me? Why didn't Daddy tell me about him? Where is he now? I want to meet him, right away!" Amber's mind was racing and her questions were nearly too much for Inez. She made her way to a chair and sank into the fine leather.

"Lance couldn't find the boy Amber. That is why he never took him to raise. He looked for the child for the first ten years of your life."

"What do you mean, couldn't find him? What did you do with him, Inez? Tell me!"

Inez stood and turned her back to Amber. She nearly shouted her reply.

"I sold him Amber! For fifty thousand dollars, I sold him on the black market. That is what Lance would never let me forget."

Eric decided that Amber's color was actually gray. He was afraid to even move. Tears stung his eyes and never had he seen so much pain written on a person's face. Not even the day they laid Lance to rest."

Amber could feel herself losing control of every emotion she ever had. She fought to regain her composure before she spoke again. Then she said, "I see." She folded the birth certificate with shaking hands. "I must say I wish I had known about this years ago. I wish Daddy had felt me mature enough to handle this knowledge. Perhaps I would have spent a little less time wishing I could get to know you." Her voice was colder than Eric ever dreamed it could be. She was visibly trembling from head to toe.

Eric spoke with caution. "Amber, take it easy will you? Lance did what he thought was best in a bad situation; and Inez was young and stupid. What is done is done. We have to look forward from now on. The past isn't important, just the future. You said so yourself a little while ago. Remember, you said you didn't think it nearly as important as"….his voiced trailed off to silence and Amber's glare caught his attention.

"You knew about his Eric?" she breathed cautiously, afraid her chest might explode. She held her birth certificate toward him.

Eric blushed, knowing he had turned his hand at the wrong moment. He stuttered just a bit, trying to weigh his words quickly and finally answered. "Amber, I was your father's friend a long time before I became your lover. He spent years and thousands of dollars looking for the child, and yes, I knew about the investigations he had conducted." He walked to her side and tried to take her hand in his but she jerked away from him as if she had been suddenly burned. "Amber, Baby, don't do this, come on, calm down."

She turned to face him squarely; she threw her head back slightly and laughed briefly. Then with a bit of sarcasm she addressed both Eric and Inez. A lone, silent tear escaped her left eye but she spoke without hesitation. "Inez, the guest room is the first room on your right. Eric, I think it is time you left for the night. You know the way out. I'm going to my room. Good night to you both." She left the room but not before walking to the fireplace and dropping the birth certificate into the fire. She watched briefly as the fire swallowed the yellow document. The she hastened out of the room without another word. Eric, shocked at his short and not so sweet dismissal, picked up his coat but realized he was much too warm to put it on. Inez sat back down in the chair that faced the fireplace and watched the fire erase all traces of her son's existence.

"Why didn't she throw me out on the spot?" she asked.

"You don't know Amber. She has to think things through. She is very much like her father. Much more than even I knew until tonight."

"Oh my God, then I don't stand a chance with her. She will hate me with the same vengeance Lance did."

"Probably," Eric said, knowing that they might as well face the truth from the beginning.

"Thank you for your words of encouragement! I should have never come back here. What on earth could I have been thinking? I should have never been honest. I thought it would be for the best and the only thing I did was make a mess of things for good."

"Don't be so hard on yourself or on Amber. You never know how she will react. Just hang on for a few hours. She didn't throw you out, so she must not want to close the doors of communication totally. She just needs time to adjust to your bombshell. She has already surprised the hell out of me."

"Maybe you are correct. I'll spend the night. The worse she can do is throw me out in the morning." She smiled at Eric. "You know you are pretty cool. Are you always so together in a crisis?"

"Yes," he said smugly, then quickly added, "However, we will see how cool I am when Amber decides to 'deal' with me in the morning." He laughed and Inez walked to him and embraced him tightly.

"Thank you for being civil to me Eric. I need for somebody to be willing to listen to my side of life."

Eric felt awkward as he placed his hands on her back. Her hair smelled faintly of fine perfume and her body was warm and soft, not made of stone or steal. "You are welcome, Inez." He held her away from him by her shoulders and looked into her eyes. Her eyes were dark and warm and sad. She was a beautiful woman, not much older than himself and for an instant he felt embarrassed about the thoughts that were racing around in his mind.

"I gotta get going before we wake the entire house. Besides you better get some sleep." He left abruptly, actually afraid of his desires. He knew if he held Inez Chandler another moment that he would kiss her; explore that mouth so soft and moist and begging to be used. Inez worried Eric, he didn't understand why, but she did.

When he finally arrived home and got into his own bed, Eric lay awake for an hour thinking about the two women at Harris Manor. In some ways they were very much alike. Was that part of the reason they couldn't possibly get acquainted? Amber retreated into herself when she was hurt, if Inez was about to suffer she left town before anyone could notice. Both women were absolutely beautiful. He couldn't think of another woman Inez Chandler's age that was as vital as she was. He wondered how many hearts she had broken through the years. He knew that if Amber had more confidence that she could turn the head of every man she met instead of just half of them as she did now. That was why it was so important for him to dominate her. He moved restlessly in his bed. He wondered what Amber would do in the morning. He started to call her but decided she might possibly be asleep and Lord knew she could use the rest. They had a big day planned for tomorrow and he hoped it wouldn't be spoiled by the events of the last couple of hours.

Eric could have called. There was little chance of Amber sleeping. Instead she paced the floor of her room. She already burned that hateful certificate and now she wished she could tear it to shreds and throw it to the wind. God how frustrated her father must have been. He had practically adopted Eric out of need for a son and all along he knew that somewhere in the world he had one of his own. One he would never see, never hold. No wonder he had forbid Inez to come near their daughter. Her thoughts ran through her head till she thought surely it would burst. And why? Why did Inez come back now? How could she trust Inez, even if she wanted to? Did she want to? No, hell no! Why didn't Inez just go away and leave her alone? She could in no way go to sleep, so she decided to go down to the kitchen for a snack. She always ate when she was nervous. She poured herself a cup of cold coffee and took a drink. She looked down at her hand. She had meant to tell Eric so much tonight. She had wanted to let him know she loved him but that she was going to have more of a say in their destiny. They probably would have celebrated with lovemaking. Damn Inez and her phone call! Amber was sure of her love for Eric and she certainly enjoyed their love affair immensely, but now she couldn't help but wonder if Eric had any other secrets that he wasn't sharing with her. Her mind wandered to her nightmares which were almost a nightly ritual now. She wondered why these things were happening to her now. Wasn't it enough that Lance was dead and she was practically alone in the world? Why couldn't she have some peace of mind with her choices as to how to fill her life. She didn't want to worry about whether she was marrying Eric to play it safe or not. Was she afraid to challenge the world on her own? She had always depended on some man; she realized that now more than ever. She wanted to go to sleep without having to face the torment of the future. She took a deep breath and left the kitchen and was about to enter the library when she realized Inez was sitting by the fireplace. The fire was nearly out and Inez was starring into the picture that the McIntires had given Amber for Christmas. Silent tears ran down Inez's face. Amber stopped in her tracks and quietly watched the woman. Did Inez really care? Did she really feel remorse for all the mistakes of the past? Amber's own tears wet her face and dripped off her chin. She walked through the doorway. When Inez realized Amber was in the room she valiantly started to dry her tears away.

"I can't sleep," she sighed. "I feel like my whole life has been worthless. I should never have come back here, especially now! I never meant to mess up your holidays. I'm so sorry and I'm so sick of being sorry for something all the time. Seems like no matter what I do it is the wrong decision."

"I couldn't sleep either. I really don't want to think about 'us' Inez. And I can't handle any more surprises like tonight's either, okay? So if you have anymore, just keep them to yourself, no matter what I say in the future. Daddy was correct, ignorance is bliss."

Inez half smiled, then said, "Do I dare ask how you feel about me now?"

"I can't really tell you how I feel right now. I guess I don't feel anything to tell the truth. For a while I was very angry. But I can't tell you if I'm angry because you sold my brother, or because everyone knew about it but me. Am I mad because you have been absent all my life or because you are here now and your presence just keeps making me face unpleasant truths about my life. You show up and I find my father and my lover have kept secrets from me my entire life. I am more confused right now than I was in fifth grade."

"Well, really Amber, you can't possibly miss someone you've never known. What difference can it make now? I know I shouldn't have conducted my life as I have and that I made one mistake after another, but can't we let bygones be bygones?"

Amber was amazed at the woman's ability to cast aside all feelings about the matter. She wondered if anyone else in the world could be so calloused when it came to their own flesh and blood. Amber was about to decide that Inez only cried because "things' didn't go her way.

"Do you hate me Amber?" Inez was looking at Amber eye to eye for the first time.

Amber decided that honesty was the best policy. "I don't know for sure. In some ways, yes, I do. I used to hate you for leaving me behind and making me feel worthless. I spent a great deal of time wondering why my own mother did not love me. I felt guilty and Christ, I didn't even know for what. And I hate limbo. You pop in and you pop out of my life and I feel like we are on an emotional roller coaster or something. Frankly, right now, I wish we had never met."

Inez blushed brightly. She dropped her eyes before she spoke. "Amber, listen to me just this one time. I am just a human. I made mistakes. Lots of them and real bad ones. I know we can't be mother and daughter, but maybe we could get to be friends enough that we might learn something from each other."

Try as she might, it was impossible for Amber to hide her anger. Suddenly she was the little girl that had never known her mother, the little girl that cried night after night for a mother who never came to see her. All the resentment of a thousand nights would not be stifled. "I doubt if you can teach me anything I care to learn, Inez. But there is one thing I would like to know. Did you ever love my father?"

Inez took a deep breath and set her jaw, knowing that the battle lines had already been drawn and there wasn't much that could be gained by treading softly now. "No, I did not love him at the time of your birth, Amber. Not really even before your birth. After he found and adopted you, I could have loved him, but by then he wouldn't give me the chance."

"He loved you, all those years, he loved you. And if you never loved him in the first place why did you commit to him so seriously?"

"Really Amber, grow up. Don't you really want to ask me why I slept with him for more than a year when I didn't love him?"

Amber blushed and had to clear her throat before she could answer. "Yes, I guess I do mean that," she stuttered.

"Amber, when I met Lance Harris he was twenty three years old. He was handsome, he was honest and in a few months he loved me. He was the first man to ever pay attention to me for more than a week at a time and frankly he was good in bed. But he was also dirt poor. He couldn't afford to keep himself and your grandmother, much less me. I was young. I looked like you look now and I had a few dreams of my own. I wanted everything Lance Harris didn't have and I wanted it fast. If we would have married, in a few months we would have hated each other. My choices were clear cut. I could leave and have him hate me at a distance or I could stay and have him hate me up close. It was a little more convenient and comfortable to leave, so I left."

"But in time Daddy could have given you anything that money can buy!"

Inez snapped to attention. "I beg your pardon!" she was shouting.

"My desertion of your father inspired all of this!" she waved her arms violently around the elegant room. "If I would have married him, he would have been content to scratch out a living and get by on corn bread and soup beans and I on the other hand would have been miserable."

"But what about your babies? ME?"

"Amber, I knew that anyone that would pay fifty thousand dollars for a child would certainly take care of it. That money was my ticket to freedom, my passport to the world I wanted. As for you, I knew that you would be taken care of by someone. I knew that you would be adopted; I just never dreamed it would be your crazy father. When he approached me with demands about the boy I nearly died. I hadn't even wanted him to know I had been pregnant. For a while I thought he was going to kill me or have it done. I know for a fact he wanted to. Instead he just shut me out. He sent me money until he had paid me fifty thousand dollars for you. He said you were worth as least as much as the boy. Things hadn't gone well for me even with the money I received for your brother and I was usually broke so I kept the money Lance sent me. He sure as hell didn't miss it. If all of this makes me a demon, then I stand guilty Amber. I am not a monster though. I came back here last year to let Lance know that I had finally located a lawyer that says he knew another lawyer that handled the adoption of a black market baby from Aston, Virginia in August 1947. Aston is so small it had to be your brother. I went to Lance's office to talk to him and was told that he was dead. That is when I got the idea to come here and meet with you. I figured there was no need in telling you of the boy since you didn't know about him in the first place."

"Perhaps you are not a monster, but I'm not so sure. Maybe it is because I missed you so much while I was young, but I'll never turn away from my babies, no matter what, I know I won't." Tears streaked her cheeks but for the first time she didn't care if Inez watcher her cry.

Probably the worst personality trait that Inez Chandler had was her temper. And when she was about to be hurt or cornered that temper flared, uncontrollable, hurtful. She lashed out at Amber mainly because she had no other way to keep her young daughter from inflicting pain upon her; pain and guilt.

"Oh really! Is that so, Miss High and Mighty. That is pretty easy for you to say. You sit here, rich and educated with a servant to serve your every whim. If you get yourself knocked up there are probably ten men in this county willing to marry you. I wasn't so lucky."

"Daddy would have married you! He loved you!"

"Well, I didn't love him!" Inez shouted now not caring who heard her rage.

Amber was shocked at the outburst and drew in her breath quickly. "Yes, I understand. You have made that quite clear. I just happen to be a bastard twin of a woman that let herself become pregnant by a man she didn't even love. How nice. I can't ever call myself a "lovechild"!"

Inez was crimson. She inhaled trying to regain some semblance of control. "This is getting us nowhere. I have made one mistake after another concerning you. I should have never returned at all, not last year, not now. I'll get my things and leave. Take care of yourself, Amber." She paused only an instant at the door. "Merry Christmas, Amber."

Amber stared into the fireplace. She couldn't speak. She was still looking at the dying embers in the fireplace when Inez walked out the front door of the Manor House. She handed an irate cabby a slip of paper with an address written on it. "You know where this is?" she asked. The cab driver hated 3 a.m. calls. They were usually drunks or some dame cheating on her husband.

He growled a "yes," and Inez was on her way. From her purse she brought a small flask. She swallowed the contents in two gulps. Her nerves were shattered all to hell and the straight whiskey burned her throat but at least it gave her something else to think about. Why did Amber anger so quickly? Why did she go crazy every time Amber confronted her? Was she jealous? Hell, maybe she was. The heat in the cab and the whiskey were taking affect, and she was beginning to feel a bit silly. It was a welcome change. The cab pulled up in front of an ancient apartment building. It was brick and two angry looking gargoyles guarded the entrance. Inez got out of the cab and cold air momentarily took her breath away. She paid the cabby and made her way up the walk way till she found apartment number twelve. She rapped the brass knocker and waited. She knocked again and started to shiver. On her third try, she finally heard some movement inside. The occupant came to the door in his robe. He stood looking at her in amazement.

"I know I should have called first, but to tell you the truth, I was afraid if I let you think about my coming you would say no." She started to shiver uncontrollably. "The hotels really are full. I honestly have no where else to go, Eric. Please help me."

The cold air cut through his robe and brought him out of his dazed condition. "Come on in, Inez. Did Amber throw you out after all?" His surprise was obvious.

"No not exactly. We couldn't sleep and we tried to talk and things went poorly as usual. In fact awful. It is just better for both of us if I get out of her life and stay out. I didn't want to look at her in the morning." She shivered again.

"Come on over here by what is left of the fire." He took her coat and overnight bag. When he leaned forward he could smell the liquor on her breath. "Wow, did you and Amber have a party after I left?"

"Very funny. I needed something for my nerves when I left Amber. I am coming unglued. I really am. You got anything around here worth drinking?"

"All I have is Scotch. You surely don't want to mix this stuff up in your system do you? Besides it is past three in the morning, aren't you ready to go to sleep?"

"No, I can't sleep now, I'm too hyper." Her voice was shaking and she added, "Why do we always fight?"

"Probably because you are alike. In some ways very much so." He handed her a glass of straight scotch. He couldn't imagine he was doing her any favors.

"Ha!" she nearly shouted. "We are about as much alike as night and day. She has everything and I have nothing. Nothing and nobody!" She swallowed her drink in one gulp and held her glass to Eric for a refill. She was hell bent on feeling very sorry for herself very fast. Eric obliged knowing it was a mistake. "You had better slow down," he warned. "Your head will explode come daylight."

"Who cares?" The liquor affected her speech now. "You know what I am Eric?"

"It doesn't matter now, Inez. Come on, I'll show you where you can lay down and rest whether you sleep or not." He tried to maneuver her toward the bedroom. She stumbled over her own feet and Eric caught her around her waist. She was tall but was dwarfed by Eric's stature, much like Amber.

"I'll tell you, Eric. I am lonely. I am lonely and you are right, it doesn't matter. Not to a damn soul does it matter." She leaned into Eric's chest and began to sob.

"Right now you are also drunk and we have got to get you to bed so you can rest. You will sleep soon and things will look better in the light of day, I promise."

"Where will I go from here?" she asked almost child like and near drunken stupor. Eric was glad Amber didn't drink very much.

"Let's worry about it in the morning. Let's get you to bed and get some sleep. That is what you need most right now. I know I certainly do."

He carried her to his bedroom. He put her on the bed and loosened her blouse. He took her shoes off carefully, noticing the slender ankles and shapely legs. He watched her as she nuzzled into his pillow near delirium. She looked so much like her daughter. She was beautiful. Again it hit him that there were but a few years between their ages. He placed a quilt over her and walked back to his living room. It was 4:30 a.m. Christmas morning. He stretched out on his sofa and tried to relax. His mind raced with thoughts of the woman now lying in his bed. Amber came into his mind. She would have a fit over this; there was no doubt about it. But then he couldn't leave a human out to freeze to death could he? God how could things get so confused in such a small amount of time. No wonder Amber was an emotional wreck. His mind refused to sleep for at least another hour. When he finally drifted into slumber he was awakened suddenly by Inez's moaning. She was in the bathroom. She was sick, not only hangover sick, but really ill with chills and fever. Probably weakened resistance and the bitter cold outside last night. When her heaving finally stopped Eric helped her back to bed. He touched her forehead with his lips and was shocked by the heat emitted. She was snow white and her lips had a blue tinge. Christmas Day, there wouldn't be a doctor in town, much less in an office. The nearest emergency room was thirty five miles away and Inez clearly needed some serious attention. Eric's mind thought of Lillie. She knew a lot about home remedies. She also hated Inez and she would never get Amber involved. In a couple of hours he was to announce to the world that Amber Harris thought enough of him to be his wife. He wondered just how angry she would be about this. Well, one bridge at a time, he thought as he dialed the phone. Lillie's voice was happy when she said "good morning." Her mood changed instantly as Eric explained his dilemma. Her voice was restrained as she told Eric about the hot brews she guaranteed to break Inez's fever. Inez moved only slightly in the bed and looked forlornly at Eric. She shuddered and Eric went for more covers as soon as he hung up the phone. He returned with another soft cover, one that he had laid on many times with Amber. It was velvety blue, Amber's favorite color.

"Thank you for being so kind, Eric. Go on to church. I know this is a big day for both you and Amber. I will be alright in a little while. Then I'll get up and out of here and be on my way again. And I promise, no more surprises, ever. You take good care of Amber, okay? I'll be out of your way by the time you get home from church."

"You are not in my way, Inez." Eric was more than a little nervous and it showed.

"Well, we must admit that I can't be the most welcome guest you have ever had." She smiled that smile.

He went to the kitchen to search for the ingredients of Lillie's magic brew. "I'll go to church as soon as I fix this for you. Promise that you will drink it and take your time getting out of here. There will be no problem, I promise. Amber will understand, she is basically a kind person, Inez. It is

just that when you two are together you bring out the worst in each other."
He carried a tall cup to her. She shivered again. "I just need to get warm,"
she said. "Then I'll be fine. I really will. Other than these chills I don't feel so
bad now." She took the cup and sipped the bitter brew. She leaned back
against her pillow and sighed.

"I'm going to get ready for church. You just sip this and rest."

Inez was already asleep by the time Eric finished his shower. He dressed
quietly and looked in on her one more time before he left. She was still
fevered but resting quietly and her breathing was noticeably easier. Maybe
she did just have a touch of the flu combined with a hangover from hell, and
she would be better soon. He relaxed a bit and crept out the front door and
walked through the snow to his car. He arrived at the church just in time to
greet Amber on the steps. "She is so beautiful," he thought as soon as he
saw her. Then he added; "I hope she doesn't go nuts before she lets me
explain about Inez." He embraced Amber and kissed her on the forehead.
"Merry Christmas, Ladies!" He tried to sound happy. His reception told
him Lillie had already filled Amber in on his overnight guest. They were
inside the ancient church and he had to whisper. "I've got to talk to you," he
told her.

"Oh really? I figured by now you would be all talked out," she nearly
hissed at him. Eric had never seen her so angry, not even last night.

"Oh, for heaven's sake. What was I suppose to do? Did you have to
throw her out in the snow on the coldest night of the year?" His voice was
accusing and Amber could hardly sustain her rage. " I DID NOT throw her
out! Her leaving was her idea but frankly I thought it was a very good one.
I might have known she had plans for the rest of the evening."

"Just what does that mean? And for your information she is very sick.
Should I have let her freeze to death on my sidewalk?"

"Why did she come to your place? What gave her the idea she would be
welcome in your bed?"

"I don't know! What exactly are you trying to accuse me of?"

"Nothing. I just don't understand any of this, that's all. You keep secrets
from me for a life time, treat me like some kind of child and then spend the
night with a tramp and I'm not supposed to mind."

"Will you lay off? I didn't sleep with her and for pete's sake will you give the woman a break? There wasn't anywhere in this town to go last night, you know that."

"That's good! Go ahead and take up for HER."

"You are acting like a spoiled brat, you know that?"

Amber looked at Eric for the first time since their conversation started. She was so furious she could no longer speak. Her anger disturbed her which only served to make her more angry. Damn Inez anyway. Oh Lord, now she was swearing in church. Why couldn't Inez just go away. She was pretty good at disappearing when Amber was born, why not now?

Mass was starting and Eric had to punch Amber twice to get her to pay attention. Lillie and Mr. Templeton had sat in the back of the church to allow Amber and Eric some privacy and Eric was beginning to wish he hadn't come at all. He had never seen Amber so totally consumed in anger. She didn't touch him, she wouldn't look at him, and she didn't speak again during the entire service. Eric wished he had kept his own temper in check. He knew his last remark to her had cut her to the core and he was sorry. He just didn't know how to handle Amber when she was like this, and he felt he was losing control. Losing control always frightened him.

When the service was nearing an end, Father Keiner came forward and both Eric and Amber realized that her was about to announce their forthcoming marriage. Eric leaned to her, his voice somewhat resembling an Army drill sergeant's her said, "Now straighten up and at least act happy for a few minutes."

Amber's look was mixture of despair and hate. She was angry and embarrassed and her face was crimson. She shook with rage. When she spoke it was barely a whisper but she might as well have been shouting.

"Me straighten up? You spend the night with my bitch mother and I should straighten up?"

"Amber, you are in a church!" Eric admonished her hoping no one was looking at them.

"Oh yeah!" she was louder now. "Won't you please excuse me?" She stood up and walked out leaving Eric standing in the aisle. He heard a couple of whispers and blushed brightly. He excused himself and followed Amber outside. "Amber, what is the matter with you?"

She plowed on in the snow nearly loosing her footing but none the less ignoring Eric's attempts at reasoning with her.

When Eric finally caught up with her, he grabbed her arm and harshly spun her around to face him. "Amber will you listen to me for just one minute? What was I supposed to do, leave her outside to freeze? What happened anyway, why the hell did she leave the Manor House in the middle of the night?"

For the first time all morning he looked at Amber and really saw her. What he saw frightened him. She was ashen. Her face was marked with dark circles under her eyes and her eyes were swollen from crying half the night. It was obvious she had not slept. Anger literally boiled from those green eyes that usually smiled before her lips did. There was a coldness present that Eric had never before seen in Amber. He felt that if this matter were not settled immediately that he would loose Amber for good. His own fear of such a thing angered him. He tried to grasp at some sort of calmness before he spoke again. Just as he thought he was regrouping in his own mind, he was again caught totally off guard. Every fiber in Amber's body was tense with rage. She was nearly insane with a mixture of anger and the grief she was feeling over Inez Chandler in the first place. She jerked free of his grip and backed about two steps backward from Eric. She screamed for the first time.

"Don't touch me! Inez Chandler breezed back into my life after twenty years of total neglect, turns my thoughts upside down, tells me I have a brother somewhere in the world that was no more than a quick meal ticket to her, you spend the night with her in your bed, and you tell me that I am acting like a spoiled brat. If I am such a spoiled brat, then I suggest you go home and spend some more time with your house guest. I am sure you can find something to talk about and she probably isn't nearly as spoiled as I am."

She was trembling all over. Her entire body was rigid by the time she finished speaking. Her face was as white at the snow that was dancing in the wind around her. The cold of the December day was nothing compared to the coldness that she was feeling in her heart right now.

"Amber!" it was almost a gasp. "Amber, Baby, let me talk to you. Listen to me for just a moment. Baby let's not fight, not today. It's Christmas. We have planned this day for weeks."

"I know what day it is, thank you. I wouldn't dream of fighting with you today, in fact I wouldn't dream of speaking to you again today so we can not possibly fight. I am going home Eric, and I suggest you do the same. Leave me alone and I mean that. You just leave me alone!" She was walking as fast as the piled up snow would let her. Eric pleaded once more but she ignored him, tears nearly freezing on her face. By the time she reached the Manor House she was hysterical. When she entered the house she got worse. In the back yard the pups she had purchased for Eric romped in the snow. She watched them and sobbed uncontrollably. After a few minutes she began to pull herself together. This "thing" with Inez had to stop once and for all. She would go to Eric's apartment and have one last talk with Inez. She didn't ever intend to feel this way again. As for Eric; well, Eric knew she had a temper and she would apologize. She had to get hold of herself where Inez was concerned and surely he would understand that. She bathed her face in the kitchen sink with some cool water. She patted her forehead dry and felt the nausea that had haunted her for over a month now. She barely made it to the back door before she threw up. Her nerves were getting the best of her she guessed. She cried some more. She picked up her coat and purse and carried them to the hall closet. She decided to make some coffee. Lillie would arrive any minute now and Amber didn't want to ruin the day for her and Mr. Templeton. They deserved to be happy. She looked at the ring on her finger. It was so beautiful and she was so sure Eric loved her, why was he acting so stupid about this situation with Inez? Damn Inez. Why did she have to "drop in" now and start spreading heartache and pandemonium all around? Amber wished she hadn't fought so fiercely with Eric. She walked to the phone and dialed Eric's number. No answer. Perhaps he was on his way over. She placed the phone back in its' cradle and stared out the kitchen window at the puppies. She felt lonelier now than she had in all her life.

Eric stomped through the snow back to his car. Lillie was standing there waiting for some kind of explanation. Eric looked at her and took a deep breath. "Amber was not at all understanding about my house guest."

"I am not at all surprised, Eric. Inez told her about the little boy, you know."

"I know. I was there," he sighed. He was suddenly very tired.

"That Inez, she is no good for you and Amber. You know that. She means nothing but trouble no matter where she goes. You would be real smart to steer clear of her for good."

Eric was frustrated and angry and tired and Lillie Hasglow was the only person present so he yelled at her. "Damn it, Lillie. I don't need you or Amber to tell me who I should or should not see! For God's sake, the woman is sick. Should I go home and throw her out in the snow to make you guys happy?"

"Eric Tolliver, you don't talk to Lillie that way! I have been your friend since you were a brat in blue jeans. Inez has never done a good deed for a living soul in her life and you know that to be true. You were there! You saw what she did to Lance year after year. You see how she affects our Amber! She is tearing the girl to shreds right before our eyes. Just when Amber was about to get over some very real emotional problems Inez comes waltzing back in to stir up a mess of problems again. We are all sick of it, Eric. She has got you and Amber fighting; if Amber isn't crying, she is throwing up and now, on this most holy day of the year, neither of you can concentrate on the sacraments. I tell you it is just like old times; she just comes prancing in, tears everybody to pieces and she'll be on her way as soon as she is bored."

Eric listened to Lillie's words earnestly. He knew Lillie was wise and probably correct about most of what she was saying. His heart ached and he didn't want to fight with anybody anymore. He was exhausted and he was oddly hungry. He bowed his head and moved a pile of snow with his left foot. He was very near tears himself. "I'm really sorry for the way I spoke to you, Lillie. Can you forgive me? I'm going home and straighten this mess out right now. Please tell Amber I have come to my senses and I'll be over for dinner within the hour." Lillie nodded her reply as he started to open his car door. "Oh, Lillie!" he was enthusiastic. "Here, Merry Christmas!" He pointed to a brightly wrapped package on his front seat. Lillie was worried.

"That's beautiful, but you just bring it to dinner."

"No!" Eric protested. "Take it now and put it under the tree. I'll be by the house soon."

Lillie took the present with reservations. She had the feeling that Eric would need an excuse to come by the house and this present would have been a perfect one. As she and Mr. Templeton walked toward the Manor he could read the worry on her face.

"Is there something bad wrong between Eric and Amber?" he asked sadly.

Lillie sighed. "Yes, my dear. I'm afraid that this last twenty four hours have witnessed some pretty serious mistakes. Very serious and very sad."

By the time Eric reached his apartment his mind was a mass of confusion, touched in spots by anger, but he knew he had to make things right with Amber and that would be his first priority. He had realized the root for part of Amber's anger was really despair and now he was really sorry he had helped to hurt her feelings so badly. He had been shocked when he had realized Amber's actual physical condition this morning during their argument. He wished he had looked at her closer when they first met at the church. He also knew that Inez needed someone once in a while and he wished he could be on everyone's side. He hated choosing and leaving anyone hurt.

He unlocked the door gingerly in case Inez was still sleeping. She was. He crept into the bedroom to find her almost exactly as he left her. He touched her forehead lightly. She was still on fire with fever. "Damn, how could things get so screwed up?!" he thought as he walked to the phone. He called the only doctor he knew and no one answered. He decided to call the emergency room at Bayview Hospital and stood waiting for the hospital operator to track down the duty nurse whose only suggestion was to try and reduce the fever with aspirin and an alcohol bath. He was to coax the patient to drink lots of fluids and bring her in for treatment, preferably tomorrow, since there were no "in house" physicians available today unless there was an extreme emergency. "It's Christmas Day, you know?" she added a bit too coyly for Eric's liking. Eric didn't curse but he did slam the phone down as hard as he possibly could. Inez roused in the bed. She opened her eyes and looked up at Eric. She tried to rise up but was quick to lie back down.

"Eric, I am so sorry. I meant to be gone by the time you returned." She was breathless over the effort it took to recite the sentence.

"It's okay Inez. Just rest, will you?"

"How is Amber?"

"Furious."

"At me?"

"Ha! At you, at me, at the world in general right now. Now, about this fever you've got and getting back on your feet." He was talking from the bathroom now, where he was looking for aspirin. He brought back two pills and a glass of water. Inez dutifully took them and rested back against the pillow. "I should have stayed away."

"Probably should have," Eric murmured. "But, hind sight is twenty-twenty. The fact is that you are here and we have to make the best of what "is," not what should be."

"You are amazing, Eric. Don't you ever hold a grudge?"

"I try not to. I watched my mother kill herself because she never forgave my father for dying. I watched hatred eat at my best friend till the day he died. I could never see that all that hate did either of them any good."

"Are you talking about Lance?"

"Yes, I am. You have no idea what you did to Lance Harris."

"I guess I don't," Inez sighed. "But Eric, I swear it was no picnic for me either. Why doesn't anybody want to hear about my side of all this? It isn't very fair you know?"

"The world is not fair, Inez. You are plenty old enough to know that by now."

Inez smiled. "Yes, I guess I am."

"I am going to fix you something to eat. You think you can tolerate some soup?"

"I think so, I'm so cold."

"Well, lie back and snuggle up. The soup will help warm you up. I'll be back in a few minutes."

He went to the kitchen and opened a can of soup. He heated it and poured it into a bowl. He poured milk in a glass with water spots on it but he didn't think Inez would care if she noticed at all. He searched the cabinets till he found some crackers and then made his way back to the bedroom with "food for the sick." He made his announcement in his most cheerful voice. Inez had made it to the side of the bed. Her face was moist and she was shaking. Her ebony black hair was in disarray and she was attempting to smooth it back. She looked incredibly young for her age. God, how Eric loved young women. He sat the tray on the stand beside the bed and walked to the bathroom to get a cool washcloth. He sat down beside her on the bed and wiped her face gently. Inez smiled and then reached out to take hold of his free hand. She held it tenderly. Her touch was light and she held on to his hand for a moment before pulling it to her lips and kissing the back of his wrist.

"You are the kindest person I have ever known." Her eyes met his, the suffering of twenty years written on her face. Actual eye contact with her took Eric's breath. No wonder Lance never got over her.

"Your soup is getting cold," he said with no more confidence that a school boy. His mind raced and his pulse quickened as he thought about and looked upon the woman in his bed. He was going to marry her daughter, for God's sake. Was it really possible that he wanted her. "I am going insane," he thought to himself with only a small amount of disgust. Inez noted Eric's uneasiness and released his hand but not before she squeezed it gently. He felt the warmth of her small hand on his. He wanted to hold her in his arms. Age had been so kind to her in spite of her fast lane living. She knew how to be a woman, it was obvious in every move she made. He couldn't take his eyes off the silken skin beneath her slip, which was now all she had on. He wondered when she had removed her bra and panties. Some silly notion even wondered where in the room the underwear was laying. He wanted to touch her skin and see if it felt as smooth as it looked. His hands trembled as he passed the soup to her.

Her fever broke, bathing her body in sweat and she lay with her legs exposed to the thigh. Eric stared at legs that were long and slim and smooth. He wondered if they would part easily if he were to try and make a serious pass at Inez. There eyes met again and Eric wondered if Inez could read his mind. He felt transparent in her company.

"I am beginning to feel much better. The soup was magical. You may have saved my life today. I know I would have never made it through this on a bus or a plane. Thanks again for everything, Eric. I will be out of your way just as soon as I can."

"You are not in my way. I wish you'd stop saying things like that." Actually he didn't need to be reminded of the explosive situation they had created. Inez finished her soup and Eric glanced at his watch. It was two o'clock already and dinner was at four. What was supposed to be a day devoted to the woman he loved had turned into a complete disaster. Hell, he didn't even have Amber's other Christmas presents wrapped yet. He wondered if Amber would call to see if he was coming to the house for dinner. He decided she was probably too stubborn and would wait right up to the last minute if she called at all. He wondered what she was doing. Was she still as upset as she had been at church? He certainly hoped not. What would she think if she knew Inez was still in his bed with nearly nothing on? What would she do if she could note his quickened pulse and the ever present urgency of his groin? "My God, what is the matter with me!?" He cursed at himself for fifteen minutes.

Another hour passed and Inez roused. "I'm really better, Eric. You should be with her today. Why don't you go on over to the house as you are expected?" He noticed she didn't mention Amber's name.

"I don't want to leave you alone." He really wanted Amber to call and ask him to come.

"Nonsense. I have been alone for most of my life. I will be fine. I would like to take a long hot bath. I know I would feel better if I could do that. Would you mind?"

"Not at all. I'll show you where everything is located." He helped Inez out of the bed, showed her the clean linens and started to carry the dirty dished back to the kitchen. Inez got clean underclothes from her overnight case and locked herself in the bathroom for a renewal project. Eric now spoke to her through the bathroom door. "I'm running over to the Manor, I guess. I'll back in a short while. If you need anything or get to feeling worse or anything, call me there."

Inez couldn't help but to chuckle at that thought. "Okay, you go on and have a good time. I am really fine. I found a whole new body in here."

"Ha, there wasn't anything wrong with the old one if you ask me."

"Why, thank you Eric. You are determined to make my whole day."

Eric started to say something else but the phone rang. It was Amber. Her voice was soft and hesitant. Eric suddenly felt guilty.

'Eric, I'm really sorry about this morning. I'm just so damn confused where Inez is concerned but that isn't your fault and I shouldn't take it out on you."

"That's okay Baby. I was just on my way over to beg your forgiveness. Let's just forget it ever happened. Has Lillie got dinner ready yet?" Eric was happy to let Amber share the guilt for this morning's fight.

"Yes, Lillie has the kitchen in full command. Everything smells so good. I can't wait for you to get here. I have some surprises for you!" Then just as an after thought Amber asked, "Eric, is Inez still there?"

Eric was instantly defensive and too quick to flare. "Yes, Amber, she is still here."

"I see. What is she doing?" Anger flooded her soul but she wanted to be reasonable.

"Well, right this minute she is soaking in a tub full of hot water."

All reason left Amber's mind. "What is she doing in your bath tub? I thought she was so sick."

"Damn it Amber! She is sick but she feels better and she is taking a damn bath. What the hell is so wrong with that? I thought you wanted her out of here. Well, she is trying to get ready to get out of here." He was too angry and he wondered if it showed. He should have just played it cool and he should have never used such an accusing tone with Amber again. He knew it, but it was too late. Amber snapped and it was also too late for her to practice any kind of restraint.

"Nothing is wrong with that Eric. Not one thing. Perhaps you should go and wash her back and when you are finished maybe you can tear yourself away long enough to come to dinner. Or better yet, bring her with you if you want."

"Amber, please, let's don't start this again. Why are you so jealous of her anyway?"

"Jealous? I am not jealous. I just don't think you should be so willing to hang around with someone that you know caused my father so much pain and has done nothing but cause me pain and humiliation ever since I met her."

"Amber, I am man enough to choose my own friends and I am not hanging around with her but if I choose to do so I will do so!"

"Oh, she can be classified as one of your friends?"

"She may very well be just that, Amber."

"Well, your tastes certainly have changed, Eric."

"Oh, Amber! I'm tired, I'm hungry. Can't we just knock this thing off for the time being?"

Amber soul flooded with rebellion. "Yes, Eric, I will knock it off. Completely off! Good bye!"

She hung up the phone with a loud bang. Eric stood in shock for a moment and then placed the receiver back on the phone. She would surely call back. He waited. He sat down and tried to comprehend what was going on. It was obvious that there was no talking to Amber about Inez. He wasn't really surprised so why did it frustrate him so? He was miserable. He wanted to go to Amber and hold her and forget any of this day ever happened. He wanted her warmth, not her contempt; he wanted to share Christmas Day with her, what was left of it anyway. He nearly cried. The season had been so lovely and they had planned today for weeks. How could Amber hang up like that and just ignore what "today" was suppose to be to them. He fixed himself a scotch and water and swallowed it in one choking gulp. He could feel the coldness of the liquid as it hit his empty stomach. He fixed another drink, this time with more scotch that water and drank it quickly. Once he had prepared his third drink, he lay back on his sofa and sulked. "Women! They are nothing but trouble," he cursed to himself or to the world or to anyone that would listen. Nearly every woman he had ever really known had ultimately caused him nothing but trouble. His mother was a whining mass of nerves all her life and cheerleaders were bitches that pranced around just hoping to give every male in the world an instant erection and he hated them all. Amber had driven him insane for several years and finally when Lance was no longer around to protect her, Eric had finally won her but now because of another damn woman he was about to loose Amber. Another woman…God how Inez Chandler was plaguing him. He had consumed nearly half the bottle of scotch by the time Inez walked out of the bathroom in a towel. She was lovely. The bath had done wonders for the color in her face and she had applied new makeup. Eric raised up to look at her. Inez feigned surprise and tried hard at modesty too. "Eric, I thought you had already left the house."

"I'm not going anywhere. We talked it over on the phone and Amber thinks I should stay here and wash your back." He laughed and reached for another drink.

"Why, Eric Tolliver, I do believe you are drunk."

"I am not drunk; however, I am extremely relaxed. I have never had scotch for breakfast before, and I think I may like it."

Inez laughed out loud. "Come on. Let's go to the kitchen. It's my turn to fix you something to eat." She stood over him and extended her hand toward him to help him up. He took her hand and heaved himself off the sofa. When he stood up he was only inches away from her. He took hold of her arm and pulled her closer to his body. "Do you know how damn beautiful you are? It's no wonder Lance Harris never got over you." He leaned down to kiss her on the neck. He held her firmly against him revealing to Inez that liquor does not always kill a man's ardor. She pulled free of him and lowered her eyes not wanting to look into those handsome eyes that she had only moments ago thought about flirting with. Suddenly she was ashamed of the position she had placed Eric and Amber into. Eric read the thoughts almost mystically and pulled her back to him. Inez struggled only slightly.

"Eric don't. I am not worth your losing Amber for good. We've done enough harm. You are half drunk and right now you are hurt and angry. You don't really want me; you just want to hurt Amber because she disappointed you today. She is a woman and she has the emotions of a woman. Women are naturally dubious of another woman invading their territory. And I am just another woman to Amber, not her mother."

Eric shook her gently before he spoke. "Do all you women know what I want? You always have all the answers. Well, you come prancing in here in a towel, showing off about an acre of skin, and you tell me what I want is to run to Amber and beg her forgiveness for something I am not sorry about. Well, you are wrong. Right now what I want is you and what I want is for you to not be so damned shocked about it. Hell, I think I wanted you last year. I dreamed about you for a month." He held her tightly, his heart pounding in his throat, his head swimming with every movement. He could feel Inez tremble. He liked what he felt.

"If Amber finds out she will hate me forever. She might hate you too." Her voice was barely a whisper.

Eric chuckled. "She has probably made up her mind to do that anyway. I don't ever see her nominating you for mother of the year. And she doesn't have a lock and key on me. Not yet anyway."

"Eric, this isn't right." She protested quietly and not strongly at all. Her mouth found his and her tongue parted his dry lips with bravery he had never know a woman could possess.

He picked her up and walked to his bedroom. His voice was deep, his breath heavy with the liquor that he had consumed too fast. He placed her gently on the bed. He stood over her. "How long has it been since a man made love to you, Inez?" he asked.

Inez laughed. "Eric, Lance was the only to ever 'make love' to me and that was over twenty years ago. Everything else has just been sex. I'm afraid I didn't have enough sense to take advantage of my good fortune with Lance."

Eric was looking her in the eye. He kicked off his shoes, pulled off his shirt and she watched his hands reach for his belt buckle. He smiled and spoke confidently. "Well, you have got sense enough to take advantage of me haven't you?" He unzipped his trousers with deliberation noting that Inez was a little surprised at his boldness. He wondered if most of her former partners allowed her to take charge; he would teach her that she was not granting him some favor by letting him use her body, but in fact it would be the other way around. He would do her the favors. He would delight her. He enjoyed watching her reactions. She gasped softly when his throbbing manhood was finally free of all confinement. He stood before her, his fine body completely naked. She was used to looking at men on their backs, with sheets to hide under and in the dark. He smiled and climbed into the bed. He was proud of the way he looked and he was elated at the affect he had on Inez. His ego soared when he took possession of her body. Through some fog in his brain he had heard Inez ask something about Amber and his reply had been calculated and to the point. "She will never be a daughter to you. You have nothing to loose. I will take my chances with her later, but right no I am going to take you!" He kissed her hard. His tongue found her mouth moist and sweet and she groaned with pleasure when he pressed her small frame close to his body. He drove himself into her soft flesh without caution, demanding relief. Inez was exotic and she knew how to please a man, just like he had dreamed she could. Their primal pleasure was glorious and he pounded himself into her flesh with delight.

Once drained, Eric lay beside Inez on the bed, his body bathed in sweat.

He kissed her softly now and to his surprise she responded with a take charge attitude. Her hands found his stomach muscles tight and firm. She traced tiny circles over his skin with her fingernails. When at last her fingers reached his groin area she avoided actually touching his penis. Instead she teasingly traced lines up and down his thighs, her fingernails causing sensational chills to run the entire length of his body. He felt his arousal slowly returning and when her hand actually grasped his organ, it was Eric that ached with desire. She was kissing his stomach and moving slowly down the middle of his torso. When she placed her mouth on his penis, his head spun. Never had a woman been so daring, so bold with him. When she finished teasing him beyond his wildest fantasy, she lay back down by his side and waited for him to mount her. He climbed atop her and positioned his narrow hips between her legs. He kissed her with new hunger and with one swift motion plunged himself deep into her again. She met his thrust eagerly and with their second climax came total exhaustion. They lay limp and breathing hard. They didn't speak. Eric kissed her gently and raised himself on one elbow to look at her. When he raised up he caught a reflection in the mirror on the wall opposite his bed. "Oh, Jesus Priest!" he gasped.

Amber turned to run from the doorway of the bedroom. She cursed herself for getting caught. She had just stood there watching her world crumble before her eyes and was absolutely helpless. She couldn't say anything, she couldn't cry, she forgot to breath. She just wanted to run but her legs wouldn't carry her fast enough.

Eric grabbed a sheet to wrap around himself and caught up to her in the living room. He caught her by the arm just enough to throw her off balance. She managed to jerk her arm free of Eric's grip but at the same time tripped over a large throw rug. She fell hard against his coffee table; so hard that Eric cringed at the audible "crack" her skull made when it hit the table's edge. She was blinded by the blood from the cut above her eyebrow, but even so was back on her feet before Eric could stumble to her to help her up. She tried to walk but again her legs and feet refused to move.

"Amber wait!" he pleaded. Amber stopped and turned to face him. He expected her to scream at him but she didn't. Her eye was already swelling shut from the nasty cut and it was turning an angry purple mixed with black. Her mouth was bleeding from where she had bitten her lip when she fell.

She was shaking all over and gagged noticeably when she tasted her own blood.

'Oh, God, honey. Let me help you!" he reached toward her but she stepped backward so he couldn't reach her. In a voice that was barely audible she spit words through fresh blood. "Don't touch me, Eric. Not now, not ever. Don't touch me.!" She took two more steps backward on legs that were refusing to support her.

"Oh God, baby, don't try to go outside. Jesus, you need stitches, I know you do. Please honey, I can explain this. I know this is awful." His voice trailed off into the air. Amber reminded him very much of a wounded animal. She backed farther from him. Blood ran freely down the side of her face into the neck of her blouse. She could no longer keep her left eye open. She stood with her back to the door and her hand finally found the door knob. She turned around, opened the door and tried to take a step. Her world was going black. Her knees buckled and the last thing she saw was Eric's face, ashen with guilt. He caught her just before she hit the floor again. He laid her on the sofa. Inez had finally emerged from the bedroom and stood by his side. "Oh my God, Eric, what have we done to her?" she asked.

Eric didn't answer. He was too busy trying to get dressed so he could get Amber to the nearest emergency room. He cursed the scotch, her cursed Inez and he cursed himself. The knot on Amber's forehead was as big as his fist now and her eye had completely disappeared. She was still bleeding from the cut and now her left nostril had started to trickle blood. Eric was panic stricken. Once he was dressed, he wrapped Amber in a blanket and opened the door so he could carry her out to his car. It was then that he noticed the package standing beside his television. Taped to the bright paper was a note and he recognized Amber's handwriting. "Being a redhead makes me crazy. I'm sorry. I love you. Amber." Eric fiercely wadded the note up and threw it across the room. "My God, she had come to make up with me. God what have I done?"

He wanted to weep but knew there was no time. He bent over Amber and lifted her as gently as his trembling arms would allow. He was weak all over and for a moment thought he might just pass out himself. Amber didn't rouse, instead her neck let her head fall limply to one side almost as if were broken. Her breath came in short shallow gasps. The nausea that gripped Eric was almost overwhelming. He started his car and drove for what seemed like an eternity toward Bayview Hospital. For thirty five miles Eric cursed one minute and prayed the next. He pleaded with God and all the saints to help him save Amber. Snow poured from the sky again and the road was nearly impassable in places. When he finally drove his car into the parking lot of the hospital it had been almost two hours since Amber had lost consciousness.

Eric staggered under Amber's weight now and he was nearly in shock himself when he carried her into the deserted lobby of the hospital. He yelled for help and a duty nurse came briskly around the corner. She had already started to admonish his boisterous entrance when she saw Amber's face. Realizing that the girl was unconscious, and from the look of Eric's own condition, the nurse became a little more compassionate. She guided him to a gurney and helped him lay Amber down gently. "What happened? How long had she been unconscious? What is her name? Age? Who are you? Who is her next of kin?" The questions flowed for what seemed like an hour and Eric answered them mechanically, never taking his eyes from Amber's face. She was deathly pale except where the angry purple had invaded. In fact the entire left side of her face was now a massive bruise. The cut above her eye lay gaping open and a white trace of bone shone through the blood and flesh. Eric heaved when he realized he was looking at her skull. The nurse wheeled Amber into a small treatment room, called the x-ray department and asked Eric to be seated just outside the door. She promised to keep him informed and would be back out just as soon as the doctor finished examining Amber. Eric sat alone in the dim hallway and fought to keep from sobbing. His thoughts tortured him. How could he have been so stupid, so cruel? Lillie had warned him. Hell, even Inez had warned him. Oh, God, Lillie, he had better call her. How would he tell her? If possible, his misery multiplied. He found a pay phone, dialed the number and waited for Lillie to answer. The phone had barely begun its' first ring when an annoyed Lillie said "Hello!"

Eric's throat was so dry he could hardly speak. "Lillie, it's me, Eric."

Lillie was angry. "I know who you are Eric Tolliver. Where are you two anyway? Dinner is ruined! What is going on?"

"Lillie, I'm at the emergency room of Bayview General."

"You are? What is wrong with you?"

His grief apparent, he said, "It isn't me Lillie, it is Amber. She fell Lillie, and she is hurt really bad. Maybe you should come down here. I'm scared, Lillie. It's all my fault, she will never forgive me." Eric was beginning to loose control and Lillie wanted off the phone and to be on her way.

"I'll be right there Eric. Mr. Templeton will bring me right now. You tell Amber that Lillie will be there as fast as she can."

Eric hung up the phone and stood there looking at the dial for just a moment. He was numb all over. He made his way back to his chair and waited for someone to tell him news of Amber. He was still waiting when Lillie and Mr. Templeton walked into the hospital nearly ninety minutes later. Eric tried to stand up to greet them but his legs wouldn't hold him up. Lillie had a hundred questions to ask him but the moment she saw him she recognized before her a man about to break so she held her tongue.

She begged a nurse to let her peak in at Amber and wished she hadn't. Amber lay with I.V. solutions running into each arm and her entire face was swollen and grotesque against the pillow. It had taken fifteen stitches to close the wound above her eye and there was talk of surgery to "relieve pressure" if she didn't wake soon. There was talk about pressure from blood leaking inside her head between her brain and skull. Her legs were propped up on pillows. Lillie was confused and frightened. After another hour of waiting she could stand it no longer and ask Eric gently, "Can you tell me about what happened, Eric?"

He nodded weakly. "This is all my fault, Lillie. Amber and I have fought all day over Inez."

"Inez!" Lillie hissed. "That woman is no good! Surely you know that by now."

"Well, I'm not much good either, Lillie. Anyway Amber and I were fighting, she tried to leave and I caught her arm to try and stop her. I threw her off balance and she tripped over a damn throw rug and fell against my coffee table. She got up and walked a few steps. The she just fell over and she has been out ever since. Oh God, Lillie what if I have killed her?"

Lillie was furious but she tried to soothe Eric. It didn't help much though. After the third set of x-rays on her head and neck were completed,

Amber was moved to a special observation area. Lillie and Eric were allowed to set with her there. The minutes were endless. A young intern walked into the room at last, and ask for Amber's family. Lillie jumped up from her chair. "That's me," she answered. "I mean I raised Amber. I am her house keeper and friend. This man is her fiancé."

The physician looked at Eric and instantly came to several wrong conclusions and it showed. Any other time Eric would have floored the man but right now he figured he deserved any disgust anyone might have for him even if for the wrong reasons.

"You the gentleman that brought Miss Harris in?" The question was curt. Eric nodded his affirmative answer. "I see. Can you tell me exactly how this happened?" The physician had already decided that he didn't like Eric.

Eric repeated his story and knew the tight lipped intern thought he had hurt Amber on purpose. And why not? He still smelled like a brewery and he needed a shave. He had acted half crazy ever since he arrived at the hospital. The tension building between the two men was so obvious that Lillie had begun to chew her lip. She spoke cautiously. "Doctor can you tell us what is wrong? Why doesn't Amber wake up? Is she going to be okay?"

Obviously directing more sympathy in Lillie's direction the physician answered her. "As for question number one, I can't be sure about the extent of her injuries. The x-rays aren't much help. They don't show enough damage to justify the fact that she doesn't come around. Number two, frankly I do not know why she doesn't wake up and question number three, God only knows at this point if she is going to be okay or not. We just have to wait and see what the rest of the night brings. I don't want to rush into surgery if there isn't any more swelling inside her head and right now we have that under control with the steroids. I am sorry I can't be more optimistic for you." He squeezed Lillie's hand gently, then turned and faced Eric again. "Mr. Tolliver, you know of course if Miss Harris were to actually die I will have to turn this over to the authorities."

For Eric the statement was the last straw. It started an avalanche of emotion that he could not control. He grabbed the internist by the collar and screamed in his face. "You listen to me you smart bastard! You do not let her die and is she does die, the AUTHORITIES can do what they damn well please with me but only after I kill you with my own hands."

"Eric! Enough of this!" Lillie grabbed him and with the help of a nurse they freed the doctor of Eric's grip, and sat Eric down in the chair. Eric shook visibly.

The doctor gathered his emotions and said simply, "Violence will do nothing to help here Mr. Tolliver. Would you like for me to order something for you take for your nerves?"

Eric was broken, weak with despair. He refused the offer of medication. "I don't want to be drugged up if Amber wakes up."

"As you wish, Mr. Tolliver. If you change your mind, talk to the charge nurse. I'll leave orders with her."

"Very well," Eric sighed. Lillie wiped her eyes and brought her rosary from her purse, sat in a chair beside Eric and began to pray quietly. Mr. Templeton sat in the corner, saying nothing to anyone. He would save judgment he until later when he had more facts about the situation. The older man could not help but wonder what terrible tragedy had taken place this day. He wondered if the whole truth would ever be public knowledge. Eric was suffering so badly yet seemed so resigned to suffer; as if he knew he deserved his anguish. Mr. Templeton felt everyone concerned with this tragedy needed prayers. He would provide some of those.

At two a.m. Amber stirred for the first time. Her head was bursting and it hurt to open her eyes. In fact she could only open one eye and that one only partly. The left one was completely imbedded in swollen flesh. She couldn't take a deep breath without severe pain in her chest. She moaned slightly as the memory of her last vision of Eric flooded back into her mind.

She wept quietly as the thought broke her heart over and over. She finally forced her eye to stay open long enough to survey her surroundings. Even the subdued lighting made her head ache. She moaned again. She was confused and didn't know where she was. She wanted to know what time it was but couldn't focus on the clock. Surely Lillie was upset over dinner. She turned her head only slightly and it felt like a thousand horses galloped across her brain making her cry out softly. She saw Lillie only for an instant before she closed her eye tightly trying to block out the pain in her head. The pain centered directly behind her eye and was so severe she began to panic. "Lillie," she managed to whisper. Lillie was at her side immediately. She stood close to Amber's face and bent to kiss her gently on the forehead.

"Oh Amber, we have been so worried. Thank God you are awake at last. You lay still and let me get the nurse. I promised I would get them as soon as you woke up. That is the only was they would let me stay with you the whole night." Lillie was thrilled and woke up half the patients getting to the nurse's station. "Come quick." she cried. "She is awake. Come quick. She knew me and she spoke my name." The nurse snapped attention and followed Lillie back to Amber's room. She shined a small light in Amber's eye and made notes about the pupil activity. She took Amber's blood pressure and then quietly questioned Amber. "Can you see me plainly? Can you count my fingers? Can you raise your right hand? Now the left one?"

Amber responded and told her of the tremendous pain in her head.

"You have a frontal concussion, Amber. You are going to be down a day or two. We have been really worried about you, but I think you're going to get better now. The doctor will be in to see you soon and I'm sure he will want to examine you just a little further. I'll get you something for the pain in your head and if you need anything else, just ring for me or tell Lillie and I am sure she will let us know all about it." She cast a warm smile in Lillie's direction. Lillie smiled and bowed her head just a bit embarrassed. She hadn't really meant to give the staff a rough rime but she certainly had demanded their attention where Amber and her care had been concerned. Amber tried to smile and looked toward Lillie. The entire room seemed a little lopsided. Amber read the worry on Lillie's face. "What time is it, Lillie? How long have I been here?"

"It's two a.m. past, and you have been here for more than ten hours. I've been so worried. And Eric, poor Eric. He is on a couch in the hall way. I'll get him." She started to leave.

"No! No. Please don't Lillie." Her voice was urgent and Lillie halted at the foot of the bed. She looked at Amber with questions written on her face but said nothing. Amber continued weakly, "Just let him rest. And really you should go home too. I am okay. I really am." She actually wondered if she would ever be okay again in her lifetime. "They will take care of me here. I will be better off if I don't have to worry about you dropping over on me, honest. I'll need for you to be strong for me when I get well, you know I will." She tried hard to smile.

Lillie thought about her words for a moment, then admitted, "I am tired.

But are you sure, honey? I don't want to leave you alone."

"I won't be alone. There are a dozen nurses out there and here is a call button. All I have to do is to push the buzzer and here they come. Now go on home and get some rest. I'm so sorry I messed up your Christmas Day." Amber fought hard not to cry.

"You stop that. Listen I'll go now, but I'll be back early and I'll bring you some cinnamon rolls, okay?" Lillie's cure all. Amber smiled.

"That would be great Lillie. Don't forget….REST!"

Lillie kissed her gently avoiding the huge mass on her forehead. She woke Mr. Templeton and told him the good news. They drove back to the Manor House still wondering what had happened between Eric and Amber but both too courteous to question the situation out loud. At four a.m., Lillie fell into bed but not before thanking her God for Amber's recovery.

In the lobby of Bayview General, Eric woke up when the nurses and their aides starting changing shifts. His body was stiff and his muscles ached. The unkind couch had not been long enough to allow him to even stretch out on but his body had finally given in to total exhaustion and he had slept like a dead person. He got up slowly and walked to the nurse's station. He was afraid and he looked like a mad man. His throat refused to help him speak but he finally managed to be heard. "Miss Harris? Has there been any change?" He was almost afraid to listen to the answer. He hadn't meant to sleep so long?

"Good news, Mr. Tolliver! She came around at about two this morning."

"I have got to see her, please!"

"That will be fine, Mr. Tolliver, but you have got to be careful about upsetting her at this point. We want no excitement, no sudden changes in blood pressure. And don't say anything to her about losing the baby, she doesn't know it yet. We didn't tell her this morning because we felt it more important that she rest peacefully. You understand, don't you?" She paused when she noticed Eric's ashen face. "Are you alright, Mr. Tolliver?"

"The baby," he whispered. "My God, I didn't know she was pregnant!"

The young nurse was stunned. "Oh, Mr. Tolliver. I'm so sorry. I just assumed they told you in emergency last night. Gosh, I am really sorry. Please forgive me." Her face reddened as she stumbled through the words. Eric hardly noticed. He walked toward the door of Amber's room not really knowing what to say or how to say it. He paused at the door not knowing what he would do on the other side. Amber had carried his child. Something he had dreamed of for years! Every time he had ever touched Amber, he had hoped "this time" would be the time he would leave her with child. Now the child had been ripped from her body because he had been such an idiot! It was some kind of justice he told himself. Why hadn't Amber told him of the baby! Had she known? He cursed himself.

He crept to the side of Amber's bed. She looked terrible; even worse than when he had laid down. The swelling had traveled down her face into her neck and her whole face was blue and green and even black. The huge cut above her eye had seeped blood around the stitches, and the blood had dried leaving an ugly mark across her forehead. Her legs were still elevated slightly and she had intravenous solutions connected to needles sticking from both arms. Eric had not eaten anything except Johnny Walker Scotch for over thirty hours. He was dehydrated and exhausted. The sight of Amber lying on the bed nearly made him physically ill. His audible gasp woke Amber up. She immediately turned her face to the opposite wall. Eric tried to speak but choked. After a two minute struggle he finally managed to whisper, "Amber, Baby, please at least tell me to get lost."

Amber turned back to face him. Her tears caused more pain in her head and it took every ounce of strength she had to keep from screaming. Silent tears flowed and fell off her cheek to her shoulder. She had realized she was bleeding heavily and that Eric's baby had been thrown from her body. Her heart was breaking into pieces and she just didn't have the strength to get angry any more. Finally she whispered, "Okay, Eric, Get Lost!" She turned her face back to the wall and sobbed.

"Oh, no, Amber, don't!" He wanted to touch her, hold her.

"Eric, please. I'm jut not in the mood to fight anymore. I've been kind of moody lately, and I know I'm a bit hard to live with sometimes and I am sorry for that. I've had so much on my mind; now everything has changed in my life and I am just not up to even listening to you right now. Just leave me alone, Eric. Just go away and let me think."

"Amber, baby, please, I am so sorry. God knows I never meant to hurt you."

"Eric, did you hear me say I do not want to listen to you and I really don't want to discuss your conduct; not now, not ever."

"I don't blame you," he tried to take her hand gently but she pulled it away as fiercely as she could without harming one of the tubes or needles sticking out of the back of her hand. She winced with pain and Eric hated himself for making her move.

"Okay, okay. We can talk later."

"No Eric. We can never talk about this. I don't intend to discuss it with you ever. Now will you please just leave me alone."

"Honey, don't talk that way. I can make all this up to you. I will, I swear."

"You owe me nothing Eric. I learned a lot from you this past year and I am thankful for the lessons. I'll never forget them. However, I will never give you the chance to hurt me again. Now, please go away."

Eric wouldn't give up. "But I do owe you, Amber. You were pregnant with my child." Amber looked him. He continued. "The nurse told me. Why didn't you tell me, Amber? I should have known about the baby from the beginning."

Amber laughed. "Would that knowledge have kept you out of bed with my mother, Eric? And I was going to tell you New Year's Eve. Foolish me. I thought I would make a real romantic event out of the announcement. Neat way to start the New Year and all that. My mistake."

She could barely speak loud enough for him to hear and her head was pounding. "Now, just get out Eric. Get out of my room and get out of my life."

"No, Amber, no! You don't mean that!" His voice was desperate. "I love you, Baby. You know I do. We can straighten this mess out with some time and understanding."

Amber began to weep. She pushed the call button and her nurse was by her side within the minute. "Make him leave me alone," she begged the nurse. The nurse turned on Eric instantly and ordered him out of the room. "I told you not to upset her! What are you saying to her anyway? Did she ask you to leave? Then get out, now!"

Eric whispered, "I do love you, you know I do!" The nurse had a tight hold on his arm and was guiding him firmly to the door. "Mr. Tolliver, go home and look at yourself in the mirror. Take a shower, get something to eat and get some rest. Then maybe you can be more yourself and try to talk with Miss Harris again. Now I must insist, leave!"

Eric traveled slowly back to his apartment. He dreaded confronting Inez. His "dread" was wasted. Inez was gone. No note, no message, nothing. Just gone. Eric looked around his living room. Blood stained the plush carpet and his sofa. There was still dried blood on the corner of the coffee table. The bedroom was a wreck. Obviously Inez had looked around before she left. Probably for money. She hadn't even called to see if Amber was alive or dead. Actually Eric was glad she was gone. At least he didn't have to relate the details of what their hideous deed had caused. And he couldn't admit to anyone that he had lost Amber, not even to himself. He laughed out loud. This was so typical of Inez. He cursed her and himself. The world just fell to pieces and Inez was no where in sight to help pick up the pieces. He picked up the empty scotch bottle and slung it across the kitchen bracing himself for the splash of glass that followed its' impact against the wall. He exited the room and threw himself on the sofa. At this point his eyes focused on the present from Amber and he knew he was going to be physically ill. He headed for the bathroom and heaved until he was weak. Seeing himself in the mirror was his next shock. His hair was a tangled mess, he was two days past needing a shave, and his eyes looked like road maps that were about to bleed. He decided a shower and a shave might help and they sure couldn't hurt anything. By 7:30 a.m. at least he was clean and looked a little less subhuman. He was about to eat when his phone rang. He answered while praying it would be Amber. His caller was Lillie.

"Eric, if you need to talk to anyone, I'm available. My loyalties are with Amber, but if you need help, you call me. We have been friends since you were a little boy, and I hate to see the both of you in such pain.

"Thank you, Lillie. I need all the help I can get right now, but I'm afraid there isn't much anyone can do...But, I really do thank you for calling me. You are sweet. No wonder Amber loves you so much."

"I love her Eric. Like she is my own daughter. It pains me a lot to see her in pain and all bruised up like she is. She must have been terrible mad."

"She was Lillie. Actually I guess she was more hurt than mad."

"You intend to tell me about it, Eric?"

"Not yet, Lillie. I'd really rather Amber told you about it anyway. I deserve whatever she dishes out Lillie, but how I hope she will give me a chance to make things right with her again."

"Well, Eric, if you need me, just call. Remember now. I mean it. I'm going back to the hospital for now. Any messages for Amber?"

"Just tell her that I love her, okay?"

"Sure, Eric. Well bye now."

He hung up the phone wondering if Amber would tell Lillie the truth about his stupidity. Lillie would hate him. Life for Eric would never be the same. He knew that now. He tried to eat and began to straighten up his apartment. He had to do something to keep from going absolutely crazy.

"At Bayview General Hospital, Amber Harris would not be remembered at a model patient. Once the pounding in her head had stopped she felt she was ready to leave and made no secret for her distaste of hospital routine. When her doctor finally came in to see her, she practically attacked him because he wouldn't discharge her immediately. His only response to her begging had been short and to the point. "No!" Then he added, "Miss. Harris, you are in no condition to sulk. You have just lost a baby, your head has been caved in, it took seventeen stitches to put your eyebrow back together, and you are lucky to have no more problems than you do. Now, I think I know a little bit about what is best for you right now and I can't believe that you haven't got just a few days to spare for the sake of your health. After all some day you may want to carry a child full term. Give your body a chance to heal, please." Amber calmed slightly.

"Can you tell me why I lost the baby?"

"No, not for sure. The initial shock of the fall and your unconsciousness may have caused severe shock and trauma to the fetus. You may have lost the baby anyway. You were severely dehydrated on arrival here and you lost a lot of blood. I honestly cannot tell you why with any real validity. I can honestly tell you that research has proved that most of the time when a woman miscarries, it is for the best. I know that doesn't make you feel any better mentally, but it's the truth." He smiled and tried to imagine how pretty she would be if she were not mutilated by the swollen tissue.

"Will I be able to have a healthy baby, ever?"

"Absolutely. But let's just concentrate on getting better for now. You know what they say, one day at a time."

"Okay, but seriously, when can I go home? I'd like to spend part of the holidays at home. Not that you people aren't real nice and all, but my Christmas stocking is at home you see."

The doctor smiled warmly. "That's my girl. You are going to need a sense of humor. Seriously, if you do not hemorrhage today or tomorrow and you can walk Monday without the top of your head exploding, then you can check out of our elegant establishment on Tuesday morning, I promise. But you have got to take it easy, even when you get home. And I mean easy for several days."

"Okay, I promise." She sighed but at least she had a goal in mind. She would count the hours until Tuesday morning. Her doctor left to visit with his next patient and Amber hated being alone. She didn't want to think about her pain and all the reasons she was confined to this bed.

It was nearly noon when Eric came back into her room. He approached the bed quietly and when Amber moved it startled him.

"Hello, Baby." He was hesitant. She looked at him as well as she could with only one eye to open.

"Hello, Eric." She tried to make her voice emotionless.

"Amber, are you strong enough to talk to me?"

"Really, Eric, I don't think I'll ever be that strong again. And besides I told you this morning, I don't want to talk to you."

"I guess you hate me."

"I guess I do, Eric."

"That is short and to the point at least."

"I hope so. Now would you please get out?"

"Amber, we can work this whole mess out. I know we can."

"Eric, I do not want to work it out. Can you hear me? I said 'no'. That is it. I call the shots now Eric, and I say we are done!"

"Amber, please…"

Amber was in a rage. "Please??? Please what Eric! Please trust you, love you, need you. I DID! And look where it got me. Forget it. I don't need this. You know if it had have been ANYBODY else in the world in bed with you, I might have handled it. But you and her…My God in heaven, Eric, you have been around our family all these years, watching her destroy people's hearts, so what do you do? Climb into bed with her the first chance you get. Jesus Priest, you were one of the people that demanded that I have nothing to do with her when she first buzzed back into town a year ago."

"Can I try and explain how this hideous thing happened to us."

"Okay, Eric, your happiness is so damn important. You explain it to me. I need a good laugh right now anyway."

"I got drunk, Amber. Real drunk. I hadn't had anything to eat and after our last fight on the phone I started drinking and I swear I never intended to touch her. By the time she got out of the tub I had consumed most of the bottle and I was bombed."

"Is that what I would have to look forward to if we were to get married? Every time something doesn't suit you, you'll get drunk, bed some whore and then expect me to feel guilty because I don't understand? You're damn right I don't understand. Have you stopped to think that Inez Chandler is the first and only thing we have ever disagreed about…Our first fight and you go berserk. I will NOT live like this Eric. And I don't ever intend to let you touch me again, so I repeat, leave me alone. Just get out of here and out of my life."

"Amber, this isn't like you. I've never heard you so harsh, so cold. Please don't talk this way."

"Don't tell me how to talk, Eric." She pulled the diamond ring from her finger. "Get out, Eric, and take this with you. I won't be needing it."

"Amber, Baby, don't do this. We can't just drop everything we've started to build."

"We are not just dropping everything. We are ending a relationship that should not have begun in the first place. We should have remained friends and kept the relationship sacred. Now everything is ruined." The tears were beginning to choke her. "This mess is as much my fault as it is yours. Will you please leave me alone, Eric? I have a headache and I am really tired."

"Baby, please, I love you. I have always loved you."

"No more, Eric. No more sweet talk. We should have never tried being lovers."

"Amber! We didn't TRY to become lovers. We were lovers."

"That is correct, Eric. And the important word in that sentence is 'were'. Past tense."

"Amber, honey…," he tried in vain to touch her, take her hand.

"No! Did you hear me? I said NO! I'm tired of your tying to tell me how I feel about this. You have controlled my moods for so long you think I can no longer decide anything for myself. Well, you are wrong. Our love affair is over. I will not marry you now or ever. For God's sake, let's not spoil what little there is left of our relationship as friends. Please, Eric, get out of here and leave me be. You make me very tired!"

"Amber, you know how much I need you. This isn't fair."

Her temper flared. "Your needs can be satisfied by the nearest available skirt! What about my needs? The need to know my lover and intended husband is trustworthy, even under pressure. Eric, I mean this. I DO NOT want to see you right now. Will you please, just this once, let me have the last word? There really isn't any reason for us to see each other until I am ready to come back to work. Now go before I ring for a nurse."

"No Amber, you have to listen!" Eric had begun to perspire and wondered if the room were really as warm as it felt to him.

"I have listened to you for the last time Eric Tolliver. I have listened to you for several months and look at the shape I'm in." Amber didn't even know she was shouting and tears escaped even the swollen eye. A nurse had entered the room.

"Miss Harris, it is very important that you remain calm at all times."

"I want this man out of my room and he won't leave. I don't want him back here under any circumstances."

The nurse looked at Eric and spoke with a tone that could not be misunderstood by anyone. Her announcement was short and to the point. "Miss Harris is to remain calm at all times. It is my job to see to it that she does remain calm at all times. To ensure that I will most definitely have you thrown bodily from this building. This girl can not afford for one minute to be this upset. You will have to settle your personal affairs at some other point in time and it will have to be when she is ready and much healthier."

"Okay, okay, I'm going. But Amber, we must talk about this." His exit was swift and angry. Amber turned her face to a pillow and cried some more.

On Tuesday afternoon, after taking an oath that she would take it easy for at least another week, Amber was released from the hospital. She could open her injured eye but her stitches would be in place for another four days. Amber looked at her face in the mirror as she fluffed her auburn mane. She touched the bruised skin gingerly and sighed. "If only the bruises on my heart would mend so fast," she thought. She breathed deep to ease the lump forming in her throat. God, how much had she cried? It had to end. No more time for tears, her head hurt enough already. She needed some fresh air. She was glad to be going home and she was sure if her doctor knew how very dizzy she was he wouldn't hear of releasing her. She had to make her escape good before she fell flat on her face. She hadn't seen Eric since the day her nurse ordered him out of her room and she was grateful. She didn't want any further battle with Eric. She was weak and tired and didn't know how long she could resist his persistence. She refused to let Eric ever know again how hurt she was, she still had her pride at least.

Lillie was hovering over her like a mother hen. If she was aware of the miscarriage she kept it to herself and Amber was glad for that. Amber tried hard no to think about the lost baby. In fact, she tried hard not to think about anything at all. Her mind ached as much as her body did.

On the way home in the car Amber laid her head back against the head rest of the seat. Her head was throbbing and the movement of the car made her stomach lurch. Lillie noticed the tears creeping from under the closed eyelids, running silently down pale cheeks. Lillie could hold her tongue no longer.

"Are you going to be okay, Honey?" Lillie knew full well that her young friend was not okay and that it might be a long time before she would be okay again. Amber nearly laughed before she spoke. She took a deep breath and exhaled very slowly. She wiped the escaped tears from her face. "I am going to be fine, Lillie. It's very good to be going home. I feel as I have been gone for a long time."

"You want to tell old Lillie about all this? Or do you just want me to mind my own business. I can do that you know, mind my own business, that is."

"Oh Lillie, I don't know if I can talk about it or not. Everything happened so fast and it is all so crazy. So needless!"

"What everything?"

"Lillie, when I went to Eric's apartment on Christmas Day I found him in bed with another woman."

"You aren't serious!"

"Oh yes, I am quite serious."

"Who…Who would he be with? Especially since you and he. I mean.why!?" Lillie hadn't meant to embarrass Amber. She spoke kindly.

"Amber, I don't judge anyone's actions. I've known for many months that you and Eric have been intimate so why this close to your marriage would he do such a thing?"

Amber was weeping openly now. Her pale cheeks were flushed and her voice barely a whisper. "Lillie, the woman was Inez Chandler."

"Oh my God, Amber." Lillie was stunned. She felt like she was frozen in time. She was so shocked that she wasn't even sure she should be trusted to drive the car. Then she angered; angered as only a person who loved Amber from nearly the moment they had met could be angered. Angered as only a woman that quietly been in love with Lance Harris could be angered. For years she had stood by and watched the damage Inez Chandler had done to Lance and now she had started in on Amber. She wondered why a woman such as Inez is allowed to exist while a man such as Lance is struck down in his prime. She prayed silently asking God to forgive her question of His wisdom and to show her the ways of His will.

For the thousandth time Amber sniffed into a hanky. She sat up straight again and then slowly stated with every ounce of determination she possessed, "That is it, Lillie. I don't ever want to or intend to discuss this mess again. And don't tell anyone else, please. Promise, Lillie. Promise you will not tell another soul."

"Okay, my dear. NO ONE, I will talk to no one about this." Lillie patted her on the shoulder and continued the drive home in silence.

Once home, Amber went to her room. The room she had so loved Eric in. The room where he claimed her virginity. She lay across her bed and stroked the pillow that so often had cradled Eric's head. Everything she looked at had been touched by their love affair. Only a week ago this room had served as their own hiding place from the world. She had learned so much from Eric and now the room felt like a tomb. She looked around once more and tried to laugh. She thought about redecorating and wondered cynically how many men you could "redecorate" out of your life before you actually died of a broken heart. Lillie hustled into the room with hot coffee and fresh cinnamon rolls and sat them beside the bed. Amber looked at the fresh rolls and cried immediately. Lillie rung her hands but said nothing. She left Amber with her thoughts and went downstairs to clean the kitchen and to pray for Amber. Amber finally slept and when the morning sun filtered into her room she was wide awake and felt somewhat rested. She lay on her side and looked out the window wishing she could float away on one of the snowy white clouds that looked so close to the ground. A snowflake occasionally danced into view but the weatherman had promised no more snow until the weekend. Amber eased from the bed hoping that is she moved slowly her head wouldn't throb and the dizziness wouldn't take over. She didn't dare let Lillie or her doctor know about this but she wished she could do something for it. She felt confident that time would heal the inside of her head. She wasn't so sure about her heart.

She stood upright and nothing happened; no pain, no dizziness. Great! She snuggled up in her favorite robe. She tiptoed downstairs. Lillie was gone but there was fresh coffee on the stove. The kitchen smelled of baked bread and coffee beans. She poured herself a cup of coffee and dialed the number of the downtown offices of Harris-Tolliver Enterprises. Eric's secretary was delighted to hear that Amber was home and "No," she was sorry but Eric was momentarily out of his office. She would be glad to see that he called her as soon as he returned. She did NOT tell Amber that he was nearly drunk when he left the office and would probably be incoherent by the time he returned. She had hopes that now that Amber was back on her feet, things between the young Miss Harris and her boss would "straighten out" and life would return to normal. Of course her boss had not told her why he and the fair young lady had so suddenly split up.

Amber placed the phone back in place and sighed. Pain filled her head and her heart. She sadly wondered if she should forgive Eric's foolhardy betrayal but she immediately knew there was no real way she could forgive his actions with Inez. It wasn't just his sexual conduct that she resented. Her bitterness was mixed up inside with anger over Eric's total abandonment of respect for Lance's feelings. Had he suddenly forgotten all loyalties? Amber had compromised all she had been taught to carry on a love affair sans marriage with Eric. He had cast their relationship to the winds to satisfy his carnal tastes with Inez. Inez; the known enemy of all that love holds dear. Well, she would not COMPETE for Eric or any other man, damned if she would. She walked toward the library. She passed the beautiful tree that she and Eric had decorated together. "She and Eric," everywhere she turned there was something to remind her tortured brain of him. As strange and as painful as all this was, Amber was not surprised. From the very beginning of their affair, Amber had feared losing Eric. She thought about the nightmares and wondered if they were indeed some kind of premonition. She tried not to believe in premonitions.

As she neared the library, she passed the hall table and took note of the unopened mail lying in stacks. She smiled. There wasn't anything that Lillie did that she didn't do neatly. She picked up the mail and leafed through it absentmindedly. As she was about to toss it back on the table she noted a letter addressed to her in long hand. The envelope was blue onion skin paper and her name was written in old fashioned script, much like that written by the scholars of the middle ages. There was no return address.

She opened the envelope to find matching stationery that smelled like British Sterling after shave lotion. Her heart leaped. How many people knew how much she loved that fragrance? Not even Eric knew it. She read the note quickly. It read: "The statue is perfect. I had the date engraved on the base at Calhoun's Jewelry. Benny Calhoun tells me you are absolutely beautiful and that you always sniff the British Sterling samplers. Merry Christmas, Miss Harris, and seriously, Thank You. The statue will be treasured. Sincerely, "Shadow" McIntire. P.S. I'm looking forward to actually meeting you. Jason."

Amber couldn't stop smiling as she re-read the note. She breathed deep as the sniffed the paper again. She giggled. "So Benny Calhoun thinks I'm beautiful. How sweet."

She moved into the library and decided to pen a note back to Jason McIntire but changed her mind. She really didn't know what to say anyway. Instead she reached for the phone and dialed the phone number of the McIntires. Ada's voice was pleasant and mild as usual. After some small talk, Amber asked if Jason were present. She told Ada about the gallant note she had received and explained that she as looking forward to meeting him. However, as always, Jason was not present. In fact he was at one of the barns tending a mare that was about to foal. Ada could sense Amber's disappointment. Never during all the time that Amber had been visiting them had Ada McIntire thought about her son being a viable companion for the young lady. Funny, Ada didn't really know why. Amber was pretty, sweet turned, honest, hard working; it just had never occurred to her to try and arrange for the two of them to meet. They were after all, from two different worlds. Or were they? Ada thought about Amber's father and his humble beginnings. "Shall I have him call you?" Ada asked. Amber lost every ounce of courage she had and replied quickly, "Oh, no, no. That isn't necessary. I'll see him when I come out to visit. Don't bother him while he is doing something important. But do tell him that I appreciated the note and that I am really pleased that he enjoys the statue."

"Alright dear. You have a Happy New Year."

"Happy New Year to you too, Ada." Amber hung up the phone and thought to herself, "Happy New Year indeed. It couldn't be any worse that the last one, that is for sure."

On the opposite end of that telephone line Ada McIntire stood looking into the receiver of her phone before placing it back into its' cradle. She wondered about her young friend. She had sounded so unsure of herself and sad. Ada had never imagined Amber in that light during the entire time they had begun to know each other again. Amber sounded so distant and so alone. Ada wished Jason had been present to receive his call.

Amber heard Lillie enter the house. She was busy "shushing" Mr. Templeton until she realized that Amber was up and about.

"Oh, there you are. We were afraid we would wake you."

"No, Lillie. I am up and Dear Lillie, I am not sick, okay?" She hugged Lillie and Mr. Templeton. "I want everything around here to get back to normal."

"Good. That is what I want too." Lillie scurried to the kitchen to fix lunch for the three of them. The phone rang and Amber answered knowing that Eric would be on the other end of the line.

"Amber, Baby! God, I am glad you called. I'm sorry I was out. Hey, how you feeling?" He was rushing his words and Amber sensed he had been somewhere besides a business meeting.

"Eric, please listen. I just called to tell you I am fine and that I'll be back in the office in a couple of days. I didn't want to just walk in."

"Amber, I'll be at the house in ten minutes. You have to let me talk to you."

"Eric, NO! Don't start with me. Don't come out here."

"Yes, yes I am. We can't go on like this." He hung up.

"Damn him! Why can't he take no for an answer?!" She threw the phone back into place and stomped into the kitchen.

"Lillie, I'm going for a drive. When Eric gets here in a few minutes just tell him I said to back off for once in his life."

"Amber, you should not drive."

"I'll be okay. I'll drive slowly. I just don't want to fight with Eric right now. I'm just not up to it. I'll be home soon and I'll call you in a little while."

Lillie gave up quickly knowing that Amber wasn't really in any condition for stress from anyone. "Okay, but please be careful," she begged.

Amber was dressed in record time and when she eased her car out of the drive way she turned opposite the way she knew Eric would approach. She shifted gears smoothly one to another. It felt good to be in control of something. Why was it that no matter what the situation, someone was always trying to take over for her. Damn Eric, why couldn't he be reasonable about all this? After all, it was his conduct that was questionable. Why couldn't he be a gentleman enough to at least let Amber have her own way for once without a fight? Why couldn't he just bow out gracefully? She began to get more angry with each passing mile. She found herself heading out of town toward the countryside. The trees along the road were heavy with snow; their branches hanging close over the road, forming a silver and white tunnel. The skies were pale blue with silver clouds dotting the horizon. The crisp clean air was just what she needed to clear her thoughts and to ease her anger. She drove slowly, observing the iced beauty of the woods. She drove around in circles for nearly three hours. The sun was sinking in the west when she realized that she was pulling into the driveway of Aston Acres. She was startled by the fact that she had driven so far without even realizing it. The time had just disappeared and she felt uneasy about the new falling snow that peppered the windshield. She should be on her way home but since she was all the way out here she might as well at least say hello to everyone. She could call Lillie from inside too. She stood for a moment by her car and looked over the snow blanketed fields surrounding the farmhouse that had served as her home so many years ago. It seemed like at least a hundred years ago that her father's dump truck had sat in the drive where her own car sat now. She breathed deep. A cup of hot tea with Ada would help, she knew it would. She stepped lightly to the porch and knocked on the door. There was no one home. Disappointed, she turned to go back to her car. Then she thought of the mare Ada mentioned earlier and wondered if the little foal had arrived yet. It couldn't hurt anything if she looked in the barn could it? There was a neatly shoveled path through the snow to the barn. Amber made her way to the barn gingerly and tiptoed quietly inside. In the very first stall, there she was; a magnificent brown mare and her new born colt. Amber edged to the door of the stall and peaked through the boards at mother and babe. The new hay smelled good and the gentle mare seemed calm; very much used to human intrusion. Amber scratched the soft nose and soon discovered that the animal would stand there as long as she would scratch. Amber smiled and apologized for moving on. "I really have to get going, but I sure am glad I met you pretty lady." She paused before she muttered to herself, "Oh Lord, I'm talking to a horse." The next stale housed a smaller, obviously younger mare of equal beauty to the first one. Amber petted it and talked softly to it before moving back outside the barn. She closed the door securely. She walked softly through the snow. The setting sun spread warmth over the fields like a soft coverlet. Amber breathed deep and again the smell of the baled hay in the barn loft filled her nostrils. She wished she lived here again. It would feel good to call this place "home." She thought about those first years of her life and how good it had been to have her Grandmama to hold on to. She missed Lance and Sarahlou and now Eric had…tears stung her eyes. The pain over Eric was the worst of all. "Enough!" she thought. "I came out here to relax!"

Amber caught sight of a rider coming toward the barn. As the rider approached it became obvious he was quite handsome. From his height in the saddle Amber decided he must be about eight feet tall, but in fact Shadow McIntire was six foot two inches tall and tipped the scales at exactly 225 pounds. He was muscular, broad shouldered, had dark hair, hazel eyes, and his skin was golden tan even though it was the middle of winter. "Oh my God," Amber mused, "now I know what all those authors meant when they said tawny colored skin." His complexion was smooth and shone even in the fading sunlight. Amber envied the easy way he set his mount as if he were practically part of the horse. He enjoyed riding, that was obvious and right at the moment he was also enjoying the way Amber Harris was staring at him. Realizing that he enjoyed her admiring stare just a little too much,

Amber snapped herself out of the near trance she was in. Her face flushed making her eyes, even the bruised one, sparkle.

He was the first to speak as he brought his horse to a halt just inches from Amber. He liked the way Amber stood still, not afraid of his mount and careful not to startle the animal. She had to look up to see him and he noticed the color of her eyes was as green as any Mountain Laurel that he had ever seen. Her hair shone like cooper in the setting sun, and her skin was alabaster white, at least where it wasn't a mass of bruises. He liked most of what he saw before him. He wondered how she had been so injured.

"Hello, I'm Shadow McIntire. I'm the working foreman here. Can I be of service to you?" He literally slid from the horse's back with such grace that it was hard to tell when he actually touched the ground. His horse nickered to him, then nuzzled his arm affectionately. He smiled and patted the animal's neck with strokes that told Amber that he loved the animal very much. Amber was breathless. This man was as gorgeous as any character in any romance novel she had ever read.

"Well, hi! I'm Amber. Amber Harris. I came out to visit your folks but they aren't home. I started to leave but I wanted to see the new colt your Mama told me about. I hope you don't mind the intrusion Mr. McIntire. I didn't bother anything. I just scratched a nose or two. Your horses are truly lovely. You must be very proud." She was breathless and starting to get really dizzy. Probably from the exertion and cold air but frankly she was inclined to believe she was dizzy over the giddy way she was feeling. The young man standing in front of her was about to cast a spell over her that she hoped she would never get over. She extended her hand to him and added, "I'm truly glad we have finally met Mr. McIntire." She didn't get to hear Shadow's reply because that is when the lights just went out for Amber. Her world turned black and she no longer saw the sparkling snow nor smelled the fresh hay. Without warning she felt herself sink into the drowning blackness of unconsciousness. She had tried to fight it for an instant but the power was beyond her. When Amber regained consciousness she was in familiar surroundings. Shadow had caught her before she hit the ground. He carried her small body to the house and placed her on Ada's couch. The fire in the fireplace burned brightly and the only other light was a small candle on the coffee table. Shadow was sitting on the floor beside the couch.

He pressed a damp cloth to Amber's aching forehead.

The realization of what had happened hit Amber full force and she tried to rise. "I'm so sorry," she apologized; embarrassed by the fact that she needed help to survive. His strong arm held her down against the couch and he smiled. "No problem. Now you lie back and relax young lady. You got no business running around with that knot on your head, you know that, don't you?"

"What time is it? I need to call Lillie. She will be frantic."

"Hold on, you have only been out for about ten minutes. Suppose you tell me what happened to you anyway. I was going to ask you before you started your nap." His smile was warm.

Amber leaned back on the sofa and stared at the fire. "It is a long story. Actually I fell."

"I see. Listen, if you promise to take it easy for a few minutes, I'm going to run back to the barn and take care of the horses. You stay right here, please. I'll only be a few minutes."

"May I use the phone?"

"Sure, help yourself. But I repeat, please take it easy! I'll be right back."

Amber called Lillie and swore to her that she was doing fine. She assured Lillie that she would home in just a little while.

"Where are you?" Lillie inquired.

"I'm at the farm right now. I drove around for three hours. Just mostly thinking and enjoying the scenery. And they have a new baby colt here on the farm and I am visiting with Jason McIntire right now. I'll leave here in just a little while. Don't worry, okay?" She added slowly, "Did Eric show up?"

"Yes and I might add that he is not too happy either."

"Well, I am sorry about that but I'm just not ready to see him. And don't tell him where I'm at, okay? I'm sorry to drag you into all my personal problems, Lillie." She didn't dare tell her that she had fainted. Lillie was more than sympathetic.

"Don't worry about that, Amber. Just be careful and don't overdo."

"There's no chance of that. I'll see you later." Amber smiled as she hung up the phone. She watched the fire dance and felt relaxed by the flickers that burst forth from the flame.

Shadow returned from the barn. He had raced his favorite dog back to the house and when he entered the living room he was still breathless from the exertion in the cold air. He stomped the snow from his boots by the hearth and peeled off his coat. His hatless hair was covered with new snow and as he brushed the snow into the fire it caused little hissing sounds. Amber sat up on the couch. "I appreciate you kindness, Shadow."

"Would you like some brandy?" His breathing was even now and he was so totally relaxed that Amber envied him.

"I'd really prefer coffee or even hot tea if have it."

"Sure, I'd like coffee myself." He was on his was to the kitchen. Amber got up to follow him. She realized she was barefoot. Apparently Shadow had removed her shoes when he placed her on the couch.

"Do you need any help?" she asked expecting him to refuse.

"Sure, but only if you feel up to it."

Pleasantly surprised, Amber took over at the sink. "Really, I am fine. I'm a bit shaky still and I guess I over exerted a little. I think the walk in the snow tired me more than I expected."

"You going to finish telling me what happened to your pretty little face?"

"Where are your parents?" Amber smiled at him. It was easy to smile at him.

"Do you always answer a question with a question?" he smiled back. His teeth were perfect.

"Do you?"

Shadow laughed out loud now and noticed Amber's smile showed off beautiful teeth too. She blushed enough now to put some color into those pale cheeks. She certainly was pretty and he wished he hadn't avoided meeting her for so long.

"Let's start over. My parents are visiting my mother's sister. They will be gone for a couple of days. They go visit her every Christmas and they come home with a truck load of presents that no one can use but I wouldn't trade Aunt Em for anything. She is almost as wonderful as Mom. I usually go with them but I'm afraid to leave Shoebare. She's the mare that just had the colt. You never know when something might go wrong. Now, what happened to you? You actually got some stitches there."

Amber sobered immediately. "I told you I fell and I really did." Tears brimmed the beautiful green eyes. "The whole story in a nut shell is really kind of dumb. My fiancé…My EX fiancé and I got into an argument at his apartment. I started to leave in a hurry and he tried to stop me. He knocked me off balance and I tripped over a rug. On the way to the floor I made some pretty heavy duty contact with the corner of a wooden coffee table and I guess the rest is obvious. Anyway, I'm okay now. I'll get the stitches out in a day or so and I'll be back to normal soon. Actually I've always been ugly so the scar won't make a lot of difference." She almost laughed but when she finally looked into Shadow's eyes her laugh faded. His face was sober now, his eyes clouded with concern. His lower lip was drawn tight because he was biting the inside of his cheek the way he always did when he was upset about something.

Amber was genuinely surprised. "What's wrong?" She looked behind herself expecting to find something there to cause this change in his mood.

He took hold of her shoulders and gently turned her to face him again. "You are wrong," he said. "You have probably never been ugly in your life." He touched her chin with one finger before tucking a stray wisp of hair back into place at the nape of her neck. "You are in fact a very beautiful woman." He was standing just inches away from her.

"Well…well, thank you. I'll get the cups, our coffee is ready." She turned to move toward the stove but he caught her arm. His fingers were strong yet gentle and his touch sent tiny chills over her entire body.

"Did he hurt you a lot?

Amber lowered her head a moment, then threw her head back with pride, looked Shadow in the eye and spoke softly but firmly.

"Of course he hurt me a lot, but frankly, I will get over him. Honestly, my pride is wounded almost as much as my heart."

"Really?" His hands were on her shoulders again. "Would you mind terrible if I tried to help you get over him?"

"What do you mean?" Amber asked. She hadn't gotten over the surprise of his real concern before his mouth covered hers. His tongue parted her lips and searched out the sweet depths of her mouth. His kiss was gentle and longing. Instantly there was a warmth between them that thrilled Amber. His hands stayed on her shoulders but he pulled her body close to his. Shadow was shaken by the instantaneous desire he felt, and released her as gently as he had held her.

"I'm sorry Amber. I'm not usually so forward. You just."

Amber put her finger to his lips and smiled. "SHHHH. I'm not at all offended. Surprised but not offended. In fact I am a bit flattered that you care about the way I feel." She smiled again and looked deep into the hazel eyes that were so friendly. So kind. "I can use all the help I can get." She was only slightly flirtatious and Shadow loved it. She moved to the coffee cups. "Why do they call you Shadow when your first name is as pretty as Jason?"

Shadow smiled. "In his younger days my Dad never missed a rodeo. I followed him everywhere he went. We took in fairs and horse shows all over the east coast. The name caught on with most of the hands around the stables and it just stuck."

"Do you still travel the shows a lot?"

"Not so much now. I'm content to stay here and raise horses for someone else to show."

Amber poured the coffee into cups. "I've never been to a horse show."

"You're kidding. Well, come early spring, we'll fix that."

"We will?" She handed him his cup of coffee.

"Sure, and if you like the first one we will make an entire summer of it." She smiled as they made their way back to the living room. It was totally dark outside and the only light in the room came from the fireplace now. It filled the room with beautiful images that danced on the darkened walls. They sat on the couch with their legs crossed Indian fashion staring into the fire and alternately at each other. Shadow spoke first.

"I really like the statue that you bought for me. Thank you again."

Amber smiled. "It was hard to buy a gift for someone I'd never met. It took me days to find something that I liked well enough to send you. I know horses are a big part of your life. Tell me, why haven't we met before?"

"If I tell you, promise you won't be angry?" He was embarrassed and it showed.

"I never get angry. Well, almost never."

He sat his cup of coffee down on the table and slowly turned to face her. "Let me say right up front that my Mama told me I was wrong, but I wouldn't listen to her and believe me for the last couple of hours I've been kicking myself."

"You were wrong about what?"

"About you. Amber, I've seen you around. The first time I saw you was about two years ago. There isn't a prettier woman in all of Aston, hell, maybe not even Virginia. Any man would be proud to set claim to you. You and I are worlds apart. Compared to your wealth, I am a poor man. You were educated in the best schools, about politics and social graces. The only thing I want to know about is the land and my horses. We have nothing in common and there is nothing a man like me could offer a woman like you. I doubted you would even give me the time of day. And I didn't want you being nice to me just because of my parents."

Amber smiled. "You mean you were away on purpose all those times I visited?"

"Yes, when I knew you were coming. Sometimes I'd just disappear on the farm or just stay upstairs in my room till you left."

"Well, for heaven's sake. I'm really shocked."

"Don't be angry. Sometimes I'd listen to you laugh with Mama and Pops and I would tell myself I am a fool, but I'm a stubborn fool. Then, when I opened your Christmas gift I was really convinced that I'd been wrong. You see, I had figured that you were probably a rich man's spoiled brat. But, spoiled brats are not sensitive to another person's pleasures; especially without even having met them. Spoiled brats think only of themselves. They rarely know what other people enjoy, much less care. I do humbly apologize for judging you without even knowing you. I hope you can find it in your heart to forgive me."

Amber bowed her head slightly forward. "Apology accepted and I hope you have learned your lesson well!" She was smiling and when she brought her head back up Shadow's face was only an inch away from hers. He didn't move, just looked into her eyes as they mirrored the firelight. His voice was nearly a whisper.

"I've learned that you are truly enchanting."

Amber leaned forward and kissed him. She needed to be cared for by someone like him. Someone that wouldn't demand her soul, her mind. He could have claimed her body and soul right then but the spell had to be broken because Amber still had coffee cup in her hand. She drew back in an effort to regain her composure. She smiled. "That's really nice! However, if I spill this coffee on your Mama's couch, she may just beat us both."

"We can't let that happen now can we?" He took the cup and sat it down on the table. He turned to her and took her into his arms.

"Shadow wait!" Amber started to panic. He had already stretched fully on the couch and pulled her down with him so that they were lying on the couch side by side. Actually Amber was lying more on Shadow's body than on the couch.

"Wait for what, Pretty Lady? Wait to lay here and enjoy the firelight on the ceiling? Wait to listen to the quietness of the world? Why?"

"I'm sorry. I thought…."

"You thought I am ready to rape you. I am, but that's really not my style. Relax. Watch the ceiling."

Amber giggled and snuggled into the broad shoulder that was supporting her head. She suddenly felt a peace that she hadn't known before in her entire life. She lay there and thought about the past few months, the changes in her life, the turmoil with Inez. Could her life change still more, maybe now for the better? She thought of the handsome stranger she was lying with. She was so comfortable, so at peace. How was this possible? She wondered what he was thinking about and looked up at his face. She wanted to ask but she didn't want to disturb the peacefulness of the moment. Shadow's eyes were closed as if he were asleep. In fact he was asleep. Shadow McIntire rose at four a.m. daily and worked hard all day. His last thoughts before sleep had been about Amber. What better way to end any day that by lying with a beautiful woman relaxing in your arms in front of a warm fire? Amber was still smiling at him when she fell asleep, her head resting on the strong shoulder of her new friend.

It was two in the morning when she awoke. She was chilled. The fire had died down leaving only a few glowing embers in the fireplace. The room was dark and it took a minute for her eyes to adjust to the darkness. When they did adjust her heart leaped with fear. At the end of the couch was a tall dark figure. It wasn't moving; it just stood there, as if waiting for one of them to stir. Amber tried to convince herself that she was dreaming but the renewed ache in her head made her know this was no dream. The figure began to move finally, and was coming around the side of the couch. A hand reached down and grabbed Amber by the shoulder, throwing her from the couch to the floor. Amber screamed and began to strike at her assailant. Shadow woke and was on his feet instantly. He had the intruder by the coat and was busy pushing him to the floor when Amber finally found a light. Shadow was about to punch him soundly when Amber recognized their "intruder."

"On my God, Shadow wait!" She had him by the arm. She looked down at the disgruntled man getting himself up off the floor.

"Eric! What on earth are you doing here?"

He was in a jealous rage and he had drunk way too much scotch.

"You little bitch! It's obvious what you are doing here. How long has this been going on? Ever since you have been coming out here?" He was swinging his arm toward the couch and kicked at the cover now on the floor.

"Eric, what are you doing here and how did you get in?" She was bending to pick up the cover he had his foot tangled in. Her head throbbed with the action. "And nothing is going on here. We fell asleep, that is all." She took notice of Shadow's angered face and her own flushed a deep crimson with embarrassment.

Eric was having nothing to do with reason. "You are a damn liar. Wait till I tell your sweet Lillie what all these visits to the farm were all about. You must be made of the same stuff your mother is. One man ain't enough for her either, ya know!" Amber looked as if someone had slapped her. Even the bruises on her face paled as the blood drained from her face. Shadow wondered if she was going to pass out again. When she spoke it was barely a whisper. "Eric, please!" She was near tears and fighting hard not to cry. Shadow stepped forward and took over the conversation.

"I am guessing that it is safe to assume that you are Eric Tolliver. You are no longer engaged to Miss Harris and I guess that means that it is no longer any of your business who she sleeps with. And please do not call the young lady another off color name."

"You stay out of this you misplaced cowboy! As for her, I'll call her any damn thing I please." His words hissed and it was getting harder to understand anything he said.

Shadow grabbed him by the lapels on his coat. "Now YOU listen. This is MY house. You broke into MY house. This young lady is a guest in MY house and if you open your mouth one more time in MY house, I am going to personally shut it for you and it will be a while before you will be ABLE to open it again. Do I make myself clear? Now get out of MY house before I am forced to forget that my Mama taught ME to be a gentleman."

Eric was furious but didn't want to take on Shadow McIntire under the best of circumstances. When Shadow let him go, Eric turned to Amber and spat words at her that were barely audible. "Let's go Amber."

"She's not going with you!" Shadow had never been surer of anything and his assurance was rewarded when he looked into Amber's grateful eyes.

Eric straightened himself as much as his drunken balance would allow. "Amber, it is now or never for us!" Amber laughed out loud. Could this nightmare become funny she wondered. Then she spoke. "Eric, I told you last week that we are through. And we are."

"Very well." Eric directed his next remarks to Shadow. "Mr. McIntire, you can have her. Actually, she is pretty good, too. I taught her everything she knows." That was the final blow. Amber gasped and ran from the room. Shadow stepped to Eric and with more anger than he had ever known over anything in his life, he back handed Eric Tolliver hard enough to send him reeling over the back of a chair. Shadow helped him up, pushed him to the front door and threw him out onto the porch. All the while Eric cursed the world and women in general. He made his way to his car in a drunken fury, spitting blood every few steps on the way. Shadow rubbed his hand and straightened the furniture before he went to look for Amber. He found her on the back porch, barefoot in the snow, shaking all over and sobbing quietly in the darkness. He walked up behind her and placed his hands on shivering shoulders. He turned her around and pulled her to his chest and wrapped his arms around her. She sobbed harder.

"Aren't your feet cold?" he asked while he rubbed her back gently. She didn't answer, she just cried.

"Come on back into the house. Let's talk a while."

"No, I can't."

"Sure you can. What you can't do is stand out here in the snow for the rest of the night. Just looking at your feet makes me cold. Now come on, I'm not about to leave you out here." He nudged her forward with him and they sat down at the kitchen table. She was crying into the paper towels he handed her.

"Amber, listen to me. That guy is a jerk."

"He is a jerk, alright, and I am a fool. A fool for loving him in the first place. And a fool again for thinking I would ever be free to love again in the second place."

"What do you mean? Why can't you love again?"

She raised her head and looked at Shadow. Tears flowed silently as she spoke to him. "Shadow, for a little while tonight I actually fantasized about what loving someone like you would be like. But would someone like you want me now? What Eric said was true. We were lovers. I thought we would never part. I thought we would marry. I thought we were different, that our love affair was made in heaven. God, I was so wrong. Our love affair didn't withstand the test of our first fight. It's been awful!"

"Do you hate him, Amber?"

"What?" She was so surprised by the question she almost stopped crying. She thought a moment and said, "No, I don't guess I do. I don't feel much of anything but embarrassment and humiliation."

Shadow sighed and grinned. "Great! If you hated him, it would be because you still cared. Now, let me tell you something. Nobody's perfect." He smiled again and touched her cheek gently, wiping away tears. "Hell, I'm no virgin. I've made a few mistakes along the way, serious mistakes. But it does no one any good to dwell on them."

Amber was shocked by his candidness, but only momentarily before she laughed through the tears. "Jason McIntire! You are something!"

"Yes, I know." He was grinning. Then, in a more serious tone he added, "Amber, I have to see you again. Please say yes."

She looked into those kind hazel colored eyes. "You really mean that? After all that Eric said?"

He stood up and took her hand and pulled her up. He stepped close to her and put his arms around her waist pulling her body to his. He leaned forward and kissed her gently. He pulled away and asked, "What do I have to do to convince you?"

Amber smiled and answered. "You're doing it." He kissed her again and her heart leaped with joy. She knew she could leave the past behind and start fresh. Jason McIntire's kisses convinced her of that truth.

They talked for another two hours before Amber insisted on leaving.

They had talked about everything from childhood fantasies to the painful realities of the previous week. Finally after finishing what must have been her tenth cup of coffee, Amber stood to leave. "I've really got to leave. Lillie will be furious with me and I don't blame her. I've never been so inconsiderate of her in my life. She may kill me."

"Can I call you after while?"

"Yes, I am hoping you will."

"Oh, I will, Pretty Lady, there is no doubt."

Amber smiled. "You are blind, but I could love you for it."

He kissed her on the forehead, avoiding the stitches above her eyebrow. "Can I kiss you again?" he asked leaning toward her mouth.

"About a hundred times," she answered as she sought refuge in his arms. The sweetness of his kiss was unforgettable. That unmistakable hardness in his groin nagged at him again as he held her gently. Never had he so suddenly wanted a woman, yet never had he wanted to be so careful with a woman. In no way would he offend this woman. "Drive careful," he ordered her before letting her go.

"Oh, I will." She paused and looked at him once more. She touched his cheek. "I'm so glad I came."

"So am I, Amber, so am I." He helped her on with her coat and walked her to her car. He brushed the snow from her windows and she drove away from the farm house feeling more and more alive. She also felt a little as if she were leaving home.

There was no such thing as sneaking into the house. The pups she had purchased for Eric were now in residence in the kitchen and when she opened the front door, they bounded to her and happily announced to the world that she had arrived. And right now the entire world was sleeping on the couch in the living room and woke up immediately. Before Lillie could speak Amber was apologizing. It was no problem but Lillie did wish that it wouldn't happen again and she had been very worried because she was afraid Eric might have found her and caused some trouble.

"He certainly did find me and he was awful."

"How so? Didn't you make up?"

"Make up!" Not hardly! He was so drunk and he found Jason and me on the couch asleep and he immediately jumped to all the wrong conclusions.

146

He was rude and loud and he and Jason nearly fought right there in the living room. Eric said some pretty terrible things to me, right in front of Jason, too. I tell you Lillie, Eric and I will never be lovers again. I wonder now if we can even be friends. I'm going to talk to him when he is sober but I'll never trust him again. At least not with matters of the heart."

"Are you going to be all right, Amber?"

"Yes, Lillie. I am glad Eric and I are finished. And I am glad I met Jason McIntire, too. Very glad."

"Well, I see. If you are glad, then Lillie is glad for you."

Amber was yawning. She was tired and her head ached although she didn't want to admit that to Lillie. "Lillie, I was up most of the night. I am going to lie down for an hour or so. Will you please wake me up about eight or so? And call Richard Fargo's office and see if it is possible to see him today. I'd like to see him before he leaves on his honeymoon."

Lillie was puzzled. "What on earth for?"

"Nothing to worry about. Just some unfinished business." Amber climbed the stairs to her room. She showered quickly and laid down to rest. She slept peacefully. Lillie woke her at eight and she got up feeling more rested than she had in weeks.

Richard Fargo's office was decorated for Christmas and smelled like a pine forest. He was glad to see Amber as usual and thanked her for the exquisite Christmas gift. "Now what can I do for you today? I take it that this is a business visit."

"Richard, Eric and I no longer plan to marry and I no longer want to take an active part in the business. Has Eric got enough money to buy me out of the company?"

"You must be joking. No Harris in Harris-Tolliver. That can't be."

"Yes, it can be and I intend for it to be. I don't need to continue to work there and I don't want to be in Eric's life in any way. Now, does he have enough money to take me up on my offer?"

"Yes, I am sure that he does, but I don't think he will approve of this plan any more than I do."

"I don't need his approval, or yours. Just his money and the business is his. I will work at something else, maybe full time journalism. I can certainly pick up more hours than I do at the paper. I made a serious mistake thinking

Eric and I could plan a lifetime together. We can't. My working with the business will only lead to more problems. I want out and right away."

"Does Eric know about this?"

Amber smiled. "He will know about it as soon as my good friend and lawyer tells him about it. The sooner; the better, today even. I want $500,000 for my two thirds and that is dirt cheap. Eric has enough sense to know that. Tell him he can keep the Harris in the name if he wants to. Most of the companies we have contracts with are used to dealing with my father and trust the Harris name. If he doesn't want to use the name that is okay too, it makes no difference to me."

"Amber your father worked a long time building that company, I wish you would think about this for a time. Perhaps you will reconsider."

He suddenly felt very old and very tired

"I know exactly how long, Richard. Any legacy that I leave my children will include stories of how hard he worked. And any legacy I leave my little ones I will have earned for them. I don't need those coal yards to know that my daddy loved me and I intend to do some building of my own. Trust me, Richard. Part of the first things my daddy taught me was to think for myself, and I know what I am doing. Finally. It is the right thing to do."

"Very well then, my dear. What if Eric doesn't agree to this idea? What then?"

"If that happens I'll cross that bridge when I come to it. He will agree, he really doesn't have much choice."

"I will call you in the morning to let you know the final plans. I can't imagine anyone besides a Harris in charge at that company though.

"It will be fine. Eric was nearly family. Groomed by Daddy himself for years. You know that. He does love the company and I know he will uphold Daddy's dreams and principals."

"As you say. I'll call Eric now. Might as well get started since we are all in a hurry. My wife has been packing for a week and we are scheduled to leave New Year's Day. I want to have this wrapped up by then."

"Thank you, Richard." She stood and hugged him tightly, feeling good about herself. After leaving Richard Fargo's office Amber stopped at the Aston News offices. She asked to see her editor and answered questioning looks about her bruised appearance as briefly as she could. She didn't have to wait long to see Miles Edwards, Editor in Chief, Aston Daily News. He was a man of nearly sixty. He was a huge round man with white hair and a salt and pepper beard. He reminded Amber of a department store Santa Claus. His handshake was firm and he was jovial. "Miss Harris, I am pleasantly surprised. Is this business or pleasure? My God, what happened to you?"

"Strictly business, Mr. Edwards. I fell over a throw rug and hit a table on the way to the floor. I want a full time job and when can I start?"

"Well, young lady, we do have a couple of openings. You are qualified for either of them. Your weekly is received well. Do you want to expand in that area or do you want to tackle something entirely different? Pardon me, I don't mean to be bold, but didn't you take over your father's business? I heard you were doing quite well."

"I did take an active part in running Harris-Tolliver for over a year, but my life has changed somewhat, and now I want to just make it on my own."

"I see."

"I appreciate your giving me a chance here, Mr. Edwards. When can I start?"

"Oh, save the thank you. I expect you to work your tail off. Why don't we just start you the day after New Year's? Start off the new year with a brand new job."

"Oh, that would be wonderful. I'll be in bright and early on the 2nd then. Thank you Mr. Edwards, thank you very much."

"I'll see you then Miss Harris. Take care of yourself."

She was half way out the office door when she paused and turned to face Mr. Edwards again. "Mr. Edwards, could you do me a favor? Could you just call me Amber?"

"Fine. Amber. Amber it is and fine name too." He smiled and watched the young woman leave his offices. She was busy asserting her own self worth and he liked that. She wasn't just the daughter of Lance Harris anymore. She was out to set the world on fire in her own right, and that's a good start at being a good reporter. She would be good, he knew she would.

Amber sat patiently as her physician removed the stitches from her eyebrow. She lied when he asked her if she had been dizzy or had lost consciousness since she'd left the hospital. Once the last stitch had been removed, he bathed the area with cool gauze. Almost as good as new. A little cocoa butter once or twice a day for a month or so and there won't even be a noticeable scar. He handed her a mirror.

"Is everything okay, Miss Harris? I mean with your life and all?"

She smiled for the first time since the young doctor had met her. "Everything is just fine, good doctor, and doctor, please will you just call me Amber?"

"Okay, Amber. If you need anything for a headache, just call me. You know you look different today. I mean besides the swelling being nearly gone."

She cocked her head to one side and smiled again. "I am different. I'm glad you can see it. I feel great!"

"Well, something must be going your way. You look great too."

"Thank you. See you never, I hope." She marched out of his office with more confidence than she had ever thought possible. All she needed was to close her eyes to see the smiling face she had dreamed about while she slept. Her new friend. "Nobody's perfect," he had said. "Can I see you again?" he had asked. He certainly could see her again, Amber thought, and she hoped how very soon that might be. Her green eyes sparkled. She caught the image of herself in a plate glass window. She did look good but even better than that she was making choices. Decisions. She was setting down the rules and people were listening to her. They heard what she was saying and what she was saying seemed important to everybody. For the first time in her life she felt in control of her destiny.

Amber returned to the Manor and was greeted not only by pups, but, by Lillie, who had just about had it with the pups. Something had to be done about them. They were destroying the entire house. Amber's mind clicked. "Give me fifteen minutes." She bounded up the steps two at time and entered her room with a flurry. She found her favorite jeans and pulled them on. She took a soft flannel shirt from a hanger. She put the shirt on over her braless torso. She went to the mirror to brush her hair. It shone like a new penny in the sun. She skipped the makeup; nothing matched the bruises that were left on her face anyway. She bounced back downstairs to put on her boots. Lillie was in the hall fighting with the pups over the broom.

The pups were winning. "Now where are you going?"

Amber laughed and hugged Lillie impulsively. "Back out to the farm. I'm taking the pups out there where they will have a good home." Lillie eyed her suspiciously and Amber confessed to her knowing there was no way Lillie would miss her real intent. "Of course if I see Mr. Jason McIntire while I am there I won't be at all disappointed." She and Lillie both laughed while Amber wiggled into her coat. Lillie spoke as Amber was about to leave. "All right, but you get back here at a decent hour so I don't have to worry my head off over you, you hear me?"

"Yes, I do hear you and I do promise that I'll never be so inconsiderate again, okay?"

Amber loaded the pups into her car and left for the farm. She pulled into the drive just as Jason was walking to the house from the barn. He waved as she approached and pulled the car to a stop. When she opened the car door the pups tumbled out into the snow. They yapped with glee and Jason's dog, Trapper, came immediately to attention to check them out. Amber came up the walk breathless. "Can they stay here, please? I'll buy their food if you don't want them for your own."

Jason smiled. "They can stay here and I'd love to have them for my own. Where did they come from?"

"It doesn't matter, but they can't stay in town; they would be miserable."

"Can you come in for a while?"

"I thought you would never ask." They made their way carefully over the squirming puppies. The house was warm and smelled like pine trees and fresh baked bread. The fireplace held a blazing fire and there was fresh coffee simmering on the stove.

"Will Trapper be jealous of the pups?" Amber asked concerned about the way the older dog was stalking the pups.

"He is just establishing his territory with them. He has to let them know who the boss is." Jason laughed. "Come on in. They will be fine, I'm sure of it. They aren't really old enough to be a threat to Trapper and he is smart enough to know that."

"Well, if you are sure," Amber said. But she was still eyeing the three dogs through the window; not at all sure Jason's judgment was trustworthy in this matter.

"Hey now, you are supposed to trust me and that goes for my judgment about dogs too. Besides I was hoping you came to see me." He was turning her around to face him. She looked into his eyes and smiled. "I do trust you Shadow," she said. "God help me, I do. That is why I'm back here already. Please don't make me sorry."

He leaned down to her and kissed her warmly. His hands traveled down her back to her waist. He pulled her close and her breasts burned into his massive chest. "It has only been hours since you were here and I missed you. Is that possible?" he whispered.

"I think it must be, because I missed you too." She looked at him now and watched his warm smile. She liked his smile. He was looking at her closely. "Hey, your stitches are gone. I thought it would be a few more days."

"I was in town on business and dropped in on my doctor and he said they were ready to come out. They itched something awful and I was ready to be rid of them. Anyway, here I am, good as new."

Shadow leaned down to kiss her again. "You are better than new. You smell like the spring violets that grow down by the pond."

"You are a hopeless romantic."

"A romantic yes, but I dare say that I am NOT hopeless."

He was moving across the kitchen to pour a cup of coffee for each of them. "Can you please stay a little while?"

"Yes, but not nearly as long as last night. Lillie was really worried. And I feel guilty. She slept all night on the hall couch waiting for me to get home."

"You like Lillie a lot don't you?"

"I love Lillie. She helped raise me. As a matter of fact she is the closest thing I have to a mother. She is family to me. All the family I have now." She thought briefly about the lose of Eric's friendship.

"I see," Jason said.

They walked to the living room and sat on the floor in front of the fireplace.

"Does it hurt?" Jason asked.

"Does what hurt?" Amber answered.

"Your head."

"Oh, no, not at all."

"That's good. Do you ever wear a bra?" he asked matter of factly.

"Not very often." She tried to be as casual as he was.

"Do you know you can make a person crazy that way|?"

"Are you crazy?" she teased.

"Come here and I will show you how crazy I am." He pulled her close and kissed her again with the gentle sweetness she already had come to expect from his kisses.

"I like the way you kiss me," she said, leaning back from him. "Your kisses don't demand anything."

"Only that you enjoy them." He kissed her again.

"I do," she whispered. She was unable to catch her breath, her soul was on fire.

She lay back gently against the cushions on the floor. Her hair lay in soft waves at her shoulders forming a blanket beneath her head. Shadow looked down at her and smiled. She touched his lips with one finger and said, "You smile more than any person I have ever known. I think that is so nice."

"You make me want to smile, Amber."

"I do?"

"Yes, I just feel so good when I'm near you. I just feel happy inside."

"I'm glad, Jason. I really am."

"That isn't all that you make me feel, Amber." He leaned closer to her now and placed his arm across her waist. Amber focused green eyes on his face. Her cheeks burned and for a moment she thought she would cry. He touched her soul with his tenderness.

"What do I make you feel, Jason?"

"It shouldn't surprise you that I want you very much. I think it has been apparent every time I have been near you." He kissed her forehead, her nose, her throat. She shoved at his shoulders. He didn't move. Her pulse quickened and she spoke not at all with confidence. "I shouldn't have come back here today. I'm really sorry. I don't mean to be a tease, honest. But I can't go on. Please let me go. I just can't jump into bed with you now. We've only just met. Believe me I'd like to but I just can't."

Shadow sat up abruptly. "Amber, I know that!" He was almost angry and it showed. "I didn't mean to imply that I thought you should jump into bed with me." He suddenly laughed out loud. "You have to admit that it isn't a bad idea though." The look on Amber's face was one of distress and

Shadow recognized her pain. He got serious quickly. "Amber, listen to me. Before yesterday I was as foot loose and fancy free as they come. I've spent my adult life doing as I please. When you fell into my arms in the barn I don't really know how to explain what I felt. For the first time I was really worried about someone's welfare. Oh, I love Mom and Pops but they have got each other. But, with you, I felt suddenly responsible and I like it. I've thought about it all day. If you hadn't have come out here today, I would have found an excuse to come to you tonight. I want your company. I'm not going to lie to you and say I wouldn't make love to you right this minute if given the honor, because I certainly would, but I am willing to wait for you. I'll wait till you want me, till you can't live without me. Until being with me sexually is the most important part of your day. But that may take a year to happen and it may never happen. I've got sense enough to know that. But in the mean time I just enjoy being near you. I'd like to be a real friend to you. Know all about you. Share part of your life with you. Strictly at your pace of course. Don't be afraid of me, I'll never hurt you, Amber."

"Shadow, you sound so futuristic and I am so unsure of my future. Every time I think I have my life mapped out, something happens to turn my entire world upside down."

"Maybe you have headed in the wrong directions or perhaps even had the wrong leaders."

"Maybe so, but I intend to be pretty cautious from now on. I really don't think I can handle very many disastrous love affairs, Shadow. I don't like for people to walk all over my heart." Her face clouded with a slight pout and Jason McIntire knew that the next man to win this woman's heart would have it for life. And he already knew that he wanted to be that man.

"Hey, don't get dreadful on me." He pulled her to him with one strong arm. "I promise that I'll never walk on your heart. Your toes maybe, but never your heart. And by the way since we are talking about toes, would you want to go to an old fashioned barn dance on New Year's Eve?"

"That's tomorrow!" she protested.

"True," he smiled.

"You don't give a girl much notice."

"I haven't known you long enough to give you notice. How much notice do you need anyway? Have you got plans for tomorrow night?"

"No, I do not have plans, but I also do not have a thing to wear to a New Year's Eve party."

"Whoa, there. You're going to a barn dance, not a premier opening at the palace. Wear anything! Just say you'll go with me."

Amber laughed and hugged him. "I wouldn't miss it for the world."

"Fine, then it is settled. I will pick you up at seven. Mom and Pops will be home tomorrow. I'll bet they will be surprised to see us together."

"I hope they don't object."

"Object! They will be delighted. They love you dearly."

"Well, I had better head home. I'm sure Lillie will be waiting up for me. The roads aren't bad now but as long as there is a snowflake in the air she worries."

"Okay." Shadow stood up and extended his hand to her to help her stand. Once on her feet, he pulled her close to his body. His hands on her shoulders held her firmly against his chest pressing her breasts into the inviting warmth of his body. He kissed her gently yet passionately. Heat flowed through her veins at his very touch. His hands drifted from her shoulders, down her back, rubbing gently as they traveled to her waist. Her shirt had long ago pulled free from her jeans. He soon discovered this new freedom and when he actually touched the bare skin of her back little thrills of excitement raced through both of them. His fingers traced small lines up and down her skin causing chills and excitement to run through her body. She pulled away from him, her cheeks glowing with desire. She smiled and looked up into the hazel eyes she had grown to trust. "Wow," she whispered.

"I know. Isn't it wonderful?" he spoke softly, almost a whisper. His hands traveled up her sides now, gently stroking her warm, tender skin. She felt so soft to his fingers. He leaned toward her and rested his chin on top of her head. "I love the way your hair smells."

"I'd better get home, Shadow. It is already dark."

"Do you really want to leave?"

"No, I don't, but I have to go."

"Okay," he sighed. "No pressure tactics, I promised. I'll see you at seven tomorrow." He kissed her once again. "Goodnight, Sweet Amber."

"Goodnight.", she whispered. It took real willpower to walk out the door. Shadow hadn't said another word while he helped her with her coat and walked her to her car. Amber didn't speak either. They didn't need words to communicate the things they were feeling. Light from the porch lamp danced on the snow. The entire yard looked like a winter wonderland. There was a sincerity about Shadow McIntire that Amber wanted to hold on to for the rest of her life.

Already this man was in her thoughts and in her dreams. She wondered how her own mind could accept the thought of another man to love so soon. Was what she felt indeed approaching love for this man? He could make her feel so good about herself without even trying. She wondered if her mind could stand all this confusion. But, there was no doubt that she did want Shadow and he wanted her. The chemistry was certainly there for both of them; it had been from the moment they met. Amber smiled up at Shadow again. She tiptoed to kiss him quickly. "Goodnight." She slipped into her car and left Shadow standing in the snow. He waved once more before he turned to pet Trapper and to kick snow at the pups he'd just acquired. He laughed out loud in the night and looked at the sky to count the snow clouds. There were but a few stars to be seen, but it didn't matter. For Jason "Shadow" McIntire the lights were shining from within and all the stars were lucky ones. He felt good about himself, he felt good about being alive, and he felt absolutely wonderful about Amber Dawn Harris.

Lillie was waiting up for Amber in the kitchen. Amber stomped the snow from her boots and hung he coat in the hall closet before joining Lillie in the kitchen for hot tea and toast. Lillie looked smug and toyed with her napkin waiting for Amber to tell her more about Jason McIntire. "Well, young lady?"

"Well, what?" Amber teased.

"You know what!" Lillie acted as if she was getting up to ring Amber's neck if she didn't start talking and talking fast. Amber laughed but quickly sobered.

"Lillie, Jason is a truly nice person. He is kind, strong, honest, self controlled, demands nothing and is willing to give everything. Lillie, from day one Eric told me I would be his. Jason asks me if I will consider being his and is willing to wait until I'm ready for that." Tears stung her eyes. "Gosh, Lillie, am I awful? I feel so guilty because I am not miserable. Am I a tramp, Lillie? God, I am so confused." Tears fell freely, making Lillie's heart ache for her young friend. She took a deep breath and patted Amber gently, much like one would pet a wounded puppy. Then she spoke slowly. There was a sparkle in her eye and Amber knew that what she was about to say had probably happened to Lillie in her own life.

"Child, there are no laws that govern how many times you can fall in love or to what degree. Some people are more lovable than others and some people have several other people in love with them at the same time; like maybe your Daddy." Lillie paused for a moment and Amber knew for sure now that her suspicions that Lillie Hasglow loved her father were true indeed. She loved Lillie even more when Lillie began to speak again. "Perhaps you didn't love Eric as much as you thought you did at first. He moved in on your emotions while you were still in mourning and very vulnerable. Maybe that is why you are able to get over him without lying down to die. And that is the way it should be. There isn't any use in suffering over something that can not be changed. You don't have to feel guilty because someone can make you happy. That is what makes this old world go round and round. Young people falling in and out of love. Now, the best thing for you to do is to proceed with a little caution so that you don't get hurt again, and so that you don't cause someone else to get hurt. Always be honest and fair, just like your Daddy taught you. Those principles work in love as well as they do in business, maybe even better. The best way in the world to get over a lost love is to find a new love."

Amber was smiling now. "Lillie, I'm glad you're so smart and sweet and understanding. I feel so lucky. Not many people come as close to making the kind of mistake I was about to make and come away with just a scar over their eyebrow. How could I have been so blind about Eric all this time?"

"You weren't blind, Amber. I think you knew all along that you two weren't exactly right. Eric moved in on your heart at a time when you needed someone to lean on the most. He made it easy for you to fill a new void you were feeling. You needed someone to concentrate on so that you wouldn't feel so empty all the time. Eric knew how to use that for his own benefit and before long he could practically command your thoughts. If you had been ten instead of twenty years old, I could have bought you a new puppy to hold and cuddle in bed and that would have helped mend your broken heart. As it was you had to pick your own "cuddle material." Something warm and responsive for you to hold and love. You picked Eric and for a long while I thought him a good choice too. But I think Eric has some emotional problems of his own and you are not strong enough to help him." She paused a moment and surveyed Amber's distant gaze. She touched her hand gently. "You are going to be fine, Amber. Follow your instincts. Trust yourself. Well, I must get to bed. I have an early day tomorrow."

Amber hugged Lillie, holding her tightly for a moment. "Thank you Dear Lillie."

"Goodnight, Amber. Sleep tight honey."

Amber sat at the table and looked around the kitchen. Thoughts raced through her mind one after another. "Seems like I'm always making decisions in the kitchen," she mused. "This house has been my home for so many years and now suddenly I want to be somewhere else." Her mind drifted back to the days when she would get up in the farm house and make a dash for "her spot" behind the wood burning stove to get dressed. Seemed like that was the only warm place in the entire house. Her feet would always freeze until she got to that spot. One year Grandmamma had made her house slippers but she lost one of them the very first week she owned them. House slippers just slowed her down anyway. She was always bare footed. She remembered a campaign to shame her into wearing shoes. Her father had told her that when she grew up her feet would be hard and ugly and she would be embarrassed on her wedding night when she took off her shoes and her groom got a look at her ugly tough feet. As a matter of fact, he doubted if a girl with really ugly feet would even find a boyfriend by the time she was thirty. Amber had listened, not knowing for sure whether to really believe him or not. She didn't want to wear shoes, that was something she did know for certain. But she hadn't been so certain about the boyfriend part. Most boys were a pain in the neck but then there was Lenny Landon from the next farm. She would hate for him to think her feet were ugly. Just in case her Daddy was correct, she started coating her feet with white Vaseline at night when she went to bed. If anything would keep a person's feet soft, Vaseline would. This plan had stayed in effect until the day Amber jumped out of bed forgetting about the gel on her feet and hitting the hardwood floor in a hurried run. She had made it almost to her bedroom door before fate turned on her and both feet flew out from under her. She landed soundly on her bottom, much to her distress. Her Daddy laughed so hard at the breakfast table that tears streamed down his cheeks. Sarahlou had not laughed at the breakfast table or anywhere else. Especially after she got a good look at the bed clothes and the mess they were in. She had threatened Amber with several days' punishment but Lance had intervened saying that it was as much his fault as Amber's. Amber sighed. She wondered how many times her Daddy had protected her from harmful consequences. It had been only in these last few months since his death that she had come to the full realization of how much Lance had protected her. She missed them so, Lance and Sarahlou. She took a deep breath so that she wouldn't cry. She got up to put her coffee cup in the sink. She longed for the days when life was so simple, so easy for her. She was sleepy. Tomorrow she would solve her problems. "There will always be a tomorrow," she thought. "There has always been a tomorrow."

Amber slept well. No nightmares, no waking up and being afraid to go back to sleep. Her phone rang at 7 a.m. It was Eric. Amber listened for a brief moment and then hung up. He dialed furiously and her phone rang again. She picked up the phone and without even answering it she hung it up. Eric threw his phone against his living room wall. "Damn her!" He walked to his liquor cabinet and poured his breakfast into a tall glass. He swallowed most of the contents with one gulp and poured more. He cursed women, he cursed his mother, his father, and the world in general. He threw himself down in a chair and cleared his table with one sweep of his arm. He sent everything on the table crashing to the floor. His apartment was a mess. There were dirty clothes everywhere and what Eric had eaten at home could be identified by the dirty dishes scattered here and there, some of them broken after being hurled against a chosen wall.

He talked to himself in drunken logic. He had just about had it with that little bitch, Amber Harris. He had damn near helped raise her. He had always loved her. He had been her friend. The ungrateful wretch. One mistake and I'm out! Just like my Ma! One mistake and you're out on your ear, the hell with how you feel. Ma blamed me for Pa dying. Said I should have been home to help her get him to a doctor. Jumped all over me after the funeral like I didn't love him or something. The she kills herself rather than live to finish raising us kids. And that's my fault too, my sister says. Damn women! I helped Amber all these months; I've been good to her and one mistake and she turns her back on me. She will be sorry. She could have been my baby for always. She will be sorry.

He finished his drink and staggered toward his bedroom. He fell across his bed and cursed some more before he finally passed out. It was only 8 a.m. Harris-Tolliver Enterprises went on with its' business day as usual without Eric. His secretary took messages and relayed whatever information that she could to the public. At the end of the day, she was glad to be going home. She couldn't help but wonder how long the business could stand this kind of neglect. She decided that she would call Miss Harris and talk to her about the recent problems. Thank God Miss Harris would be back to the office in a few more days. Maybe she would be able to better deal with Eric. And she could trust Miss Harris not to tell Eric where she got her information about his recent neglect of duties. Her mind was made up. She would call Miss Harris from home so that no other employee would have to know about the call and have to cover up for her if questioned about her loyalty.

Amber dressed for the New Year's Eve barn dance with all the energy she possessed. She chose a white off the shoulder blouse and a blue full skirt supported by several crinolines. Actually Shadow hadn't seen her in a dress yet. She was anxious to see if he would approve. Her hair shone in the bright hall light as she bounced down the steps to greet him. He stood and looked at Amber. He leaned forward to kiss her gently. His admiring looks told Amber all she needed to know about his approval.

"You look perfect. Nothing like a city girl at all."

"Yes, now you be careful. I got some grass roots of my own you know."

They laughed together and when Lillie entered the room Amber took her hand and led her close to Shadow. "Lillie, I want you to meet Jason McIntire. Known better as "Shadow" McIntire. Isn't he just as gorgeous as I told you?" Jason blushed immediately at Amber's teasing. Lillie mused a moment and agreed. "In a pinch he would certainly be my choice."

"Am I at the mercy of two lecherous females?" he paused. He then added, "I'm very glad to meet you Lillie. I've heard a lot about you. Quite a girl you've got here. And I'm really sorry about the other night. Please don't blame Amber for being so late. We didn't mean to worry you."

"My, how sweet you are. Well, just don't worry about the past. Just concentrate on the future, and don't keep my Amber out so late without letting me know, okay? I know she is a grown up, but I do worry." She was smiling at the young man and he knew already he had an ally if he needed one in Lillie Hasglow. He liked her; no wonder Amber adored her.

"Fine, I promise." He turned to Amber. "I told Mom about us."

"What did you tell her? What did she say?"

"I told her we are going to be married and she said great!"

"Oh stop your teasing." Amber was laughing out loud. He was helping her on with her coat when he replied. "Okay, you ask me a question and I answer it. Can I help it if you won't believe me? But Mom believes me. She has already started baking wedding cookies."

Amber giggled and slapped him on the shoulder. There festive mood was interrupted by the phone ringing. Amber answered it and her smile faded. She listened as Eric's secretary related the disastrous way Eric had been behaving for the past few days. She didn't want to cause trouble but she was genuinely concerned. Amber thanked her sincerely and assured the woman that she had done the proper thing by calling her. She was obviously troubled and Shadow was moved with concern.

"What's wrong, honey? You look awful."

"There is some trouble at the offices. It seems Eric has practically stayed drunk since my accident."

"Good Lord, that has been nearly two weeks."

"Shadow, I know this is a lot to ask of a man on a first date, but I need to drop by Eric's and talk with him. Just a moment. There are a lot of people that work at Harris-Tolliver. They have got families and they depend on their jobs. We can't let something this stupid cause the company to go down the drain. My Daddy worked all his life for that company. So has Eric. I can't believe he can be this shallow."

Shadow had reservations. "Are you sure he won't try to hurt you? He was awful nasty out at the house."

"Surely he has settled down by now. Besides I am just going to tell him what a mess the office is in and remind him that for twenty one years that business has been his life and that he had better do something positive before it all goes down the drain. I'll survive without it but I don't know if he would or not. I'll be okay and besides you'll be just outside and Eric will know that."

"Okay, if you're sure. But we have to hurry. I don't want to be late for our first dance."

Shadow eased his car to the snowy curb and hopped out to open Amber's door. His tall handsome form could be observed by anyone, including Eric Tolliver that happened to be looking out his bedroom window. Rage flooded his soul.

Amber walked to his door and started to knock. The door flew open and Eric grabbed her arm, pulled her into the room and slammed the door shut behind them. "Why didn't you use your key? Doesn't your new boyfriend know you have one?" He frightened Amber but she fought for composure.

"Eric, I didn't come here to trade insults with you. I came to talk with you about Harris-Tolliver Enterprises. You have got a business to run. You can't stay here drunk all the time. You have got several people, to say nothing of whole companies depending on you. Do you want our reputation to go down the drain after all the time and effort you've put into it?

"What do you care? You want out. Fargo told me so!" He was shouting.

"Eric please calm down. You don't have to shout at me. I came here as a friend, as your partner. You have got to pull yourself together."

Eric looked at her and breathed deep as if trying to extinguish some desire to scream. "I want you. He can't have you Amber. Not now, not ever." His eyes were glazed with anger and hatred. Amber shook, but she willed the strength to stay calm.

"Eric you are talking silly. I don't know who you think you are but you don't own me. No one does. I can go out with any one I please. You know that. Can't we be civilized about our affair? It is over. It should never have begun in the first place."

Eric moved closer to her. "Take off your coat," he ordered.

"No Eric, I'm not staying." She moved toward the door. He grabbed her and swung her around to face him pulling the coat from her shoulders as he did so. Her bare shoulders enraged him.

"SO, that is what you wear to tease him on, is it?" He stroked her neck with one hand while pinning her against the wall with his body.

"Eric, let me go and stop this foolishness. You are so damn drunk, you're not even yourself. Let me go!" She fought against him. He tried to kiss her but she twisted away from his mouth. The smell of stale liquor on his breath gagged her and tears began to escape and trickle down her cheek no matter how hard she tried not to cry.

"Well, look at that. Tears. Real tears. You want to leave that bad? I'll tell you what. Let's make a deal. You come to bed with me one more time and I'll let you go. Let me put my seed in your belly one more time and then you can have your cowboy." His tone was mocking and Amber had never heard such crude language. He was breathing raggedly and she could feel his desire for her as he stood pressed against her. She struggled and he laughed at her.

"Eric, you are sick. You need help. Let me go and I'll stay and help you. I really will."

"Oh, you are going to help me. You are going to help me right now." He pushed her roughly toward his bedroom. "I'm going to show you how much you can help me. Remember how good it was, Baby? Remember what it was like when I took you?"

"No Eric, no more!" She managed to free one arm from her coat sleeve and with her free hand she picked up a brass lamp and heaved it at the window they were passing. She tried to scream but Eric's hand was over her mouth nearly suffocating her. She felt dizzy and prayed she wouldn't pass out. The lamp met the window and crashed through it exploding into pieces and causing fire to fly from the severed cord. Shadow saw the lamp and leaped from his car. He ran to the door and pounded it for less than ten seconds before he kicked it in. The sight of Eric's hand over Amber's mouth was all he needed to make his decisions. He grabbed Eric from behind and with one crashing blow sent Eric to the floor. Amber had fallen when Eric lost his grip on her and she lay in the floor gasping for breath and fighting to stay conscious. Her head ached and her blouse had blood on it from her lip. She was visibly shaking all over. Shadow rushed to her and helped her up to her feet. "Let's go!" he ordered. On the way out of the building he handed the super a twenty dollar bill to cover the cost of the lock he had broken. Once in his car he took Amber in his arms and held her tightly.

"My God, Amber. Don't every go near that maniac again. I'm begging you. He could have really hurt you and I think you know it."

Amber sat for a moment and then noticed her bloodstained blouse and began to cry. "I can't go anywhere like this! I'd have to change and there isn't anything I can do about my lip. I look awful! I have ruined your whole evening."

Shadow grinned for the first time since they had returned to the car.

"Oh, sweet Amber. You damn near get yourself raped or killed or both and you worry about my evening. Listen, let's just pick up something to eat and go for a drive. It's a gorgeous night."

They decided to dine on hamburgers and fries but the salt on the food stung Amber's freshly cut lip and she didn't consume much. Shadow eyed her quietly for some time before he spoke. "Would you like for me to speak to him for you?"

"Oh, NO!" Amber was definite. "I'll get this whole mess cleared up soon. I will! I am going back to the office after the holiday and take some really affirmative actions. I hate to delay my job at the newspaper, but I will if I have to.

"I wish you would stay away from him. He is really dangerous, Amber. You have got to believe that. I am beginning to think he is capable of anything."

Amber raised one eyebrow. "I'm beginning to think so too. I've never seen him like this. He has never consumed so much alcohol and he has never been violent in his life. Shadow, I have known Eric all my life. I just can't believe this is really happening to us."

"Well, believe it Pretty Lady. Besides, he has always had his way before; did you ever think about that?"

Amber sat silent. She hadn't considered it before and now that she did think about it she realized that their entire relationship had been always on Eric's terms. He only tolerated her opinion and Amber knew that a subject of debate was never really closed with Eric unless he got his way. Even little things like insisting on calling her "Baby" after all the times she had asked him not to call her that. He had often treated her like a possession but denied any such actions when Amber tried to confront him about it. And now he was absolutely beyond reason.

Shadow spoke again, breaking into her thoughts. "Would you like some more coffee? That is the only thing you have actually swallowed." Amber smiled at him. "That would be good." He left the car and walked back to the carry out window to order more coffee. Amber watched him cross the parking lot. He walked with an easy grace for a man of his size. His shoulders were broad, his hips narrow. He was, in fact, just plain good to look at. She smiled while she watched him flirt with a car load of young girls cruising through the lot. He certainly was desirable.

"Can you drink while I drive?" he asked. She assured him that she could. He eased the car onto the street and turned south, out of town. He drove for several minutes before speaking again.

"Would you like to take in a movie or something?"

"No, not really. Let's just go somewhere and relax."

"How about back out home? We can build a fire and watch the New Year come in by firelight.

"Sounds good to me. I'd love that."

They rode in complete silence back to the farm. Shadow led the way to the house and opened the front door. The house always smelled the same to Amber. A combination of fresh baked bread and pine branches. Their Christmas tree stood just inside the living room and small bright lights twinkled through the darkness. Shadow hung their coats on a peg and moved through the semi-darkness to the fireplace. In just minutes he had a roaring fire and there was no need for any other lighting. He threw several large cushions on the floor and knelt down before extending his hand to Amber. She took his hand and knelt beside him and gazed into the fire. He watched her face and studied her intensely.

"You want to talk Amber, or would you rather just sit and dream?"

She smiled at him and finished sitting down on the floor. She sat close to Shadow and he put his arm around her and held her closer. She cold feel his heart beating against her shoulder. Steady, constant, strong beating that made her feel safe. Safe. Something she hadn't really felt in many months.

"Can we just sit and watch the New Year come in? It is only three hours away." She paused. "I am sorry I ruined your plans for the evening."

"Ruined! Are you kidding? I can't think of a better way to begin any year." He snuggled closer to her, pulling her to him gently.

Amber sighed softly and said, "Keep me warm. Protect me from the cold." The she added, "Please." She snuggled against his chest.

"I'll protect you from more that the cold if you will let me," he murmured. She smiled and held onto him. They lay back against the huge cushions, relaxed and watched the glowing fire dance. Before the New Year officially arrived Amber was fast asleep; snuggled against Shadow's strong chest. He had watched her for nearly an hour before he settled back and closed his eyes. He held her close and silently hoped that he would spend every New Year's Eve for the rest of his life with this woman. He couldn't explain to himself how she had claimed his heart so quickly, he just knew she had.

Jack and Ada McIntire found their son and his date resting beside the fireplace at three in the morning. Even in the now dim light of the last embers in the fireplace, Ada could see Amber's blood stained blouse. She placed a large comforter over them both knowing her questions could wait till daylight to be answered. And she had at least a dozen questions going through her mind as she readied herself for bed. The most outstanding question concerned her handsome son and whether or not he would ever settle down and marry. She wondered how serious this thing with Amber Harris might become. She could think of a lot worse companions than Amber. Amber came from good stock, at least on her father's side and Ada knew Amber valued life. That was good. Amber was good and Ada was glad her son had finally decided to pay attention to the young woman. She lay beside Jack and listened to him breathing evenly. He was already asleep. She smiled and said her prayers and then she too slept peacefully.

Amber woke at five in the morning with her neck stiff and her feet cold. She roused Shadow and he kissed her gently. "Happy New Year, Pretty Lady. I guess we slept through most of the festivities."

Amber smiled. "I guess so. I bet you think I am a pretty dull date by now." She was embarrassed.

"Not at all. In fact it is kind of refreshing to be with a woman I don't have to work overtime impressing. You want some coffee?"

"I do, but I better not take the time. I'd better get on home before Lillie sends out the State Patrol or something. I'd like to thank you for being so understanding about last night."

"My pleasure." He smiled and watched Amber as she scurried about the room picking up cushions and folding the comforter. "Calm down. I'll have you home in a flash. What are your plans for today?"

"Oh, I don't really know. I plan to spend some time with Lillie. We haven't had a decent day together since the morning I fell."

"Can I call you later?"

"Yes Shadow. You may call. I hope you call." She smiled and looked at him closely. "I hope you will call often. Anytime you want, although you may have to catch me at the office for the next few days." She caught the look of distress that crossed Shadow's face. She continued before he could voice his protest. "There are some loose ends that I have got to tie up before I start my job at the paper. I was supposed to start tomorrow but I don't want some disaster looming over my head all the time. I have got to concentrate on the future. That means clearing up the past. Don't you agree?"

He didn't agree but he didn't say so, he just changed the subject. He smiled and asked, "Are you really going to go to work? I mean punch a time clock and all?"

She laughed, and then answered with real determination in her voice. "Yes. Yes, I am really going to work. I am going to go forward on my own steam from now on. I have to make my own waves. Not just ride around on my father's. You will agree with that won't you?" Her green eyes had focused on Shadow's face and for a moment he could barely breathe. He felt himself being drawn toward this woman with more force than he had ever thought possible. She was so very real; so very different from any woman he had ever known. So vulnerable, yet so strong in so many ways. She was indeed alone in the world and yet, clearly unafraid of anything she might encounter. Finally, after postponing the urge to grab her and kiss her so hard she fainted, Shadow answered.

"Yes, I do agree with that. I'm just surprised, that's all. I mean with your money you could sit back and take it easy for a very long time. Most women would."

"Well, I am not most women and besides I would be bored to death."

"No Amber, you certainly are not most women. No contest."

Shadow smiled as she finished straightening the room. He retrieved their coats while she pulled a brush through her hair. He watched her from across the room. Her hair was indeed the most striking feature about Amber Harris. He wondered how it would feel against his naked chest. He hoped he would find out soon. He wanted Amber, more than he had ever dreamed of wanting a woman. He thought of the way Eric Tolliver had abused and taken advantage of her vulnerability and felt literally sick. He could very easily hate Eric Tolliver. Tolliver had always struck any uneasy note with Shadow. Nothing he could put his finger on, but, he had always had very bad vibes about Eric. Shadow didn't appreciate the way Eric watched Ada on the rare occasions that he had visited with Lance. Shadow knew he was comparing Ada to something. Again, there was nothing Shadow could pinpoint, but yet something very real; something very distasteful. He stood hoping that Amber hadn't bit off more that she could chew when it came to settling things at Harris-Tolliver Enterprises. Shadow would never trust Eric Tolliver.

Yet more snow had fallen and the beagle pups were nearly buried in drifts. Amber bent to pet them briefly before she and Shadow started back to town. She rode silently for some time wishing she didn't have to face Eric in a showdown. She knew some serious changes had to take place and fast. There had to be some way to correct Eric's behavior of late.

Amber sneaked into the Manor house as quietly as possible. She coaxed Shadow to have a cup of coffee with her before he left. The coffee smelled rich and there were fresh cinnamon rolls on the sideboard. They finished off a half dozen rolls and half a pot of coffee. Shadow got up from the table and put on his coat. "How's your lip?" he asked.

Amber smiled and answered, "Much better."

"That's good," Shadow said as he took her into his arms and kissed her passionately. "I'll call you later, okay? I've got to get home and get started on today's schedule. I'm already two hours behind." He kissed her again. "I'd like to just stay right here all day."

Amber smiled and whispered, "Me too." She held him a moment more before he stepped out into the snow. He turned to leave and then paused. He faced her again and smiled. "You be careful, please. I'm just beginning to know you and so far I really like what I know. You really are a very special person. I don't want to lose you."

"Thank you Shadow. You are pretty special yourself."

He touched her face carefully avoiding her cut lip and still bruised cheek bone. "I hate to leave you," he whispered. "I've never felt like this in my life."

Amber grinned and took his hand. "We can't spend twenty four hours a day together."

"Says who?"

Amber didn't argue. She just smiled and kissed him once more on the cheek. "You best get home. Drive carefully. I'll talk with you later. I am glad we spent last night together. I hope you really didn't mind missing the barn dance."

"Mind? I'd trade a hundred barn dances for a night alone with you anytime."

They laughed together and hugged once more before Shadow left the Manor and started happily home. Amber pushed the heavy door closed and whispered "Happy New Year, Shadow McIntire."

Amber walked to the phone and dialed Richard Fargo's phone number. When no one answered she starting talking to herself. "Of course no one answers, it is 8 a.m. on New Years day!" She dialed his home phone number and again no one answered, but, this time an answering machine asked her to please leave a message at the tone. She fought the urge to giggle and then reminded Richard to go forward with her proposal to Eric as quickly as possible. She related the impossibility of their reconciliation, especially after his conduct on New Year's Eve. She wished Richard and his family a happy new year and a safe journey. She hung up the phone and started to her room. All she wanted right now was a hot shower and a little rest on a real bed. She had slipped off her shoes at the door and now unfastened the buttons on her skirt ast she climbed the stairs. She hummed one of Lillie's favorite tunes and remembered that Lillie was probably at church. Lillie never missed sunrise services on New Year's Day. She entered her room, tossed her skirt on a chair and started toward her bathroom. She touched the light switch and froze.

Eric stood leaning against the door frame of her bathroom. He took the last drink from the near empty scotch bottle and then slung it across the room. It crashed against the floor sending glass in all directions. Amber screamed. Eric was on her before she could turn to run. He threw her to the floor and pinned her down with her left arm behind her back. He slapped her hard across the face. He leaned down and forced his mouth on hers with a vengeance. He slapped her again and told her to kiss him. He ripped was left of her blouse off her shoulders exposing her breasts. "Did he thrill you like I did?" He spit the words at her, lacing them with pure hatred. He tugged at one nipple with his teeth sending pain and panic through her body. She struggled beneath him but it merely delighted him and exhausted her. Amber screamed again when she felt him rip her panties from her hips. He hit her again with such force that it momentarily blinded her. Her shoulder ached from the twisting motion he used on her arm to keep her pinned down. She tried again to move and he yanked her arm so hard that she wondered if the crunching sound she heard was her shoulder dislocating. The pain was unbearable.

"Your cowboy won't want you when I am through with you this time." His body was heavy on her chest. She could hardly breathe. Her lip was bleeding again and her head felt as if it would surely burst wide open. One last time she pleaded. "Eric, please, don't do this to us." She wept openly. His laugh was demonic and his answer was to finish ripping her shoulder from its' socket. Her body arched with pain as she screamed. Knowing she could no longer make use of her arm and thinking she could no longer struggle, he let her arm go and rose to position himself above her. She felt him thrust his penis into her flesh. She screamed again and with her uninjured arm she tried to hit him. He laughed again, and, even as Amber clawed his face with her fingernails, he drove himself deep into her. The world began to go black for Amber and she could no longer force herself to stay conscious. Eric was choking her fiercely as he pounded himself into her body, stroke after vicious stroke. She thought she was going to throw up but her throat would not open enough to let that happen. She thought only briefly of the pain, and, as she drifted into blackness her mind cried out to Shadow McIntire.

Amber didn't hear the noise. She didn't feel Eric's body go limp. She had already lost all consciousness.

Amber opened her eyes slowly. Every part of her body hurt. She was gagging on the taste of blood. A nurse stood over her murmuring soft words. She was urging Amber to be calm and to lie still. Amber didn't want to move anyway. Her entire left side ached and even trying to close her fingers into a fist hurt her shoulder. Amber was confused and frightened. There was blood everywhere and she thought the nurse was giving her a bath. Where was she? How did she get here? Where did all this blood come from? Was she dead?

She tried to speak but her throat was swollen and her words turned to moans. It took several minutes for the nurse to wipe all the blood from Amber's body and put a clean hospital gown on her. She covered her with a soft, warm blanket and promised to return in a few minutes with something warm for her to drink and some medication for pain. Amber watched her leave the room before she closed her eyes and tried to remember what was happening. She drifted into a drug induced sleep instead.

It was Eric's blood the nurse had washed from Amber's body. He had been so intent on killing Amber that he hadn't even noticed the second intruder in the room. The shot had been instant death for Eric.

Inez Chandler had not been so lucky. She had lived long enough to tell why she had returned to the Manor House. Eric had left the front door slightly ajar. Inez had heard Amber's screams and had traced the commotion to Amber's room. Eric was literally killing Amber. Inez had taken the small revolver she carried from her purse and had spoken to Eric. He had been in such frenzy, he hadn't even heard her. She pulled the trigger one time, sending a bullet through Eric's temple into his brain. The bullet had ripped the life from him instantly. Amber was blue, unconscious and Inez thought her to be dead. Feeling responsible for the entire mess, Inez turned the gun on herself. She had suffered for nearly an hour when Lillie returned home to find the chaos. Lillie's screams brought Mr. Templeton upstairs immediately and together they had called the police and life squads. Lillie had tried to soothe Amber but could do nothing for her. Amber was in shock and autistic. She said nothing, she felt nothing.

Lillie had to be treated for hyperventilation and shock. Amber lapsed into unconsciousness again on the way to the hospital. Inez died saying once again she was sorry for destroying Amber's happiness. She was sorry, always sorry.

Amber opened her eyes again. Her face was swollen from the slapping she had received and she couldn't move her left arm now at all. It had been taped to her body and she couldn't feel anything. She wondered what drug could make one feel so totally numb. She moved her head slowly to look out the window. It was dark now and she had no idea what day it was. She was frightened all over again and started to cry. Her quiet sobs woke Shadow from the fitful nap he was taking in the chair at the foot of her bed. He snapped to attention when he realized Amber was awake and conscious. He sat down gently on the side of her bed and pulled Amber into his arms and hugged her. He spoke slowly trying to make sure she understood him. "You are safe now, Amber. Forever safe from anyone that will ever try to hurt you. I love you, Amber. I love you more than I even knew I could love anyone."

She did not speak. She just wept. She cried herself to sleep again in Shadow's arms and a nurse helped him lay her back against the pillows without waking her. At least she had been conscious. Shadow refused to leave her side. He sat in a chair by her bedside the entire night and long into the next morning. If Amber stirred and opened her eyes, she saw him. Ever present, ever faithful. He didn't speak. He didn't need to. The look on his face told Amber all she needed to know about his devotion. She would look at him and close her eyes and drift away again. Time after time he watched her slip back into darkness. He nearly wept himself. He sat slumped forward in a chair with his head and arms resting on the side of her bed. He held her free hand tightly. Amber woke again but did not stir. She looked around the room. Lillie and Mr. Templeton shared a small sofa, propping each other up while they slept sitting up. Ada and Jack McIntire actually sat in the floor with only a pillow between them and the wall. Someone had thrown a blanket over their legs and they held hands in their sleep. Amber laid there and watched her sleeping friends for over an hour. All these people loved her. They loved her for the person she had grown up to be not just for whose daughter she might or might not be. Life was basically good and she had to learn to cling to that thought. There weren't many Erics in the world. Mostly there were people like the ones sitting her with her now, waiting for her to mend. She would concentrate on that, but it was difficult to concentrate. Her mind was so very tired. She drifted off to sleep again, leaving her friends to grieve her condition.

Five full days passed before Amber stayed awake and conscious long enough to hold a real conversation. During those five days the only time Shadow had left Amber's side was to help Lillie arrange for funerals for both Eric and Inez. They had decided Eric should be buried beside his parents and Inez was placed in a remote corner of the same cemetery where Lance was interred. Lillie hadn't been sure she was doing the right thing, but, both she and Shadow decided it couldn't do any harm. Actually, in the end Inez had saved Amber's life, and for that Lillie and Shadow would always be grateful. Shadow and Mr. Templeton escorted Lillie to both funerals. There were a few subdued people at Eric's funeral, none of them a brother or a sister. Every one of them voiced concern for Amber and sent their regards. There was no one to mourn Inez Chandler. Her last few moments on earth were spent with Lillie and Mr. Templeton, Shadow and a young parish priest. Lillie wasn't even sure if Inez was a Catholic.

Shadow drove Lillie and Mr. Templeton back to the Manor House in silence. His every thought was of Amber. His worry was beginning to show in his dark hazel eyes. The circles beneath his eyes from lack of rest were visible at twenty paces. He spent hours at Amber's bedside blaming himself for not staying with her longer on that fateful morning. He had wanted to protect her and had already let her down. He had just begun to know this young spirit and now it seemed broken; gone; perhaps for good. He longed to hold her in his arms again, smell her fresh scent, taste the sweetness of her kiss. He had loved it when she laughed and he missed her. She was the first woman he had ever enjoyed just talking to. He wasn't a praying person, but for the last few minutes he had prayed earnestly for Amber's recovery. He parked his car and sat quietly for a moment before making his way across the lot through the slushy snow. There were two men taking down the Christmas tree in the hospital lobby. They nodded at Shadow and wished him well. He took a deep breath while waiting for the elevator that would carry him back upstairs to Amber's room. He had hated being away so long but Eric's funeral had drug on for what seemed like forever. He wouldn't have attended it at all if not for Lillie. He entered Amber's room trying hard to smile. His heart sank. Amber lay on her right side. Her eyes were still swollen and the dark circles below them made her look at least twice her age.

Shadow crept to her side. He bent down and kissed her gently on the forehead. He pulled a chair to the side of the bed and sat down so that Amber would see him if she opened her eyes. He sat for several minutes in silence. Then he started to speak to her and to make small talk. He talked about the mares and their new colts and the farm in general. He took her hand in his and held it gingerly. He took deep breaths to keep from weeping. Then out of desperation he nearly shouted, "Amber! Can you hear me? Damn it! You are not alone in this. Let us share your suffering. At least tell me if you can hear me!" He felt her hand quiver. He knew she had heard him. "Amber, honey, I don't mean to frighten you. I just want to reach you, that's all. Let us help please. I miss you so much." His words drifted into the air, his voice broke and he felt is own tears wet his face. "Amber, baby, please!" His agony was evident, his tears flowed freely.

Amber focused swollen eyes on Shadow's face. Half choking, half crying, she spoke in a whisper. "DON'T ever call me Baby again, okay?"

Shadow was stunned and fought for control. "Amber! Oh, Amber, Pretty Lady, you got it. Never, never again. I promise. Oh, Amber, speak to me again, please!" Then before she could speak he went on, "Do you want me to call Lillie? Oh, honey, please tell me you are okay. Please tell me. Just be okay again. I'll help you. We all will."

Amber shushed him softly, then cleared her throat and tried to speak again. She tried valiantly to smile, "My brain is so numb, I'm so tired. Why am I so tired?"

"You have been to hell and back, that's why! Your mind is trying to protect you. At least that is what these fancy doctors around here keep telling me. They say you sleep so you don't have to face the pain. But, honey, you are not alone. I'm here; Lillie is here most of the time. And Mom and Pops. Even Richard Fargo postponed his trip for a month just to take care of the Enterprises. Poor Mr. Templeton stands at the foot of your bed and prays for hours at a time. We all care, Amber. We all love you." He paused for the first time. "I love you Amber. I really do. I know we just met but you complete my every moment."

Amber's eyes clouded with tears. How could Shadow or anyone else love her? She felt so stupid; so used. "I don't see how," she said.

"How? I'll tell you how. Because you are you. Warm, wonderful, beautiful. Actually I can't wait to see you when your face isn't beat all to hell." For an instant he could have torn his tongue out. Amber looked at him and smiled at first. Then she giggled and then she broke into absolute laughter. She laughed until she cried. Then she said, "What if I look even worse?"

Shadow took her gently into his arms. "I'm not worried for an instant." He dried her tears and his own.

Amber sobered. She said simply, "Eric?"

"It's over, Amber," he said dropping his eyes. He couldn't stand looking at the pain he read in her eyes. "And Inez?' she added. He barely whispered, "That's over too, Honey."

Amber let him blot away the constant flow of tears. He touched her face ever so gently and she could hear him breathing deeply while trying to force his own emotions from the surface.

"She saved my life didn't she?" Amber paused. "How did Eric get so insane without any of us noticing?"

Shadow cleared his throat. "Don't dwell on it, Amber. I'm just glad you are with us now. You are okay, aren't you, Sweetheart?"

She tried to smile and answered, "I don't know if I will ever be okay again."

Shadow wanted to change the subject. "Let me go and get a nurse. They wanted to know as soon as you responded to anything."

"No, don't," she begged. "Just sit with a little while longer. I don't want them hovering about. You just stay with me, will you?"

"I'll stay forever if you will let me."

"Don't change on me Shadow. Don't turn into some sick monster when my back is turned."

"No chance. Don't worry about the past. I'm healthy and together we are going to mold a future. Just worry about getting strong enough to come home with me." He leaned back in his chair and held her hand until she went back to sleep. Their conversation seemed to totally exhaust her. Shadow watched her and again took deep calming breaths to stifle his tears.

He silently left the room thanking God for this new ray of hope for Amber. The nurse made notes and expressed delight at this good news. She went back to Amber's room with Shadow and checked on her. They left her sleeping, but this time quite peacefully.

"Can she come home now? Shadow was anxious.

"It is hard to say Mr. McIntire. She has suffered severe shock and trauma. This disaster on top of her recent accident has just about been too much for her to cope with. She may be all right now but then again, she may lapse right back into shock. The important thing is to support her without rushing her. Dr. Van Nuys can probably answer your questions better than I."

"Hey, you have done fine. I guess I just want this to be all over with for good. I'd like for her life to get back to normal. I've been so scared that I'd lost her permanently. This is a good sign though, isn't it? I mean her knowing me and talking to me."

"Oh yes. It is an excellent omen. In fact Dr. Van Nuys may want to hear about your conversation with her, especially if she should lapse back into a state of shock.

"God forbid!" Shadow murmured. All the while starring at Amber's door. He thanked the nurse again and headed for a phone. He called Lillie and shared his good news about Amber. Her response was exactly what Shadow expected and within minutes she was on the way to the hospital. She couldn't wait to speak to her beloved Amber again. She prayed for wisdom on her way to Amber's room. She entered the room quietly and when Amber turned to face her and smiled faintly, Lillie burst into tears. She rushed to Amber's side and embraced her gently. Amber shushed Lillie and caressed her dear friend. Lillie spoke through broken sobs, "Amber, we have been so worried."

"I know Lillie. I'm okay, don't cry. Please don't cry. I keep trying to think and I get so confused. It has been easier to just let the drugs keep me asleep. I know I have to get it together and face reality. I'm going to make it, I promise. I'm sorry for scaring you."

"Oh, don't you be sorry. Just get strong so that we can take you home."

"Oh God, Lillie. Home. I don't know if I can ever go back home."

"Don't say that, Honey. Time will heal. I know it will. You will feel like it is taking forever, but it won't. I have already moved you into your Daddy's room. You always felt safe there and you will feel safe again. You'll be right next to me and I'll be there if you need me at any time. We will get through this together. I know we will."

Silent tears mirrored the fear the older woman felt for Amber. She looked at Amber and smiled anyway and Amber tried hard to return a grin. "Okay Lillie, if you say so, we will get through it." Amber rested while Lillie held her hand and prayed.

The days melted into another week. Shadow began leaving for a few hours each morning to return to the farm to help his father keep things in order there. Before noon he would return and sometimes not leave the room until dawn the next morning. It had taken three days for Amber to work up the courage to leave the bed and walk. She nearly fainted form the pain in her shoulder and chest. She had suffered five broken ribs during her beating and pneumonia had settled in her lungs, causing pain with just breathing. Shadow had supported her walking three times around the room before he would give up and let her sit down. He had felt guilty when he realized she was wet with sweat from the exertion. Her pale face broke his heart into pieces. Amber kept telling him to spend more time at home but he would hear nothing of that. He brought books and flowers daily and she wondered when he had the time to even purchase them. He told her everything. He talked about day to day news, the weather, about his parents. He talked about every doubt he had ever had and bragged about his best achievements. She listened and during the second week she was finally able to speak and even laugh a little without pain to her throat. He begged her to talk to him. And she did. About Lance, about Sarahlou. About school and working in the coal yards as a youngster. They joked about Amber having to help him catch up on his farm chores once she mended. She agreed she might indeed love that kind of life. Shadow hoped secretly that she would truly adapt to farm living, for now his every thought for the future included Amber Harris.

When Amber left the hospital it had been almost a month since her ordeal; Shadow McIntire had spent less that four hours a day away from her.

The morning Amber left the hospital lobby her heart pounded in her throat as flash bulbs exploded at her. She tried to shield her face from their blinding light, but nothing could shield her from the heartless questions thrown at her as she tried to make her way to the car. "Was it really your mother that killed your lover?" "How could they call it rape, weren't you two lovers for over a year?" Yet another voice demanded, "Was this a three way love triangle?" "Where does Jason McIntire fit in?" Her cheeks burned with embarrassment and tears stung her eyes. She rushed past cameras and reporters to her waiting car wondering how they knew she was leaving the hospital today. She climbed into the back seat with Lillie. Mr. Templeton sped away. Lillie prayed for some way to help Amber, but this time there was no way. They rode home in total silence. Both women cried most of the trip. They arrived at the Manor House and the phone was ringing as they walked in the door. Amber went to the library while Lillie answered the phone. She could hear Lillie trying to persuade the caller to just leave Amber alone. Amber sat down, her body trembling uncontrollably. Her eyes focused on the picture that Ada had given her for Christmas. Seven weeks ago. God it seemed like years. How she wished she were a little girl again, with her father holding her hand and protecting her from all the bitterness the world has to offer. Her mind ached, her body ached. She wondered how much you could cry before you brain just gave up and exploded. Lillie entered the library with tea laced with honey and cinnamon. Thank God for Lillie. Amber sipped her tea, relaxed against the huge sofa and wished she could sleep for another month. She sat for some time before she became aware of someone else in the room. She looked up to find Shadow standing in the door way.

"What are you looking at?" she ask.

"Just the most beautiful creature in the state," he answered.

Amber straightened and asked if he would like tea? He wouldn't, but would like coffee and he cold pour it himself. When he finished pouring a mug full of steaming coffee he started carefully toward the couch. Amber smiled. "Don't look at the top of the cup while you walk. It throws you off balance and your hand will shake. Look straight ahead as you walk." she advised.

"Well, I guess I can learn something new everyday." he said forcing himself not to look at the cup he was carrying. He laughed when he managed to get to the sofa without spilling a drop of the hot liquid. He sat down slowly.

Amber looked a bit smug and she was smiling.

"Congratulations!" she smiled even more.

Shadow looked at her and wanted to kiss her but didn't. "How are you, Pretty Lady?" he asked instead. He was nervous and Amber could sense his discomfort. It made Amber sad for his usual confidence to be blighted. He spoke slowly.

"Amber, are you okay? I mean really okay? You didn't come back here too soon, did you? Lillie said you cried all the way home."

"Is Lillie your personal spy, now?" Shadow couldn't tell if she were angry but decided to hope she wasn't as he answered.

"Of course she is. But the only thing I ask her about is your health." He continued, "And that is just because we have all been so worried about you. Please don't be mad at me for prying, nor Lillie for telling." He eyed her not knowing what kind of reaction to expect. She studied him quietly for a moment. She was pale and looked exhausted but finally had no visible bruises. She was without a doubt beautiful as far as Jason was concerned.

She spoke with determination and resolution for the first time in over a month. "I'm going to say this once, Shadow. So please pay attention. I cried today out of anger, now sorrow. I got upset with those stupid reporters. I am supposed to go to work with some of those people. I don't know if I can walk into the Aston Daily and face those people without punching them out or not. I feel so helpless in so many situations these days and it really frustrates me. However, I can not wallow in self pity for the rest of my life. I am "OKAY" if you mean am I going to break into pieces like some piece of porcelain. I am NOT going to do that. You and Lillie can stop worrying about that. In fact, all this fuss over me just makes me nervous and I wish everyone would stop it. I have got to get back on track with my life and want to never dwell on these last few weeks again. Can you understand?"

Shadow nodded and smiled broadly. He was hearing exactly what he wanted to hear. Amber would heal; not just the broken ribs and busted lips, but her mind and soul would heal too. Amber continued, a bit breathless and obviously tiring. "I can't believe a person can get their lives so screwed up in such a short time." She shook her head and for the first time since Christmas morning it didn't hurt. That pleasantly surprised her and she suddenly smiled. Shadow was caught off guard by her change in her demeanor and looked puzzled.

"It's my headache," she said. "It's gone. Isn't that wonderful? For the first time since Christmas I can move my head and it doesn't feel like it is going to explode."

Shadow could resist no longer. He placed his cup on the sofa table and took Amber in his arms and held he close. "You are incredible. Life deals you a bad hand and you refuse to fold. No one would be surprised if you had a screaming fit or two, you know."

"I'd like to sometimes. But I'm mostly angry at myself for being so vulnerable in the first place. I don't know if I can forgive myself for being so blind."

"Well, do me a favor and give yourself a break. The almighty Sigmund Freud couldn't have foreseen what happened here." Shadow blushed wishing he hadn't brought up the horrid events that had taken place. Amber grinned and put her arms around him to return his embrace.

"It's okay, Shadow. I said I don't want to dwell on the subject but I can face casual conversation about it."

Shadow held her tightly while taking care not to hurt her ribs. "Are you sure, Honey? I can't believe you have held together so well." He released her and looked at those clear green eyes. He wondered how many tears had flowed from them in the past month. He wanted to erase all pain from her life, if only he knew how to begin.

Amber took a deep breath. "I'm going into the office in the morning."

"So soon, Amber?"

She shook her head affirmatively. "Yes, Shadow and it isn't so soon. You realize my company hasn't had a senior officer present for over a month now. She paused knowing in her heart that walking through that door in the morning would be one of the hardest steps she'd taken in a long time. She continued, "There is a power company that was interested in leasing all the companies' holdings. I'm going to find out if they are still interested; and, it they are; and if they will employ the same personnel working there now, I'm going to bail out for awhile. I hate being weak, but even under normal circumstances I couldn't run the company alone." Her voice trailed off and tears brimmed eyes. Shadow watched her; he admired her so much. She breathed deeply willing herself to stop crying. "I'm going to conquer all this before I go to work at the paper." she said smiling.

"Are you sure you want to work at all?" Shadow said.

"Didn't we have this conversation once before?" She raised one eyebrow at him and he smiled.

"Yes Pretty Lady. I guess we did at that." He looked straight into her eyes. "Amber, may I please kiss you?"

Amber swallowed the knot in her throat and blushed. "You mean after all that's happened you still want me in that," her words were barely a whisper, her face crimson.

Shadow spoke with amazement. "Amber! Please! Want you? I want you more than food and water. I wanted you the night I met you and I haven't stopped wanting you for a minute. Nothing for us has changed except for the fact that I am no longer afraid to tell you that I am in love with you. I know it seems sudden to you but I think you were aware New Years Day how I had begun to feel. I admit that now I am caught up in fear of rushing you. I promise I won't do that and I don't want to frighten you in any way. I want to be your friend; I want to be your lover. Hopefully you will do me the honor of someday becoming my bride. There, I've said it all. Not a very romantic proposal I admit, but I hadn't planned to ask you today."

Amber sat with her mouth open. Shadow continued, "Now, may I kiss you?" Amber sat for a full minute and looked at him. Then she began to smile. She touched his face. Tears ran silently down her cheeks and Shadow wiped them away. "Shadow, you do not need permission to kiss me now or ever. You may kiss me at any time and personally I hope your desire is to do so often."

His mouth found hers, eager, sweet and receptive. His hunger for her intensified by all the other emotions running wild through his mind. Any barrier he thought might have existed was washed away and their desires ran wild and free. No comparisons to anything. No hidden agendas.

Amber withdrew from his embrace and took a deep breath. She smiled and looked up at Shadow.

"WOW!" she said. "Just like before. You make my head swim and it is so pleasant. You make me feel so good all over."

Shadow hugged her and laughed. "That is the way it will always be, I promise."

"Shadow, you are such a good person. What if I can't be what you think I am? I don't want to disappoint you."

"Amber, I do not THINK you are anything. I KNOW that you are warm, kind, responsible, loyal, loving, trustworthy, sexy, honest, and fun. I KNOW I liked you before I loved you. I KNOW that I would love it if you would be by wife tomorrow but I also KNOW you have some things in your own life to settle and I can wait until you decide the time is right. NOW, I trust you to make the right decisions and if your decision for your future does NOT include me, then I will respect that decision. I won't like it, but I will respect it." He looked at her and then grinned before adding, "I'll pout, too." He bowed his head as if waiting for her to declare him a knight or something. Amber laughed and said, "Promise me one thing."

He looked up and said, "Anything!"

"Promise me that you will always have such a good sense of humor."

Shadow laughed. "No problem. It runs in our family. Our children will be born laughing instead crying. Really, you wait and see."

"Our children?"

"Yes, all six of them."

"Six children?"

"Yes, absolutely. Maybe more if you're healthy…maybe we can adopt, too."

"You're serious."

"Yes. I hated being raised an only child. Didn't you?"

Amber looked at him seriously. "Yes, actually I did. I was always lonesome. The sad thing is I am not really an only child. I have a twin brother somewhere in this world. I wonder if he was ever as lonesome as I was."

"That's heavy. I didn't know." Shadow was genuinely surprised.

"Neither did I until Christmas Eve. But there is no need to dwell on it. I just though you ought to know that those six children could come in pairs. You might want to be prepared." She laughed with him.

"Oh Amber, my beauty. It is so good to hear you laugh."

"It feels pretty good too." She paused. "Say are you hungry?"

"In fact, I am starving."

"Well, let's go out to the kitchen and torment Lillie."

"Hey, I don't want to get on Lillie's bad side. She has been a real friend to me."

"The only way to get on Lillie's bad side is to refuse to eat her beef stroganoff. And don't refuse because it is really good." They were still laughing when they entered the kitchen. Lillie looked at them and could hold her emotions no longer. She threw her arms around Amber and held her closely. "Welcome home, my Darling Amber." Lillie then embraced Shadow. "She looks better already. What have you two been talking about?"

Amber laughed and pointed to Shadow. "You tell what we've been talking about." Shadow blushed and Lillie insisted, "What. What. One of you tell me!"

"Okay, Okay. We have been talking about the fact that our six children might be born in pairs. Amber brought it up, she thought I should know so I could prepare for the shock."

Lillie didn't know whether to take the two of them serious or not. "All right," she admonished, "didn't we skip a few minor details here?" They all laughed and Lillie busied herself getting lunch on the table while Amber poured fresh milk into tall glasses. Shadow helped Amber clear the table after lunch and Lillie retired for a short nap on the living room couch. It was so good to have Amber home. She could rest easy this afternoon.

Shadow and Amber spent the rest of the day together. They watched the sunset from the back windows of the house and shared many long loving kisses. Each time they kissed desire mounted in both of them but Shadow made no attempt to seduce Amber any further. Amber clung to him when they kissed good night at the front door. "I'll call you tomorrow," Shadow said. "Sleep tight and sweet dreams." He walked to his car and drove away slowly. He wondered if Amber felt the same uneasiness he was feeling. He had left her just this way the morning this horrid nightmare had begun.

Amber did feel the same way and as she crept upstairs to her father's room to retire she wished Shadow could be with her. She brushed her hair and looked at her face in the mirror for a long time. She sighed. Mr. Templeton and Lillie were in the parlor downstairs reading Bible verses and sharing one last cup of tea for the evening. The room was warm from the fire in the fireplace and Lillie had rearranged the furniture so that Amber could see the fire from anywhere in the room. She was safe. She laughed out loud. She was looking at her hair. It was more like copper that ever. She thought out loud, "At least there are a couple of constants in my life; red hair and freckles!" She undressed and walked to the large poster bed that had comforted her Daddy and crawled beneath the heavy covers. The clean sheet smelled like the lilac powder that Lillie had dusted them with when she changed the bed. Amber held tight to the feather pillow and drifted into sweet undisturbed sleep. Her only dreams were of Shadow McIntire and the sweet way he kissed her.

Amber woke with the dawn and was dressed in five minutes. She went downstairs softly so as not to wake Lillie but she needn't have bothered because Lillie was already in the kitchen. The coffee was fresh and it seemed to Amber like an eternity since they had sat down at the kitchen table for a decent breakfast and to talk to one another. Lillie looked refreshed and ready to greet the world. "What are you dong up so early?" Lillie hugged Amber and started pouring her a cup of coffee in what seem like all one motion to Amber.

"I'm up to check on you and to make sure the house is all still here. It seems like I have been gone for a year. I was afraid maybe you had sold everything we own in a yard sale or something." Lillie laughed with her. Amber continued, "Besides I want to be awake and alert when Richard Fargo gets here. We have a lot to discuss."

"I know Amber. I wish things could be easier for you."

"Lillie, I'm fine. Don't start to worry. Shadow and I talked all day yesterday and I really am going to be okay. Don't you go treating me like I am going to fall to apart or something."

"Okay, you are fine. Actually, you look fine today. Sleeping in your own bed must have done some good."

"It is good to be home, Lillie. Did you overhear any of my plans for the company?"

"Yes and I think you are making a good decision."

"I hope Daddy would understand."

"Your Daddy would want only what is best for you Amber. I knew him well enough to know that. And this is best. You couldn't run that company completely by yourself and have any other part of a life. Your daddy didn't run it by himself. He had Eric and Richard Fargo and it was still almost more than the three of them could handle at times."

"You are right Lillie. I don't want to ruin the company's reputation while I'm finding out that I can't handle the place without help. This is no time for false pride."

Lillie changed the subject. "What about you and this Shadow McIntire? What's all this about six children?" She was smiling.

"Well, I think he is about half serious about wanting six children someday."

"Is he half serious about anything else young lady?"

"He says he loves me, Lillie. I don't know if I am ready for that kind of devotion or not. I'm frightened of failure, Lillie."

Lillie stopped moving about the kitchen and turned to face Amber. "You didn't fail Amber. You are young and inexperienced in the ways of life. Or at least you were. You were a victim. I really feel if none of this nightmare had happened, another one would have. You can not hold yourself responsible for Eric's illness. And you deserve happiness, just like everyone else in the world. Don't be afraid to take another chance. Don't turn you back on the adventures of life like your daddy did. He missed out on such much joy because he refused to take the chances again. Don't make the same mistakes he did."

"How did you get so smart Lillie?"

"I've been living for well, never mind for how long. Just believe me." Lillie laughed and finished the toast and jelly she was eating. Amber raised one eyebrow. "Are you ever going to tell me how old you are Lillie?" Lillie smirked…"No. Never."

The phone rang; Amber answered bracing herself for another attack by some reporter. She was pleasantly surprised to hear instead Richard Fargo. He was on his way to her house and wanted to make sure she was up and about. She assured him she was ready to conquer the world in fact, and agreed he should come right over.

He arrived within half an hour and before 10 a.m. any doubts Amber might have had about he decisions were erased. Northern Power and Light Incorporated had already contacted Richard and proposed an even more generous offer to lease the entire company. Harris-Tolliver Enterprises had run smoothly when other companies had fallen flat. N.P. &L. had the good sense to know a good thing when they saw it and was more than willing to be fair and generous to get their hands on the company. Amber would hold the title to the company for two more years and share in the profits while N.P. &L. did all the work. Then theirs was the option to buy the entire company for 2.5 million dollars and Amber would be free of all responsibilities. Every employee would be guaranteed a job for the next five years and thereafter depending on job performance. The employees had already had a meeting with Richard and had assured him that they were satisfied with the options. Actually their health insurance and pension benefits would be better. Everyone felt five years was ample time to prove themselves to their new executives. They felt safe. Amber was elated.

Richard left and Amber walked to the phone to call Shadow. He wasn't home and she felt a little let down because she wanted to share her news with him. She hadn't even had to go to the offices to wrap up the loose ends that had haunted her life. She walked back to the kitchen to find a snack and a cup of coffee. Lillie had walked across the yard and was conversing with Mr. Templeton. Amber wondered just how serious their relationship was. From the look on Mr. Templeton's face, Amber was inclined to guess pretty serious. The man obviously loved Lillie. Amber smiled and was happy for Lillie. She started out the back door and nearly ran into Shadow who had just raised his hand to knock on the door. Amber looked at him and waited for his explanation. He smiled and brought his hand down to rest it on her shoulder. He pulled her to him and kissed her gently. "What are you doing here. I expected to see Lillie. I thought you would be at the office or something."

"Shadow, I live here. You might find me here almost anytime. What are YOU doing here?" Shadow laughed.

"I told you I came to see Lillie. If I weren't in love with you, I'd be in love with her."

"Very funny. Now what is going on with you two?"

Lillie was rushing across the yard. "Shadow, I didn't expect you till later. I thought Amber would be gone by now."

"Okay you two. Just what kind of conspiracy is going on? I demand an answer!" She tried to look angry but could only smile at the two of them trying to think of an excuse to hide the real motive of their meeting. Finally Lillie spoke. "I plead the fifth amendment."

Amber could never stand for someone to keep secrets from her. She stomped her foot. "Now wait a minute. This isn't fair!"

Shadow laughed and led the way into the kitchen. He removed his heavy coat and hung it on a peg. He sat down and asked if might have a cup of coffee. He was obviously bent on changing the subject and Amber soon knew there was no real need to keep badgering either of them. Their lips were sealed and her frustration was of no concern to them. She decided not to waste energy pouting. Instead she poured a cup of coffee for Shadow and asked if he would like a sandwich. He refused the sandwich but munched on the oatmeal cookies Lillie had brought forth from the side board. Lillie excused herself and went to the laundry room so that she wouldn't have to discuss the real reason for Shadow's visit any further. She was obviously pleased with herself.

Shadow enjoyed his coffee and cookies and smiled at Amber. She tried to act as if she were no longer interested in the reason for his visit with Lillie. He leaned back in the big oak chair and she noticed again how very handsome he was.

"What happened to your trip into town this morning?" he asked.

Amber smiled. "Richard Fargo came out here to meet with me. It seems Northern Power and Light has wanted Daddy's holdings for some time. They want everything. The mines, the trucks, the yards, the offices, everything. They are prepared with a more than generous offer about it. Richard had already taken care of all the contracts and they complied with my every wish concerning the future of the business and the people at work there now. Isn't it wonderful?"

"That's great! You mean you don't have to bicker back and forth with these people at all?"

"That's right. Richard has everything in control and all I have to do is sign the dotted line. My employees will continue to have a job for as long as they want and their seniority will amount to something with their new company. Their fringe benefits will be even better than we could afford as an independent company. I didn't want any of Daddy's people to loose what they had worked for all this time just because my life is so screwed up."

"Your life is going to be fine, Amber."

"I know, and I want to be the last to whine about my woes, but sometimes I just." Her voice faded and she sat quiet. Shadow stood up and walked to her side. He knelt by her chair and took her in his arms and kissed her passionately. He let he go only after several seconds had passed and only then because he was afraid he heard Lillie approaching. Amber was blushing and she looked at him. "You do the nicest things to me," she said.

"I'm on my way to an auction. Would you like to join me since you don't have to go into the office?"

She smiled at him. "I do have to go to the office. I should be the one who tells these people the contracts have been finalized. And I have about one hundred other things to do too. I'd like a rain check though. Do you issue those?"

"You bet I do. How about next weekend? We can drive to Shelbyville and take in the pre-spring sales. We will stay the entire weekend. There's a dance Saturday night if we aren't too tired to attend it." He was excited and Amber wondered if would always be this enthusiastic about everything. She hesitated before she started to answer. Shadow hastened to add, "If you think we need a chaperon Lillie or my Mom or both of them can come with us. Lillie can take in the malls and Mom can show her around the food courts. She would love it. You will love it Amber, I know you will. Please say yes."

Amber thought a moment more. "Okay. Okay, I'll go." She smiled.

"That's terrific. And how about dinner tonight? Please. We've never had a decent meal together that Lillie hasn't fixed." Amber looked at him and laughed. "Shadow, we haven't had a decent outing of any kind together."

"You are correct and it is high time we changed that statistic, don't you think?"

Lillie answered him. "I think so for sure. Go on Amber. It is time you returned to being a young woman again. Enough of this mourning for things we can not change."

Amber looked at Shadow. "Well, how can I refuse? I am outnumbered on all counts. Is anybody on my side?"

Shadow looked at her closely and then kissed her on the forehead.

"I beg your pardon, Pretty Lady. We are all on your side. I will see you around 7:30 tonight. Stay hungry." He stood and picked up his coat. Amber followed him to the door. Without a doubt she had never met anyone like him. He kissed her again not even noticing that Lillie was staring at them. He left the room without a backward glance. If he had looked back he would have seen Amber watching his every movement. She did want to go out with him, but down deep she felt guilty. Almost as if she didn't have the right to be happy or have a good time with anyone. So much had happened. So much tragedy. Perhaps she wanted too much. It seemed every person she wanted to love came to some bad end. Suddenly she felt very paranoid. Lillie was watching her think.

"You should go out and have a good time. There is no reason for you to shut yourself up like a hermit." Lillie was smiling.

"I am just afraid something terrible will happen to him if I begin to really like him. I just don't trust fate these days, I guess."

"Amber, you sound phobic!"

"Well, just look at the terrible things that have happened this past year!"

"You can not control the circumstances of life. You can not let your mind blackmail you into being afraid of loving another. Several people that I have loved are dead now, including your father. I can not be afraid to love others just because this is true. If I felt that way how could you and I have any kind of friendship? Or what of me and Mr. Templeton? We are not as young as you and Shadow, but we have our good moments and we are happy. We do not dwell on those we have already lost. You shouldn't either."

Amber grinned and hugged Lillie. "As usual, Lillie, you are correct and I don't know what I would do without you." Lillie hugged her and laughed. "You would do your own laundry, that's what. Now be off with you; I thought you had errands in town."

Amber had forgotten all about the secret meeting between Lillie and Shadow. She left the house a few minutes later and had hardly left the driveway when the phone rang and Lillie answered. It was Shadow McIntire. His voice was so warm and friendly. Yes, Lillie did like Shadow.

They discussed the documents they had retrieved from Inez Chandler's purse the day she died.

Amber walked into the offices of Harris-Tolliver Enterprises and small droplets of perspiration wet her forehead. She hadn't dreamed it would be this hard. Mercifully, someone had already taken Eric's name from the door that led to what had been his office. His secretary had taken the liberty of turning the room into the office library and conference room. They had needed that for some time anyway. It was lined wall to wall with books about transportation safety and the highway limitations of every state in the Union. There were maps outlining every route that every Harris-Tolliver semi traveled. The phones were ringing on nearly desk when she entered the room. She would miss this place but it was time to move on. She asked the switchboard operator to hold all calls for ten minutes. Ten minutes. Could she sum up the lives of two men in ten minutes? She did. With tears streaming down her cheeks, she went on to vow that she would remember the employees of Harris-Tolliver now and always. They were the backbone of this operation and she knew no one had to tell them that their jobs were safe mainly because of their own conduct. She made each of them promise to keep in touch with her and if anything ever threatened the welfare of the company she pleaded for them to come straight to her. She cleaned of her desk and threw most of the contents away. She left Harris-Tolliver Enterprises with her head held high and a renewed hope for the future.

She stopped by Aston Daily News Offices and left a message for the editor. His young secretary promised he would call her promptly.

She arrived back at the Manor House about an hour before her date was to begin with Shadow. She concentrated on her talks with Lillie and tried not to get nervous before his arrival. She showered quickly and buffed her skin to a rosy glow. She was still pale but decided to skip using blush on her cheeks and relied only on soft pastel eye shadows to accent her deep green eyes. She brushed her hair till it shone in the lights. She hadn't trimmed her hair for several months now and it had grown past her waist again. She picked out a gray dress that clung to her slim body and tossed the shoes that matched it toward the door. She would carry them downstairs and not put them on until the minute she had to walk out the door with her date. She still hated shoes and she smiled as she looked down at her feet.

They were ugly, she had to admit that. But then, how pretty could feet be?

Shadow arrived at 7 p.m., a full half hour early, and Lillie had him cornered in the parlor. Lillie was busy showing him pictures of Amber as a child. Amber had to laugh and remembered how good laughing felt. Shadow walked toward her, greeting her with that already familiar smile. He leaned down to kiss her on the forehead. "You look great!" he said with real enthusiasm.

"Thank you, I feel fine." She paused for a moment and then tilted her head back and repeated almost to herself. "I do feel fine. Are we ready to leave?

"Well, I am, but I think you might be forgetting something."

"What?!" Amber looked indignant.

"Your shoes? I think you might wish you were wearing them when we dance."

"Oh really? Are we dancing tonight?"

Shadow helped her on with her coat and she slipped first one foot into a shoe and then the other. He offered his arm to her and answered, "Yes indeed, Pretty Lady. Tonight we dine, we dance, we sing, we thank our savior for our blessings."

They walked toward the big front door and Lillie hugged them both; she was so glad to see Amber smile and at peace. She listened to them laugh as they walked to Shadow's car. Lillie could have hugged herself. Her darling Amber was going to survive. She rushed to the kitchen phone and dialed Mr. Templeton. He would be glad to share this good news about Amber and he probably wanted some fresh brownies anyway.

Jason McIntire and Amber Harris became at "item" all over the state of Virginia. They saw each other nearly every day. Amber did accompany Jason on the weekend trip to Shelbyville and although they spent the night in separate beds, they shared many long loving kisses and it had been Jason who put a stop their petting, not Amber. Jason loved Amber as surely as the sun rose each day. He was patient and kind and forever considerate of Amber's feelings. He had vowed to wait until she asked him to make love to her. She felt herself drawn to him more each day and almost wished he would be more insistent, but she did not bring up the subject to him. They went to horse shows or auctions every weekend during the spring, and they camped overnight on the back acres of the farm. Ada taught Amber how to make her prize winning biscuits and breads. They shared birthday dinners for Jack and Ada. The "pups" were half grown and they took them hunting although Jason spent most of his time watching Amber instead of looking for game.

Amber's work at the Aston Daily was superior. She had earned the respect of her co-workers within weeks and no longer needed or had to prove anything to anyone, including herself. Amber Harris was to turn twenty one years old in two days and she was a success in her own right.

Jason and Lillie had been working on her surprise birthday party since the beginning of the year. To say the least it was going to be elaborate. It had taken Jason weeks to trace the leads that Inez Chandler had left in her purse that fateful morning. With these new leads, the help of Richard Fargo and the new administrator of the Aston County Orphanage, along with the

Selective Service Offices in Washington, D.C., Jason had succeeded where Lance had failed. He had found Amber's twin brother. Once he had contacted the boys adoptive parents, the rest had been easy. They proved very receptive to meeting Amber and the boy had begged to travel to Aston on the very day he met Jason. This was Jason's gift to Amber.

There wasn't anyone in Aston that didn't know of the party that was being thrown in Amber's honor. That is no one except Amber. The party proved to be the best kept secret of the century. She hadn't the slightest idea and could not believe that no one had so much as mentioned her birthday. After all this was the big one, number twenty one! She rose at 6 a.m. and thought she would fix Lillie some hot tea. She was too late. Lillie was already in the kitchen and when Amber walked in, Lillie was about to slip some elaborate looking dish into the oven. Amber smiled knowing Lillie was about to wish her "happy birthday." Lillie didn't.

"Good morning!" Lillie said smiling. No mention of Amber's birthday was to follow. Amber sat waiting, munching on cinnamon rolls and sipping coffee. She talked about the weather changes and how the years seemed to go by faster than ever. Lillie agreed pleasantly and participated in the small talk and still said nothing about Amber's special day. Amber became smug. She decided that whatever was in the oven must be for some special dinner that Lillie would prepare for her birthday and excused herself to get ready for work. Amber could wait for her birthday wishes that she was sure would come later in the day, when Lillie was serving up whatever delicious dish she was preparing. She dressed for work, kissed Lillie on the cheek before she left and drove to work singing "Happy Birthday to me, Happy Birthday to me."

She waited all day for a call from Lillie or Jason to wish her well. She waited in vain. Jason didn't even make his usual call to confirm the night's plans. She tried not to be silly about it, but deep down she was a bit disappointed. It was really her birthday this year and no one noticed.

Back at the Manor House the day was hectic. At 9 a.m., Jason had arrived with the Galloways; Bryan, Amber's twin, and his parents, James and Hazel. They were delightful people, not at all threatened by Amber's existence and glad that their only son would have family after their passing. Lillie and the Galloways spent an hour exchanging stories about the youngsters and noting similarities in their tastes. Bryan wanted only to hear about Amber as she was now. He looked at her pictures and fought back tears when he heard of the tragedies of the past year. Jason was as kind as he could be about details concerning Inez and dwelled on the fact that she did save Amber's life. At noon everyone except Mr. Templeton piled into Jason's car and headed for the small farm outside Aston. They would wait there for Amber.

Amber had mused about her birthday all day. She just couldn't believe Lillie had forgotten. Jason maybe, but not Lillie.

She drove home unable to concentrate on anything. She eased her car into the driveway only to be greeted by Mr. Templeton before she could even get out of her seat. He seemed a bit flustered.

"Lillie called. She needs for you to pick her up at the McIntires right away. Seems she has had car trouble.

"Oh really? She didn't tell me she was going to visit Ada today."

"Well, I guess she expected to be home before you got home. I'm awful sorry," he said these words with genuine concern in his voice.

"Oh there's no problem, Mr. Templeton. I'll run out there now and get her. Don't you worry."

Amber backed her car out of the driveway gingerly. It didn't occur to her to check her rear view mirror as she left. If she had done so, she would have noticed a grinning old man racing for his own car to follow her within five minutes of her departure.

Amber reached the farm a few minutes before six. The house seemed lifeless. The "pups" always frolicked the moment they saw her and she had to stop and pet them on the way to the porch. She walked up on the porch and started to knock on the door, but it drifted open when she touched it. A slight chill ran over her body and she had to force herself to remain calm. She called weakly to Ada as she poked her head into the alcove leading to the living room. Just as she was about to turn and leave, the lights flashed on and fifty people yelled "Happy Birthday!" It took Ada and Lillie to carry the large cake. It glowed with forty two candles. Amber looked at the cake a moment. Then she looked up at Jason, not sure at all if she liked the reminder of her brother. In fact she was going to tell Jason she thought the candles a little tasteless considering the circumstances. Jason was smiling and obviously bursting at the seams to share something with her. Amber embraced Jason and kissed him on the cheek. Jason stepped to one side of the doorway and a young man walked into Amber's view. She could not speak. She saw her father, only he was twenty eight years younger than the day he died. The young man's hair was exactly the color of her own and slightly wavy just like her father's. His green eyes, the line of his jaw, the cleft in his chin; he was the image of Lance Harris at twenty one.

Amber started to speak but nothing audible left her lips. Jason led the young man forward. Jason took Amber in his arms and held her only for a moment while he whispered "Happy Birthday, Darling. I love you." He released her and spoke again. "Amber, I want you to meet a new friend of mine. His name is Bryan Wayne Galloway. He is my friend, and; he is your brother." Amber sobbed as she threw her arms around the young man smiling at her. It took a full two minutes for Amber to let him go and to try to speak to him. When she did talk it was through tears and laughter at the same time. Jason stood back and watched the woman he loved find her brother. Neither Amber nor Bryan ate a piece of cake or drank a glass of wine for the next five hours. The party happened without either of them. They sat in front of the fireplace and exchanged life stories.

Except for the Galloways, Lillie and Mr. Templeton were the last to leave the party. Lillie hugged Jason and fought for the hundredth time to hold back her tears.

"I don't know how you did it, Shadow. To see those two united after all these years is just about the nicest thing I've ever witnessed." She paused a moment. "I'm sorry Amber has been so inattentive all evening. She should have at least shown her appreciation to you." Shadow smiled and shook his head negatively. "Lillie, don't fret about the way Amber treats me on any occasion. I hope tonight will live in her heart forever. She has a lifetime to discuss with Bryan. I wouldn't dream of intruding on their time together. Amber and I will have a thousand tomorrows, the rest of our lives and I hope one of the things we talk about will be how wonderful tonight was for her."

"You are a remarkable young man, Shadow. You really love Amber don't you? I mean the life long kind of love."

Shadow blushed but smiled. "Yes, Lillie. I love her. I love everything about her. I always will."

"Do you hope to marry her?"

"With all my heart I hope to."

"Have you asked her?"

"Oh, we have joked about it now and then and, as a matter of fact I had intended to give her this tonight. Of course I should have known how the events would turn out as soon as she saw Bryan."

He spoke while he pulled a black velvet ring box out of his pocket. The diamond solitaire inside was exquisite.

"Shadow, that is beautiful. She will love it."

Shadow smiled. "I hope so. I'll wait now till all the excitement over Bryan settles a bit and then I can get serious about discussing marriage with her."

Lillie hugged Jason once more, kissed him on the cheek and promised to include prayers for his happiness and future in her devotions from now on. She left with Mr. Templeton and congratulated herself on the success of the party even if Amber was hardly a participant.

James and Hazel Galloway had retired over an hour before the party ended. There had been some talk of the hotel in Aston and Jack McIntire had put a stop to that almost instantly. They slept in one of the many empty bedrooms upstairs. Ada had lasted long enough to thank the last of the guests for coming to the party. There wasn't anyone who didn't understand Amber's preoccupation. All agreed that the food and the music had been excellent anyway. Feeling pleased with themselves for their contribution to the happiness of another person, Jack and Ada retired to their bedroom. In only minutes Jack laid sound asleep and Ada rested peacefully. She wondered when her son would ask Amber to marry him and what Amber would say when he did. She hoped Amber would not hurt her only child; he was such a good person. She thanked her Lord for her blessings, including her beloved son and husband, then she turned out the lamp by her side of the bed. She snuggled close to Jack and just before drifting into peaceful sleep while hoping she would have a grandchild while she was still young enough to enjoy it.

Shadow stood in the hallway outside the parlor and listened to Amber and Bryan compare notes on their lives just another minute after Lillie left.

He wrote a large note telling Bryan where to sleep and where his parents were, then in the same note he told Amber when she wanted to go home to wake him, the time did not matter. Lillie and Mr. Templeton had taken Amber's car because Mr. Templeton had loaned his car to Galloways in case they wanted to move about in Aston tomorrow. Anyway, when she wanted to go home, "He would take her." He quietly taped the note on the door frame of the parlor. They couldn't leave the room without noticing the large white paper. He walked into the living room, pitched another piece of wood in the fire place and then made himself comfortable on the couch. It was already past midnight and he had been up since 5 this morning. It had been a good day and best of all Amber was happy. Shadow was asleep in five minutes.

Bryan Galloway had talked till his throat hurt and Amber couldn't believe it when they glanced at the clock. It was almost 2 a.m. She was shocked and suddenly realized that the party had happened without either of them. She was embarrassed and began to fret over being rude to all her guests and then she thought of Shadow. She had hardly spoken to him. IN FACT, she had not spoken to Shadow once he had introduced her to Bryan. She remembered his words when he introduced her and then he just stepped back and faded into the crowd and let her devote every minute to Bryan. She walked to the door and found the note. Amber guided Bryan to the stairway and hugged him once more. They decided to have dinner "whenever" everyone woke up tomorrow. Bryan was sure his parents were suffering from jet lag and he wasn't in the best shape himself. Amber held him tightly for just one more moment. "Get all the rest you need. We have the rest of our lives now. We don't have to ever loose touch again."

Bryan smiled at her. "You know, Jason told me you were outstanding. He didn't exaggerate a bit."

Amber blushed. "Shadow talked to you about me?"

Bryan laughed out loud. "Only for about twenty hours. He loves you very much Amber. But surely you know that."

Amber smiled at her brother. "Yes, I think I do," she said as she folded the note. "I just didn't' know how much until tonight."

"Well, good night Amber. I'll see you in the morning." Bryan kissed her on the cheek and turned to go up to the room he would sleep in for the next twelve hours.

Amber tiptoed into the living room and watched Shadow sleep. She took two large pillows from the love seat and placed them on the floor just in front of the fireplace. There were only embers left of the fire and they glowed warmly in the darkened room. Amber lay down on the floor and propped her head up on one of the cushions. Her mind danced with happy thoughts for only a few minutes before she slept.

Shadow woke up at dawn. He was cold and when he realized it was daylight it startled him. He had expected Amber to wake him before now. Then he noticed her lying in the floor. She slept peacefully in spite of the hard floor and lowered temperature of the room. He wondered how long she had been there. He covered her gently before going to the kitchen to make coffee. His mother was already on the job and the coffee was just about done. She spoke quietly so as not to wake any of their guests. "You look awful!" she teased.

"I slept on your couch! How does Pops stand to sleep on that thing?!?"

Ada laughed. "I don't know. I always say he can sleep standing up. What time did you take Amber home?"

"I didn't. She's asleep in there in the floor. I don't know what time she finally laid down. She and Bryan were still talking past midnight when I gave up and laid down on the couch. I expected Amber to wake me up to take her home but I guess she talked all night."

"You did a beautiful thing, uniting those two. I am very proud of you."

"Well, thanks Mom. But it seemed the only right thing to do. I'm just glad Lillie didn't just throw that Chandler woman's things away before inspecting the documents she had with her. Lillie deserves a lot of credit in this too."

"Maybe so, but I know how much you care for Amber and I think last night was the nicest thing you will ever do for her. You gave her family and we all know how important that is, now don't we?"

Shadow smiled. "We sure do, Mom." He knew her next words before she even opened her mouth. He spoke in unison with her;

"And when do you think you will start a family of your own?"

He laughed out loud with her. Then with a smug look he surprised her for the first time with his answer. "In fact, just as soon as Amber Dawn Harris is over the shock of meeting her brother, I intend to beg her to marry me. Do you think you can settle for a daughter-in-law with long auburn hair?"

Ada's mouth dropped open and Shadow thought he really shocked her. She was blushing and he had started to laugh at her when he realized she wasn't looking at him at all. She was looking past him and watching the reaction to his words on Amber's face. Shadow turned in his chair to see Amber. He stood up and his face turned crimson. Amber smiled and rushed to his arms. She spoke through tears of joy. "Amber Dawn Harris is over the shock of meeting her brother and you, Jason McIntire, don't have to beg for anything."

Shadow looked at her. "I didn't mean for you to hear us. I intended to ask you after…"

Amber laughed. "Now listen to him, Ada. Already he is squirming! I accept his proposal and he's trying to take it back!"

Shadow took her in his arms. "Oh no, Pretty Lady. I am not trying to take it back. I just had intended for it to be a little more romantic." He pulled the velvet box from his pocket and opened it. "This is for you if you will have me for a husband."

"Oh Shadow, I would be proud to be your wife." Then she added, "I love you." He kissed her with a passion that left her breathless. Ada tried to act like she wasn't in the room while tears streamed down her face. Shadow slipped the ring on Amber's finger and thanked her for accepting his proposal. Then he said, "When?"

"You mean a date for our wedding?"

"I certainly do. Why don't we get married while the Galloways are here so they can attend the wedding?"

Amber gazed at him for a moment. "That is sort of sudden isn't it? I mean they have to be back in Pittsburgh day after tomorrow."

"That leaves us all day to get ready. Do you think you can be ready by, oh, five o'clock tomorrow afternoon?"

"Shadow, are you serious? Ada, is he serious?"

Ada laughed. "I think so Amber. You better get used to his impulsiveness."

"This is NOT impulsive. I have loved Amber for nearly a year now and I have waited patiently for her to notice it. Now she has agreed to be my bride and I am not about to wait much longer, that's all. What is so impulsive about that?"

"And I love you too. I will always love you, Shadow. And I will be ready by five o'clock tomorrow to become your wife. I never imagined our engagement would be so long." She laughed with Shadow and Ada. "Now, you best take me home. We have about a thousand things to do between now and tomorrow. Where should we have our wedding?"

"Why not right here?" Ada spoke up.

"Fine," Shadow and Amber agreed. "And Father Keiner will be glad to meet us here. And I bet Richard Fargo will help us get the license today. I'll call him as soon as his office opens. Lillie and Mr. Templeton can stand up with us. You call anyone you want to and invite them to the festivities."

Amber smiled. "Actually, if the Galloways can stay and with your parents and Lillie and Mr. Templeton, I think that's about all we need. Ada, if there is anyone special you would like to call that's fine with me."

Ada spoke with excitement. "I'll have dinner prepared and we will have a feast right after the ceremony. Shadow, I suppose you have some plan for a honeymoon?" Amber blushed and Shadow smiled as he pulled her close to him. "Yes, Mom, I certainly do have plans for a honeymoon."

Ada scolded, "That isn't exactly what I meant young man. You watch your tongue!" She couldn't help laughing with them. Jack came into the room and asked about all the commotion. When he heard of the wedding plans he clapped his hands and whistled for joy. "Well, it's about time!" he nearly shouted. He hugged Amber and then his son.

Shadow drove Amber back to the Manor House and went inside with Amber to share their news with Lillie. Lillie cried and laughed and cried some more. Of course she and Mr. Templeton would stand with them and then she grew quiet. Amber noticed. "Lillie, is something wrong?" Lillie just smiled for a moment and then spoke.

"Amber, I raised you from a little girl. It is just hard to see you grow up and not need me anymore. I never really thought about it until now."

Amber gasped. "Lillie! Need you! I'll always need you. Who do you think is going to help me with this man's six children? They will need a grandmamma every day. And Lillie, I will need my friend always!"

Lillie smiled through fresh tears. "Oh really," she said, "six children."

"That's what he says." Amber threw her arms around Lillie and held her close.

"At least six," Shadow added.

Lillie recovered and wiped the tears from her face. "Well, we have a lot to do between now and tomorrow." She became strictly business as she pulled a pencil and note pad from a drawer and started making a list of errands. Amber and Shadow shared a kiss before he left. He promised to call her around noon. They decided they would travel to Calhoun's Jewelry to pick up wedding bands around 3 p.m. Shadow drove back to his home a truly happy man. He could hardly wait for Bryan to wake up so he could tell him they would be brothers-in-law.

Amber raced upstairs and showered quickly. While her hair dried she called the newspaper office to tell them she wouldn't be at work today and that she undoubtedly would miss tomorrow because she was getting married. She instructed her secretary to please pull on of her standby columns from her files and to submit it for this week's work. She hung up only after the entire office crew had shouted congratulations into the receiver. Amber giggled and thanked her secretary and dialed the phone again. This time she talked with the manager of the only department store in Aston. She needed something to get married in, not too fancy but something special that she could save for her daughter. Maryann Mays had known Amber since first grade and had been manager at Stiffler's Department Store for almost a year now. She could be at the store in ten minutes.

Amber met Maryann on the sidewalk in front of the store. Once inside the store it didn't take Amber twenty minutes to pick out the dress she wanted. She wrote a check for the purchase and Maryann placed it in the cash drawer of the department. Then she led Amber to her office and they shared a cup of hot tea and admired Amber's ring and talked about the past twenty four hours. Maryann made Amber promise to bring Bryan by the store on one of his future visits. Amber left Stiffler's Department Store half an hour before it was scheduled to be open to the public. As soon as she got home she would call Bryan and tell him about Maryann. She giggled. She loved having a brother.

She parked her car in the driveway and rushed into the house. Lillie was waiting to see her dress and together they hung it up so that it would not wrinkle. Its' simple beauty was just what Amber looked best in. Lillie praised her choice.

Amber called Father Keiner and asked if he would do the honor of marrying her and Shadow. She explained their rush by telling him about her brother and the demands of his schedule. She told him how important it was for her for Bryan to be present at the ceremony. Father Keiner was delighted and promised to be at the farmhouse about an hour before the ceremony. He understood the rush, but he still needed to counsel them a bit on the sacrament of marriage as was the custom of their church. Amber agreed and thanked him again. She hung up and wondered if Shadow was doing as well with his list of errands as she was with hers. She smiled and mentally hugged herself. Was it really possible to be this happy and content?

Shadow was prompt. He and Bryan arrived at the Manor House at 3 p.m. and after a fast tour of the house for Bryan, they left for Calhoun's Jewelry Store. The threesome walked in and Benny Calhoun greeted them robustly. He looked at Amber and winked at Shadow. "What did I tell you Shadow?" he said. "Didn't I tell you she is beautiful?" He paused and looked at Bryan. "And you, I heard about you when Shadow purchased the diamond for your sister. I am so glad to meet you. I know how important family is. You see if it had not for my family believing in me, I probably would still be in the streets." He shook Bryan's hand the entire time he spoke to him. The he turned to Shadow and Amber. "What can I do for you? The ring fits doesn't it?"

"Oh yes. The only things we need now are some wedding bands. We would like for them to match, but they have to be something you can size today. We are getting married tomorrow." Shadow was smiling broadly. Amber blushed.

"Well! I see. You waste no time once your mind is made up do you Mr. McIntire?" He reached into the glass case in front of them and brought out two gold bands. "These are the best gold in the store. I can size them while you wait if you want them." Shadow looked at Amber and asked, "What do you think?" She smiled and said simply, "I love them. I didn't know it would be this easy."

Benny sized their fingers and suggested that they go across the street to his favorite restaurant and have a late lunch while they waited on their rings. They agreed that was a good idea and were pleasantly surprised to find that as they had walked to the restaurant, Benny had called and instructed for their bills to be added to his weekly tab please. They ate and talked non stop of their plans for the next ninety minutes. Bryan promised to visit often and Amber encouraged him to consider a future in the state of Virginia when he finished law school. They looked at each other for long moments without speaking and Shadow could only marvel at their instant love for each other. He envied them in a way and yet felt very much a part of their happiness.

The threesome went back to Calhouns, Shadow paid for the rings and they left to the sound of Benny singing "Oh Promise Me." They arrived at Richard Fargo's office just before closing and picked up their marriage license. Richard was delighted with their decision to marry and didn't hesitate to say so. He and his wife would be present at the ceremony. In fact, he went so far as to tell Bryan that he just might be welcome in the Fargo Law Offices if he had a mind to practice corporate law. The shook hands and Bryan thanked him for all the help he had been when Shadow had begun to look for him.

Shadow and Amber were all set. All that was left for them to do was to show up tomorrow at four o'clock for Father Keiner's lecture on the sanctity of marriage and at five o'clock for the wedding. Shadow was beside himself with anticipation. He was sure he wouldn't sleep a wink this night.

The threesome stopped by the Manor House to pick up Lillie and Mr. Templeton and the five of them traveled back out to the farm house for dinner with the Galloways. Amber could hardly taste the food sitting on her plate. She really wasn't hungry but if she had been, she was sure that she was so excited that she couldn't have tasted the food anyway. Otherwise, dinner was perfect. As always Jack and Ada McIntire were the perfect hosts, with Ada's supreme cooking and Jack's friendly ways that made everyone comfortable. He played the banjo and fiddle til nearly ten o'clock and it was James and Hazel that decided that everyone should retire and get some rest for the big day tomorrow. Hazel teased Amber and said she couldn't believer Amber could stay so calm on the eve of her wedding day. She couldn't believe Amber accomplished so many planning details with such a short notice. Amber laughed and looked at Shadow and Bryan.

"Well, I had a lot of help from a man that I really think had a little bit of a head start on me. Guess I shouldn't complain though. I think things are going to move along pretty smoothly and that is my biggest concern."

"Well, tomorrow may be pretty hectic and I just want to take the time now to let you know that I am glad that Bryan has you for a sister."

"Oh Hazel, thank you for saying that to me. You will never know how important a relationship with Bryan is to me. I already love him so much. I can't thank you enough for the fine way you have raised and cared for him. And I thank you for coming here with him to meet me. A lot of adoptive parents would not have been so receptive to this situation."

"Bryan is my son, Amber, not my possession. And we love each other; no one can take that away from us. We were always honest with Bryan and we told him of his adoption. We hid nothing so we had nothing to fear." Hazel smiled at Amber, and then continued to speak. "My only regret is that the two of you didn't get to grow up together."

"We will be together for our future; Hazel…we can grow old together. That's what counts now." Amber hugged the fragile Mrs. Galloway and then added,"Goodnight. I'll see you tomorrow."

"Are you ready to drive me home, Shadow?" she asked. Shadow was smiling in her direction and held up his car keys for her to see. They hadn't been alone in what seemed like an eternity to him and he was anxious to talk to her in private; for just a few minutes anyway.

They drove for a few minutes in silence before Shadow spoke.

"Amber, I promised not to pressure you, and we have been so wrapped up in the excitement of finding your brother, I just wanted to make sure that you are sure about this marriage. I take those vows pretty seriously. This will be for all time."

Amber watched him as he tried to concentrate on the road and look at her at the same time. "Will you stop the car please?" she asked.

Surprised he pulled his car to the side of the road. "What's wrong? You aren't going to change your mind are you?"

"Shadow, I have never been as sure of anything as I am of wanting to be your wife. I admit I am a bit overwhelmed about the events since my birthday but I'm not frightened. I trust you as I have not been able to trust anyone in my life. You aren't going to change are you?"

"Never! Amber, I will always love you and we will have a wonderful, exciting life; I just know it!"

"I'm ready Shadow. I just hope I don't disappoint you. I have loved you all my life. I just didn't know who you were until a few months ago."

"Amber, you couldn't disappoint me if you tried."

"Careful, I don't want you to choke later on the words you say now." A single tear ran down her cheek. "I mean we haven't even…" she blushed and couldn't finish her sentence.

Shadow laughed while he pulled her to him and held her close.

"Are you willing to be my wife?" She answered, "Yes."

"Are you willing to be my lover?" She blushed and repeated again, "Yes!"

"And will you have my babies and love me without regret?"

"Yes, Shadow, I will! But, what if I'm not any good in bed with you or if I'm all used up?!!" She cried uncontrollably now and in spite of her pain, Shadow could not keep from laughing. When she noticed his laughter, Amber became so angry that she was able to stop crying. "What's so funny?" she demanded. "I worry about our future together and you laugh. Maybe I just shouldn't care."

Shadow sobered quickly. "Oh, Honey, that is why I'm laughing. I am happy because you do care and because you are naïve enough to worry about it."

"You mean to tell me that you don't worry about it?"

"No, Amber, I do NOT mean to tell you that at all." Then he kissed her so hard he left her breathless. He could see her pulse beating in her throat when he spoke again.

"Amber, I have yet to even kiss you without wanting to tear your clothes off you and make love to you. And I know you feel the same way. There have been times in the past few months when I think I could have taken full advantage of you if I hadn't loved you. Don't you agree?"

She nodded. "Yes, I guess I do."

"No! You don't guess, you know it. Amber, you and I are two of the luckiest people we will ever know. We are in love, not heat. And we have let that love grow between us before we got all tangled up in trying to impress each other in bed. Love making will just be the icing on the cake for us, not the entire basis for our relationship, so it doesn't have to be perfect every time. Please, Pretty Lady, don't put yourself on trial in our bedroom. No comparisons. No rivals. Just us, loving each other. I love you, so just relax and enjoy it."

He could feel Amber tremble as he held her tightly. He kissed her once more and tasted the salt of her tears. She could barely speak through the sobs.

"I just wish that I had met you first. Oh, Jason, I'm so sorry!" The walls tumbled down. The emotions of a hundred sleepless nights and days of anguish compounded into a few fleeting seconds and the torment literally shook Amber's body. Shadow held her close and stroked her hair. His own tears stung his eyes and his voice cracked with the pain in his throat.

"Amber, please don't. Today is ours and all the tomorrows of our lifetime will be spent with each other. We belong together and we didn't exist before we met. There is no past, only the future. Promise me that you will never say anything like that again; better yet promise me you won't even think it. I'm not going to worry about it so why should you? I told you the very night that we met that nobody is perfect. I'm no virgin, but that doesn't mean my heart is not purely yours. I will be faithful to you from now on and that is the only concern we have; the future."

Amber gulped huge breaths trying to stop crying long enough to talk to him.

"I think I'm turning into a basket case. Are you sure you can put up with me through times like this? I don't know what is coming over me."

"Pre-wedding jitters, that's all. After all it is a pretty big step. And I think I can handle just about anything you have to offer, Pretty Lady."

"Oh God, how did I get so lucky. I love you Shadow, I truly do. And thank you for everything."

"I better get you home so you can get some sleep before our big day." He kissed her gently on the forehead and then started his car. He pulled onto the road and drove quietly through the night. He left Amber to sort whatever thoughts she was having.

Amber sat close to him snuggling against his strong shoulder. She would not sleep tonight, there was no way. She wondered if Shadow would rest easy. In her mind she located her rosary so that as soon as Jason left the house she could begin her prayers. She would pray to her Almighty that she would be a good wife to Jason McIntire; the kind of wife a man like him deserved.

They tiptoed trough the kitchen door and tried hard not to wake Lillie from her sleep on the couch. Shadow thought about his restless night on the couch and hoped Lillie wasn't as miserable as he had been. He took Amber in his arms and held her close for more than a minute. The kissed goodnight and Shadow made Amber promise to think nothing but happy thoughts. He kissed her again this time parting her lips with his tongue, sending thrills of anticipation through Amber's body. His own desires were more than obvious to Amber as he held her close. She pulled from him and spoke softly. "After tomorrow, I'll never refuse you again. I promise that. I just hope I will always be desirable to you."

Shadow took a deep breath and smiled.

"I've waited for months to hear you say something like that Amber. Remember when I told you that I'd wait till you wanted me the way I want you?"

She smiled. "Yes, I remember and the time is now."

"I know and after five o'clock tomorrow I'll teach you all about real love, Amber. And I'll never wait longer than it takes to undress you again, I promise YOU that." He kissed her again. "Goodnight, my beauty. Until tomorrow."

Amber watched him drive away in the moonlight. There was a cool breeze and the leaves rustled on the trees. She had never dreamed anyone could be so safe and as happy as she was on this night.

Amber was correct; she didn't sleep and she had recited at least three rosaries before dawn. She and Lillie rose with the birds to eat breakfast and get ready for the day's events. It was at the breakfast table that Lillie dropped a surprise on Amber. She and Mr. Templeton had some plans for marriage of their own. They would wait till Amber and Shadow returned from their honeymoon and then they would tie the knot too. Lillie wanted Amber to stand with her at the altar. Amber was delighted.

Amber Dawn Harris and Jason Travis McIntire were married on last day of June. Lillie and Ada cried but composed themselves enough to serve a feast fit for a king after the ceremony. Bryan left with his parents but not before promising to keep in touch on a weekly basis as soon as Amber and Shadow returned from their honeymoon. They made plans to spend part of the Christmas holidays together. Bryan wanted his Galloway family to meet Amber and there would be traveling to Pennsylvania for Amber and Shadow.

Lillie and Ada were busy cleaning the kitchen when Shadow and Amber announced their departure. They would be gone two weeks and would call as soon as they arrived at their destination which Shadow refused to reveal even to Amber. They hugged everyone and made their way to Shadow's car which Bryan had found the time to sabotage with shaving cream and streamers. Amber threw her flowers to Lillie and winked at Mr. Templeton.

Ada watched her son drive away with his new bride. She felt good about his choice for a mate and wondered how long it would be before she had a grandchild. Jack stood beside her with his arm around her waist and knew without her ever speaking what his wife was thinking. He smiled and said simply, "In due time, Mama, in due time." They returned to the house and spent the evening with Father Keiner, Lillie and Mr. Templeton.

It wasn't until Shadow drove to the long term parking lot of the airport that Amber knew they were going to fly anywhere, much less Hawaii. They had been married four hours and she had thought by now Shadow would have her in some motel room claiming his husbandly rights. Instead they were on a plane bound for Hawaii and it would be another twelve hours before they were in bed together. Shadow had planned their entire honeymoon in less than twenty-four hours and this was the only flight that would come near to accommodating their schedule of the last two days. He was proud of his surprise and Amber snuggled close to him during the entire flight. Actually both of them could use a few hours rest. They both slept at intervals during the flight but it was no secret to anyone on the flight that they were newlyweds, especially after the Captain announced their marriage over the intercom. The arrived in Hawaii and were met by a limo that would take them to their hotel. Their rooms faced the ocean and dinner was waiting for them on the balcony.

Amber smiled as the bellhop left the room with a brand new twenty dollar bill and instructions not to disturb this room for the next twenty-four hours.

"I feel like I'm in a movie!" Amber giggled.

Jason laughed with her. "You aren't. You are here with me. Alone for the first times since we got married. I hope you aren't hungry." He was kissing her throat and unbuttoning her blouse. Amber responded instantly to his touch. Shadow picked her up and carried her to the bed. They didn't speak, they didn't have to. Their kisses said everything and their bodies responded in kind. The passion they shared consumed them. Shadow teased Amber to heights of desire that she had never known. Then with gentle force he took her for is own. She met his thrusts eagerly and she needn't have ever worried about pleasing him. An hour after they entered their bed, they lay thrilled and exhausted and satisfied. He had left himself deep within her; not just his semen, but his heart and soul and love.

Almost exactly nine months later Amber Harris McIntire birthed their first child. Her husband stood at her bedside and held her hand, wiped her face with cool cloths, encouraged her to stay strong. He watched with wonder while their first son forced his way into the world. He heart leaped with joy and he asked her again to love him always. She promised she would and asked him how long they had to wait before they tried for a girl. Her brother, parents-in-law, and Lillie waited just outside the delivery room to meet the newest member of the family. Mr. Templeton had walked the halls for hours while Amber had struggled to give birth. Now he was in the gift shop buying a teddy bear.

Six times Amber would lay in childbirth while Shadow stood by her side; never once did he leave her side. True to her wedding eve promise, Amber never refused Shadow again and their love making proved to be delightful in all the years to come.

Together they cared for Ada and Jack and Lillie and Mr. Templeton during their twilight years. They raised their own children and cherished every moment of their lives together. Never again did Amber doubt her self worth. Never again did she cry herself to sleep. Never again did she feel she was without love.